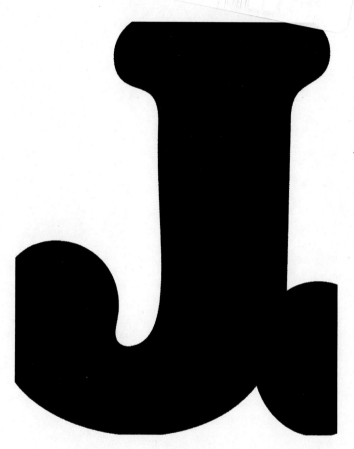

William Sanders

J

iPUBLISH.com
at Time Warner Books

For information address iPublish.com, 135 West 50th Street, New York, NY 10020.

 A Time Warner Company

ISBN 0-7595-5012-3

First edition: July 2001

Visit our Web site at www.iPublish.com

For Rick

acknowledgments

For various sorts of input and assistance, my thanks to: Geoffrey Landis, Steve Stirling, Karen Taylor, Richard Bowes, Walter Jon Williams, Doranna Durgin, and Janet Johnson. Bless them all.

Swallow Street Books
180 5th Ave., New York, NY 10010 (212) 555-5800
April 28, 1998

Dear Nate—

Thanks for giving me a look at Jay's new novel. As you know, I've always been a fan of her work. This time, unfortunately, I've got to pass.

I wish I could be more encouraging, but frankly I think you're going to have trouble selling this one in the present tight market. The narration has a kind of hallucinatory, dreamlike quality, which is fine for small-press experimental fiction, but commercial SF? I don't think so. The constant viewpoint and scene shifts made the storyline hard to follow, and I didn't feel the whole thing hung together very well.

Nate, you and I go back a long way; let me be candid with you. I'm worried about Jay. It's not exactly a secret that she's started drinking again, and you know what happened the last time. Can't you persuade her to get help, before she destroys herself both professionally and personally? I can give you the addresses of a couple of therapists, if you like; and there's always the AA.

Sorry I couldn't make an offer. See you Friday—

Hugh Leibermann
Senior Editor

P.S. And whatever Jay says, I did not "make a pass" at her at the Authors' and Editors' Reception. For God's sake, I'm a married man!

Part
One

chapter one

Dreams again, and she woke screaming.

◀ ▲ ▼ ▶

Screaming, she sat up in a tangle of sheets, eyes huge and pupils dilated, hands clawing at the empty air before her. All along the corridor, in other rooms, women stirred in drugged sleep and grumbled wordlessly into their pillows, and down at the desk the night-duty nurses exchanged looks; and after a moment one said, "Ann," and the other nodded and sighed and reached for the sedative tray, and headed down the hallway.

◀ ▲ ▼ ▶

Screaming, she jerked upright in bed, shoving aside the fur sleeping robe, one hand groping automatically for the rifle at the bedside, while the naked girl beside her cursed and tried to cover her ears. Nearby, in the tents and shacks of the little village, people listened as the scream echoed off down the hillside; and one of the men playing cards by the all-night fire said, "There goes Mad Jack again," and the others laughed, but not loudly, not loudly at all.

◀ ▲ ▼ ▶

Screaming, she rolled over and pushed herself up on one

elbow, but then her head imploded in dark-red pain and she fell back onto the pillow and lay staring up into the darkness of the apartment, tasting her own sour breath, hearing and ignoring the thumping against walls and ceiling and the shouted complaints of her neighbors. After a minute she grunted and reached beneath the bed, her hand finding with practiced ease the half-full bottle of bourbon on the floor.

In all the worlds, across all the lines, she screamed and woke; and in time, by various means, she slept again.

chapter two

A nn Lucas leaned back in the hard little chair and rested the
back of her head against the wall of her psychiatrist's office
and thought about killing him.

"Your case," he was saying, "is, well." He spread his hands on
top of his desk, palm up. "Difficult," he said, and sighed.

He was a fair young man with curly dark hair and large
brown eyes and fine, almost delicate features. A pretty boy, and
most of the hospital's female staff—and, no doubt, quite a few of
the males as well—had raging crushes on him. All the same, he
was a good competent doctor, easily the best Ann had had, and
remarkably free of the insensitivity and arrogance that seemed to
be endemic among his professional colleagues.

Ann liked him, as much as she liked anyone these days, certainly more than she liked herself; and right now she was thinking about killing him.

"This is your third stay here at Spanish Hills," he said, "in the
last five years—"

"Four," Ann said automatically. Studying the contours of his
throat, thinking how easily that pale skin would part under the
edge of a straight razor, she added, "Four times I've been here."

"Oh?" He raised an eyebrow, turned and pecked rapidly at the keys of the computer on his desk. "That's right," he said, watching the black digits scuttle across the white screen. "Two-week court-ordered admission, don't know why I forgot that. Before my time."

He pushed himself back from the desk and swung around in his swivel chair to face her square-on. "Ann, you're one of my favorite patients. Maybe my favorite. Do you know why?"

"No." Seeing the blood gushing, pouring down the side of his neck and soaking into the snowy white shirt. Carotid artery, instant exsanguination, dead before he hit the floor. "No," she said again, "why?"

"Because," he said, "you're the one patient I can actually talk with on something like an equal basis." He shrugged his shoulders minutely. "I know that sounds horribly elitist, but I can't help it. Most of these people, even the relatively educated ones, have to have everything explained in infant-simple terms, and even then they don't get it. You—"

He waved a hand at the file displayed on the computer screen. "Highest intelligence quotient of any patient in this place—past or present, I wouldn't be surprised. Damn sight higher than mine, I don't mind telling you."

He smiled, revealing even white teeth. Ann's fantasy dumped the razor in favor of a ball-peen hammer.

"I've looked at your record," he went on. "Ph.D. in physics from the University of Chicago. Did your graduate work at the Fermi Institute, stayed on for four years doing research before going to Los Alamos. NASA thought enough of your abilities to borrow your services for the early work on the manned Mars mission. I don't know much about the space program, but I'm impressed by that."

Hammer swinging, bone crunching. Blood. Ann said, "So?"

"So," he said, "we're both scientific professionals. Different disciplines, but we speak the same language, Ann."

Only, she thought in a sudden access of lucidity, I'm still "Ann" and you're "Dr. Peters." Or just "Doctor" to the mealy-mouthed head nurse. Of course you're a real doctor and I'm just a physicist. She was about to say, "Yeah, Chuck?" but then the madness rose up again within her and she clamped her lips together, trying to will it back down into the dark place where it lived. Her fingernails dug into the armrests of the chair. There was a taste in her mouth like old pennies.

"I think I can speak frankly with you," he continued, "more so than with the average patient. And I'm afraid I'm almost out of ideas."

You fool, Ann wanted to yell, you damned fool, you gorgeous child, you know so much and you don't know anything, do you? Sitting there in your damned silly swivel chair in your damned silly office, talking and talking and talking and never a clue what a werewolf you're talking to. If you could see the pictures in my head, just for half a second, you'd have me locked away forever. Or just run screaming from this building and hide yourself in the deepest mine shaft in New Mexico. "Christ," she said through tight-clenched teeth.

Dr. Peters paused. "I'm sorry?"

"Nothing." She shut her eyes for a moment. "I'm all right," she said, seeing bright flashes of light against the insides of her eyelids. "Really. Go on."

"Having another episode? If you'd rather do this tomorrow—"

"No." She opened her eyes. "It won't be any better tomorrow. Or any other time. Keep talking, damn it."

"You're sure?"

Ann forced the corners of her mouth back, trying to smile. From the look on Dr. Peters' face she guessed it wasn't a very successful smile. "I haven't been sure of anything for the last half-dozen years. Except that I'm crazy." She waved a hand as he started to speak. "I know, I know, not supposed to use the C-word in here. Schizophrenic, then. Reality-challenged. Not playing with a full deck. For God's sake, go on. It'll give me something to focus on."

"Yes, of course. All right." Ann noticed he kept his left hand on the desk now, close to the emergency button that would summon a couple of muscular and heavy-handed orderlies if things got too intense. They couldn't possibly get there fast enough, though, to stop her from thumb-gouging those lovely brown eyes out of his face. Stop that, stop it, oh *Jesus.*

"Well, as I was saying, it's not clear where we go from here. We've tried all the standard medications and several non-standard ones, and they haven't done much good, have they? Even the ones you were able to tolerate."

He put his fingertips together and made a little pagoda roof with his hands and looked at her over it. "Schizophrenia is a mysterious business, Ann. We've seen some amazing developments in medicine in the last decade, but this is one area that still has us baffled. Nobody even knows what schizophrenia is. It's just a name we give to an assortment of symptoms, that never seem to be quite the same from one patient to another, and that for all we know may have entirely different causes."

He snorted. "Oh, we've got various treatments we can administer, but we don't actually know how they work—when they do, which isn't as often as we'd like. As I certainly don't have to tell you."

"No." The fury was receding again, leaving as always a dull weariness and disgust. Ann tried to concentrate on what the doctor was saying, to understand or just give a shit.

"And now," he said, "I'm looking at an educated woman in her middle thirties, one with a fine mind—"

"Which she happens to be out of."

"If you insist on putting it that way, yes." His face registered a poorly suppressed wince. "For five years, now, your life has been increasingly unmanageable. Your career, your marriage—"

"Never mind that last item," she told him. "Let's stay with things I really minded losing."

"As you like. I was about to say, it began with the dreams. Then the delusions, the irrational destructive urges and periods of depression. The shoplifting—that was how you wound up at Spanish Hills the first time, wasn't it?"

"Yes." Caught going out the door of a Santa Fe gift shop with a pair of junk earrings she wouldn't have worn to her own cremation; after half a decade the memory still brought prickly heat to her face.

"And finally the overt violence." He looked at the screen again. "Brought in again the following year after assaulting a hotel desk clerk—"

"He was an asshole. And yes, I was out of control, I did need help. Just for the record, though, he *was* an asshole."

"I don't doubt it." Peters grinned as he scrolled the file. "And the last two times you came in voluntarily."

"I didn't see any alternative. I was afraid I was going to kill somebody. Or myself." She pushed her long black hair back from her face. "At least I'm safe in here, and other people are safe from me."

"Which was good thinking on your part," Peters said, "but it's not the real answer, is it? We want to make you well."

He made a face. "Of course as far as anyone knows there's no real *cure* for your condition—curing schizophrenia seems to be the medical equivalent of trisecting the angle or squaring the circle—but at least we'd like to give you the means to control the symptoms, let you function in the world outside." He smiled at her. "A gifted and attractive woman like you, it's a shameful waste keeping you in here."

Attractive? Ann wondered if Peters was developing delusions of his own. Mirrors were rare items in mental hospitals, for excellent reasons; but a few small ones were kept at the nurses' desk in the women's unit, to be used under supervision, and she had seen her face that morning while combing her hair. It hadn't been a cheering sight.

She glanced downward. Well, at least she didn't have a weight problem; if anything she was too thin. At five feet nine she had always been something of a beanpole, and lack of sleep and loss of appetite hadn't helped. Her long legs, that used to draw covert and not-so-covert stares from colleagues and students, were getting downright spindly. Lose weight without diet or exercise, just go mad. Maybe Peters went for the tall, pale, Gothic look.

"I don't want any more electroshock," she told him. "I've already got too many holes in my memory from last year's sessions. And it didn't do much good that I could tell."

"No. Anyway, ECT tends to decrease in effectiveness with subsequent applications. If it didn't help last year, I don't think it's worth a second course of treatments."

He paused and gave Ann a long serious look. Now, she thought, he's finally going to get to the point. He's got some big new idea he wants to try, and he had to do this dramatic buildup first, set up a regular little presentation. He may not be as big an asshole as the rest of the quacks around here, but he's still got the pretentious affectations. There must be a required course in medical school. No, they probably learn it watching doctor shows on TV.

"Ann," he said, "have you ever heard of Lomazine?"

Ah. "Another drug?"

"Just approved, as it happens. But the results have been remarkable in experimental—"

"Oh, sure. Aren't they always?" She shook her head hard. "Get yourself another guinea pig this time. That stuff last year nearly killed me."

"I explained at the time," he said, a little stiffly, "that Clozapine has some potential for dangerous reactions. You signed the consent form."

"True. It seemed worth trying. Anything seemed worth trying, the way I felt. I figured if I died, that might not be so bad." She gave a short harsh laugh. "I'll tell you something about almost dying, Doctor. It's like anal sex—you try it, you find out what it's like, and you never want to do it again."

His face went red. Proper gentleman, Ann thought, gets embarrassed when the lady talks dirty. How the hell did he make it through shrink school with inhibitions like that?

He said, "If your mind's made up, then there's no point in going on. I'm not here to coerce you into anything. Or to make a sales pitch for Lomazine."

She realized that he was about to terminate the interview and send her back to the women's unit. A vision appeared in her mind: the brightly lit arid space of the common area, with its white walls hung with bad landscape paintings, its orange couches and chairs where dull-eyed women sat watching soap operas and game shows on the old television set, while the day-shift nurses at the desk talked among themselves about diets and complained that their feet hurt.

She didn't want to go back there, not yet. It would be all right if she could go to her room and lie down on the bed and try to get a little sleep before the next attack, but that wasn't allowed in the daytime. A necessary rule, perhaps—some of the patients would never get out of bed, left to themselves—but an annoying one all the same.

Stall a little longer, then. She said, "No, please, I'm interested. What did you call this miraculous stuff?"

"Lomazine."

"Whatever." Who studied up these ridiculous names? Lomazine, Ativan, Atarax, sounded like something from *Star Trek.* "Another antipsychotic?"

He nodded. "Or at any rate it seems to have antipsychotic effects, though it was originally developed as an antiseizure medication. The chemistry's quite different from the older meds, and in fact it's not clear how it works. As usual," he said. "As I keep saying, we don't fully understand the workings of the illnesses we try to treat, so we understand even less about the mechanisms of the drugs. And Lomazine has so far proved even more mysterious than the others. A lot of people are working very hard to find out what makes Lomazine tick, because it may give us important new insights into the nature of schizophrenia."

He picked up a little box from his desk and bounced it on his palm. A sample pack, Ann guessed, from a drug manufacturer; she'd seen boxes like it before. Like those little five-cigarette packets they used to hand out in public places before the practice was outlawed. This one would be empty, a mere prop; all meds, down to the last aspirin, were kept locked away. There would have been hell to pay if Peters had kept actual drugs in his office.

"Meanwhile," Peters said, "what I can tell you about it is that it seems to work. At least it's produced impressive results in test cases, including patients who hadn't responded to anything else. I could show you reports—"

Hundreds healed in our last service. The people who used these crutches are cured and gone home. Say hallelujah. Ann said, "And the ever-popular side effects?"

"If I tell you none, you'll laugh in my face. After all, any medication will have *some* side effects. And psychoactive medications sometimes have pronounced ones, as you know."

"Yes." Like good old tardive dyskinesia; half the women in the ward had muscle twitches and facial tics from Haldol or Navane. And lithium made you bloat till you looked like something from Macy's parade, not to mention the trembling and the dizziness; and Clozapine could quite simply kill you. "Do I know," she said.

"But so far nothing serious has turned up. Some of the test patients complained of dizziness and headaches, a few experienced nausea at first. Dryness of the mouth, that sort of thing. Nothing disabling."

He held up the little box. "I'd really like you to try it, Ann. I think this might be the answer we've been looking for. Truthfully, it's just about the only idea I've got left."

For a moment she let herself be tempted. After all, she had seen other patients make amazing improvement with some of the new medications. If there was any possibility—

Watching her face, Dr. Peters said gently, "Ann, this may be your only chance."

"Chance?" All at once she felt almost too fatigued to hold her head up. "There's no chance for me. You know that. Lock me up," she said, feeling despair settle over her like a heavy gray blanket. "Put me where I can't hurt anybody, and forget about me. I've had it."

"Oh, Ann," he said sadly. "You mustn't give up hope."

"Hope's a toxin, Doctor. It builds up in your system like lead, and sooner or later it kills you. You've handed me a lot of poisons," she said, "and I've been good and taken them all. But don't push hope at me."

She passed a hand before her eyes, which hurt; the light in the office seemed to have grown terribly bright. "And I have no idea what that means, so don't ask."

She stood up. Peters eased his chair back warily, but she made no move toward him.

"I'm very tired now," she said. "May I go?"

◄ ◭ ◮ ►

All the rest of the afternoon she sat in a chair in the common area of the women's ward. She spoke to no one and made no response to the women who spoke to her; she looked at nothing in particular and, except for a couple of trips to the toilet, she did not move.

At five o'clock a bell rang and the patients began to line up by the door. Still Ann sat unmoving in her chair, until finally one of the nurses, a heavyset graying woman in gold-rimmed glasses, came over and said, "Come on, Ann. Time for our meds, and then we'll go to dinner."

Ann made no response. The nurse put a hand on her shoulder and gave it a quick shake, not very hard. "Now don't be like that," she said. "You know what happens when you—"

Ann came up out of the chair in a fast lunge, swinging both arms, slapping viciously at the stocky woman's face, knocking her glasses to the floor. Before anyone could move she had slammed the nurse against the nearest wall and was trying to choke her. "Leave me alone," she said in a low monotone, "leave me alone leave me alone leave me *alone*—"

It took two husky orderlies to separate her from her victim. Once they had her off the nurse, though, she went altogether passive, almost limp; they had to virtually carry her between them as they took her down to the isolation room.

"You be quiet, now," one of the orderlies told her. "You start pounding on the walls and hollering, we'll have to put you in restraint. Remember last time."

The isolation room was small and windowless, furnished only with a bolted-down bed without sheets or blankets. The light was kept on all night, and from time to time someone looked in

through the little Judas window in the heavy metal door. Ann
had been here many times before; it was almost another home.

She lay down on the bed and, after some time, slept, to dream
again and again of blood and fire and violent death. She woke
several times, shaking and sweating, but this night she did not
scream. Toward morning she fell into a deep exhausted sleep,
which ended much too soon when the orderlies came and
brought her back to the ward.

"I need to see Dr. Peters," she told the duty nurse as soon as
she came in. "Tell him I've changed my mind. He'll know what
I mean."

chapter
three

A burst of gunfire laced across the street and chewed divots out of the already riddled front of the abandoned store. Inside, Jack ducked and flinched as bullets whined and snapped through the shattered window. Bits of glass showered down on her and she closed her good eye and covered her face with one arm. "Fuck!" she said aloud.

The firing stopped. After a minute, moving very cautiously, she raised her head just enough to see over the window sill. It was a risk, but a necessary one; you couldn't just huddle there blind and wait for the bastards to come after you.

Anyway, she knew the men across the street couldn't see her, not clearly enough for a headshot and she wasn't going to expose anything else. The afternoon sun was full in their eyes and her side of the street lay in deep shadow. That was no accident; she had broken in that direction the instant the firefight started, by simple reflex, because that was one of the things you learned early on. People who didn't, who had to stop and think about things like putting the sun at your back in a shootout, didn't live as long as she had.

Of course not being able to see her hadn't stopped them from firing blind in her direction, but then they wouldn't have seriously hoped to hit her. They'd be trying to pin her down while they worked out how to handle the situation, and then to keep her head down while they did it.

Unless they were complete fucking idiots. She was starting to think that was very possible. Three men against one lone woman, and after all this time—she didn't own a watch, but the shadows on the sun-white street had gotten distinctly longer since the fight began—and all the bullets they'd fired, and they still hadn't managed to take her. Or even hurt her, unless you counted a couple of silly little cuts from flying glass.

Actually there had been four of them to begin with, but the fourth one wasn't a factor any more. He lay on his face, arms outspread like a fallen crucifix, in the middle of the dusty street, staring up at the bright New Mexico sky but pretty certainly not seeing it. Jack had dropped him with two thirty-caliber soft-nosed slugs through the chest—killing him twice, most likely, but she'd been in a hurry to get him dead—in the first seconds of the fight. She had hoped at first that the others would try to recover the body, but it was obvious they weren't quite *that* dumb.

For several long minutes she crouched there in the semi-darkness of the gutted store, peering out over the splintered window sill, studying the street and the storefronts opposite. Nothing moved, except for a large tumbleweed that came bounding up the street—for a second Jack thought it was going to roll right over the dead jacker, but it missed him by a couple of feet—and there was no sound but the low whine of the wind among the old buildings.

She wondered what was going on now. The last shots, she was certain, had come from the second building from the corner.

EDITH'S BEAUTY SHOP, read the half-ruined sign—but the shooters could be anywhere by now, if they'd finally gotten their fingers out, might be moving to flank or even encircle her. She considered firing a shot or two in the hope of drawing return fire, to find out if they were still there, but she couldn't spare the ammunition. Unlike the assholes across the street, or wherever they were, who seemed to have an unlimited supply; they'd already thrown enough metal to wipe out a whole village.

Which, Jack considered as she eyed the scene along the street, was just one of the many things that didn't add up here. . . .

It had begun, as such things usually did, with a chance encounter. Jack had been prowling through the little deserted town, looking for anything of value and not having much luck—the place had been picked to the bones long ago—and all of a sudden there the four men had been, coming around the corner by the burned-out bank building, bunched up and talking among themselves.

They had reacted instantly and mindlessly at the sight of her, fanning out across the street and running toward her, making high-pitched yips like wild dogs. One had fired a couple of shots over her head, apparently trying to scare her into surrendering. Another yelled, "Come here, baby, we got what you need!" and made a grabbing motion at his crotch as he ran.

She had killed that one, merely because he was the nearest and easiest target, and dived into the handiest open doorway on the shady side, while the others had holed up across the street. And there everybody had been ever since.

Easing back away from the window, Jack got slowly to her feet and leaned against the side of a smashed wooden counter.

She shifted her rifle to her left hand and brushed fragments of broken glass from her short-cut black hair, thinking. What the hell were they after? It didn't make any sense.

Oh, there was the obvious answer, endorsed by the late departed crotch-grabber; she was, after all, a woman, and there were plenty of men for whom that would be enough. Beyond simple rape—which was so basic a fact of life that the term itself was almost meaningless—there was also the slave trade; any presentable female captive would bring a good price, enough to be worth a little risk.

That was speaking of nubile girls, though, or at least reasonably young women who hadn't started to lose their looks. A leathery-faced old babe in her middle thirties, and one-eyed at that? Jack grinned to herself. It would be nice to think you still had it, enough to make men willing to risk death, but that wasn't easy to believe.

And yet that was the only reasonable answer. She wasn't carrying anything else of value, except her rifle—which they would almost certainly consider hopelessly old-fashioned—and her pistol, and they were clearly in no need of more firepower. True, she had ridden in on a horse that was worth a good deal, but he was tied outside of town, and there was nothing to stop them from taking him if they knew he was there.

Surely, she thought, it couldn't be revenge. She'd killed one of them; were they simply out to even the score? That was just too crazy. Survival was hard enough nowadays, without that sort of silliness.

Of course it was possible they *were* crazy. There was plenty of that going around. She damn well ought to know—

No. This was no time to go there. No time to start thinking about the weird stuff, the loony thoughts and the dreams, Jesus, like last night again, that scary place with the bright lights and the bars on the windows and the long hallways that went on and on, everything so white and shiny and cold, weird-looking people strapping her down and poking her with sharp things, *no.*

"No," she said in a whisper, and closed her eye for a moment, fighting down the sick confusion. Her free hand came up and one fingertip went under the black leather patch that covered her ruined left eye, rubbing the scar tissue there. It was an old and almost unconscious gesture, something she did in times of stress. It had cost her a few poker hands over the years.

Think about something else. How much ammo did she have left? She knew the answer, but it was something to focus on, to bring her thoughts back to here and now. Her fingers traveled over the cartridge loops in the bandoleer that hung over her left shoulder and between her breasts. Seventeen rounds left, plus five in the rifle; not much, considering. And six in the long-barreled .357 Magnum revolver at her hip, with another dozen pistol rounds on her broad leather belt; but if it came down to short-gun action she was in serious shit for sure.

She looked affectionately down at the old lever-action .30–30 Winchester in her left hand; her other hand gave a friendly caress to the worn walnut stock. A lot of people thought she was a fool for depending on such an obsolete weapon, but she didn't care. It might not shoot very fast, but it didn't waste ammunition, either, and it didn't jam, no matter how bad the conditions. And it would cheerfully digest anything you fed it, even old corroded brass or home-rolled handloads. Hell, it would even handle black powder, if you cleaned it carefully afterward.

Not like the fancy automatic weapons everybody else had to have, that looked cool and made a lot of noise and could maybe save you from having to actually learn to shoot straight, but quit cold if they didn't get absolutely perfect ammunition. Even one bad round would put a buzzgun out of action long enough to get its user killed. And clean ammo was getting to be very hard to find now that stocks from before the war were running low.

Although so far the jackers across the street hadn't had any problems—

It came to her then, a delayed realization that caused her to scowl and slap her thigh. Something had been wrong about that last burst of fire, something in the sound of it. "Hey!" she shouted.

And, when there was no response: "Hey! Hey, you limp-dick cocksuckers over there! What's the matter, get tired of fucking your mothers in the ass? I don't blame you, I hear they've all got crabs—"

Sure enough, they opened up again, firing blind and stupid, spraying the front of her building; and sure enough, she'd been right. Two weapons firing: an M-16—you couldn't mistake that sound once you'd heard it, and everybody had, the damned temperamental things were everywhere—and some sort of machine pistol, she couldn't identify it any closer.

Which left one weapon, and therefore one man, and where were they?

A slow smile spread across Jack's face. Moving carefully but quickly, she made her way toward the rear of the store, stepping over piles of unidentifiable rubble and avoiding the wrecked showcases with their jagged glass teeth—the place had been so thoroughly looted and trashed that she still hadn't figured out what had been sold there—and staying well out of the line of fire from the window. The crazies were still shooting and a good many bullets did find their way into the store, a couple of ricochets coming sphincter-puckering close, but she made herself ignore them and in a few minutes she had reached the door to the rear storeroom.

It was very dark back there, the windows being boarded up, and she had to feel her way to the big rear door. Groping with one hand, she found the door was barred with a heavy length of timber. She hoisted the bar from its brackets and stood it beside the door, making no sound in the process. After a moment's reflection she stood the rifle beside it.

The man coming up the alley was giving it his best, trying hard to move silently, but he wasn't very good at it. Jack heard him coming from clear down at the alley's mouth. She dropped her hand to the .357, hesitated, and then reached down and took the big knife from her boot top. A moment later she heard him coming up the back steps to the loading platform.

The door opened with a loud squeal of long-unused hinges. Jack blinked as sudden light appeared against the darkness; and then, in the middle of the light, there was the dark backlit outline of a man.

It was all over in hardly any time at all. The jacker stepped inside; Jack's left arm snaked up over his shoulder from behind and her forearm crushed his throat, choking off any outcry. The knife in her other hand went in just below his ribcage, angling upward. She held on tight as the man bucked and thrashed—he wasn't very big but he was stronger than he looked—and then there was a wet noise as his bowels emptied and his body went limp. She eased him to the floor and wiped the knife on the front of his pants before putting it back in the boot holster.

His weapon had fallen to the floor in the struggle; she opened the door to let in more light and saw it lying beside him. An old M-14, for God's sake, you didn't see them very often. National Guard hardware, she guessed; the Regular Army had quit using the piece well before the big war, back during that Vietnam thing, as had the Corps. Her father hadn't had a good word to say for the '14.

She picked it up and examined it. This one had the full-auto selector switch, which made it an even rarer item. Thinking, she slung her Winchester across her back and headed back to the front of the store, the heavy M-14 balanced in both hands.

The men across the street were firing again. She picked her way across the room and stood beside the window, out of sight. When the shooting stopped she counted silently to three and aimed the M-14 at the ceiling and triggered a short burst, and then, after a brief pause, a longer one. The racket inside the closed space was worse than deafening. At the end of the second burst she let out a long high scream, putting everything she had into it, and finished up with a single shot into the floor.

Then she waited. She didn't have to wait long. Through the ringing in her ears she heard the shouts from across the street: "Ray! Did you get her, Ray?" And, in a higher voice, "Yeah, ol' Ray got that bitch! Poke her one before she's cold, Ray!"

She heard them laughing as they came out into the street. She turned and stepped sideways, facing the window, the M-14 at her shoulder, and opened fire.

The M-14 jumped and climbed violently on full-auto, shooting high and to the right, and she realized she had made a mistake; she wasn't used to the weapon and it hadn't been properly sighted in. She did get the nearest man with a couple of rounds, knocking him down in a heap in the street, but the rest of the burst went wild. The other man stood there for half a second with his mouth open in zero-brain surprise, 7.62mm. slugs sprigging up the dust around him, and then he turned and ran, straight up the street, while Jack cursed and struggled to unsling her Winchester.

By the time she got the old saddlegun unlimbered the jacker was a good block away and running fast. He had thrown his machine pistol away, probably so he could run faster, and he was making no move to take cover, just hauling ass right up the middle of the half-buried old pavement.

Jack covered him with her sights and eared back the Winchester's hammer, but then she sighed and let the hammer back down and lowered the rifle. There was no good reason to waste a valuable round on the fool; he was no threat now, and in fact he wasn't likely to survive long in this country, alone and unarmed. There was a good chance he'd get captured for a slave himself, or simply killed on general principles—and if he ran into the wrong people he might even wind up as dinner.

Cheered by the thought, she picked up the M-14—piece of shit or not, it was valuable trade goods; she'd have to check out the dead man in back for ammo—and walked out into the street to get the guns off the others. Halfway there the reaction hit her and she stopped, shaking violently, and bent down and puked into the dust between her feet.

When she straightened up she saw that the last man she had shot was still alive. With a sigh she unholstered the .357 and walked forward to take care of that.

◄ ▲ ▼ ►

The sun was low over the big mountains to the west by the time Jack came riding up the washed-out dirt road toward the village. A cold northwest wind was blowing down across the hillside; she stopped beneath a couple of tall pines and got the thick sheepskin coat from behind her saddle and put it on, while the horse took advantage of the pause to snack on the sparse grass by the roadside. Going to be a chilly night; it was the middle of May but spring came late at this altitude. Well, there was somebody who'd help her keep warm. The thought made her hurry to remount.

The village consisted of about two dozen houses—or shanties, or cabins, or strange rough structures built around sal-vaged trailers and truck bodies and the like—and perhaps half that many tents of various sorts and sizes, all scattered untidily across the rocky hillside. Farther up the hill, a small herd of horses and a few scrubby-looking cows ambled about a big wire-fenced field.

It was, Jack considered as she rode on up the hill, all in all a pretty scabby-looking place. But then she wasn't a permanent resident here—or anywhere else, for that matter—and she'd be moving on again one of these days, so it wasn't her problem if these characters wanted to live like a bunch of half-smart pack rats.

A voice hailed her as she rode through the village: "Yo, Jack!"

She pulled the horse to a stop. "Fat Bob."

A balding, middle-aged black man grinned up at her from where he sat at a long rough-timber workbench. The bench held an assortment of tools and dies, a simple balance scale, and a bolted-down reloading press. A basket at his feet held a collection of empty brass cartridge cases, while another beside him contained a smaller number of reloaded rounds.

"So," he said, tossing a loaded cartridge into the second basket, "Mad Jack returns. Any luck?"

Jack returned his grin. Fat Bob was one of the few people who could get away with using the nickname to her face. He wasn't really fat, just chunky; seriously overweight people didn't have good survival odds these days. Even if they could somehow find enough to eat to get fat in the first place.

"Ran into some jackers," she told him. "That little town, what's the name? Down the valley, where the blacktop meets the main highway."

Fat Bob's thick gray eyebrows went up. "You got in a fight? Anybody I know?"

"Probably not. If you do, I hope they weren't into you for any credit."

She half-turned in the saddle, indicating the collection of weaponry tied on behind her. "Got some good stuff," she added. "Couple of sixteens, a fourteen—no shit, full-auto switch too, when's the last time you saw one of those? And a little Ingram chopper. Not bad for an afternoon's work."

Fat Bob got up and walked over to stand beside the horse, looking at the bundle of hardware. "Ammo?"

"Some. They used up most of what they had, shooting at me."

"I'm a son of a bitch."

"So I've heard," Jack said, straight-faced.

"Shit." Fat Bob laughed. "Four jackers with automatic weapons, and she takes them on alone. Nobody but Mad Jack . . . wait a minute."

He turned and went back inside his house, which consisted mainly of an ancient Airstream trailer and a school-bus body, both without wheels, joined by a pine-roofed walkway. After a minute or so he came back out, holding a big glass jug. "This calls for a drink," he said, and tipped the jug up in both hands and took a long throat-pulsing swallow before passing it to Jack. "Help yourself," he offered.

The home-made wine was as bad as she'd known it would be, but it felt good going down and it helped ease the cold feeling inside her body. "Thanks," she said. "Hey, look, okay if I—?" She raised the jug. "I'm about out, man. I'll pay you later."

"Take it." Fat Bob flapped a large hand. "You're good for it, I know."

"Thanks," she said again.

"Don't mention it. Hey," Fat Bob said, "there's a big swap meet up in Taos, couple of days from now. You ought to take those four pieces up there. Should bring a good price."

"Right." She tucked the jug under her left arm. "But I'm keeping the Ingram. Jennifer needs something small and light."

An odd expression crossed Fat Bob's face, as if he'd suddenly remembered something; he seemed about to speak. But then he shrugged and turned away. "The jug's on the house," he said without looking back. "See you."

◀ ▲ ▼ ▶

Jack's cabin—strictly speaking it wasn't hers, but the people who had built it had failed to return from a foraging run during the winter and nobody expected them back—was out at the far southwest edge of the village. As she slid off the horse she saw that the cabin door stood open. "Baby," she called, "I'm home!"

Quickly she unloaded and unsaddled the horse, gave him a quick rubdown with her hands, and led him over to the little corral beside the cabin. Opening the gate and slipping off his bridle, she patted him on the rump and shooed him through. "Good horse," she said without much feeling. In fact the long-legged roan *was* a damned good horse, tough and fast and steady; she just wasn't into that sentimental horse thing like some people. She'd never even given him a name, though it had been over a year since she'd stolen him from that band of desert drifters.

"Look, honey," she said as she picked up the bundle of captured weapons. "We'll take these to Taos to trade—I'll get you something pretty—"

But there was no response from within the cabin, and when Jack stepped inside everything was dark and still. "Jenny?" she said, and then realized what should have registered as soon as she came up the hill: the little mare that should have been in the corral was gone.

Feeling a sudden awful emptiness inside, she pulled the blanket curtain from the single window. By now the sun was half hidden by the mountains and the light wasn't strong, but she could see more than enough of the cabin's interior. Or rather she could tell what she couldn't see, things that weren't there any more: the clothes, the jewelry, Jennifer's things and some of her own as well—

"Christ!" she whispered, and fell back against the door frame, mouth open, unable for the moment to draw an adequate breath. A great roaring filled her ears; her vision blurred.

Fighting for control and knowing she was about to lose it, she looked around. It hadn't been a robbery or a snatch; all the weapons still hung on the wall, and there were no signs of a struggle. Besides, Fat Bob would have told her about anything like that.

She didn't bother looking for a note. Like most people her age, Jennifer couldn't read or write.

Jack pawed through half-empty clothes baskets—the little bitch hadn't taken everything, just the best stuff—and looked in vain for her good leather saddlebags. A carved wooden box, that had held her silver-and-turquoise necklace and bracelets, lay upside-down on the dirt floor. She picked it up and stared blankly at it for a moment.

Then at last the white rage flared and exploded inside her head, and a high terrible shriek ripped from her throat as she hurled the empty box against the wall, where it burst into splintered fragments. Still screaming, she lunged across the room and began ripping the fur sleeping robes from the bed, throwing them blindly to the floor and trampling on them with her booted feet, then stabbing the bed again and again with the knife she couldn't remember drawing. "Bitch," she cried, "fucking little whore, dirty cunt," and fell finally across the ruined bed and sobbed for a long time, deep wrenching sobs without tears, until exhaustion made her stop.

She got up and lurched to the door, then, seeing Fat Bob's wine jug still sitting on the ground outside. Standing in the doorway, she uncorked the jug and took a very long drink and then another. The wine hit her aching and empty stomach with boots on but after a moment the heat began to spread through her body and the booming in her ears died away to a distant angry mutter. She studied the ground in front of the cabin, reading the tracks she should have seen before: one horse had come here, not long ago, and stood in front of the cabin, and then two horses had gone away together. The rider of the first horse had not dismounted. In among the tracks, leading to and then from the corral gate, were the small footprints of a woman.

She was aware that people were watching her, none too covertly, from windows and doors nearby. The hell with them. "Go on, then," she shouted, croaked rather, and waved her free hand in the general direction of the Rio Grande valley. "I hope you'll be very fucking happy together."

She turned back toward the cabin. Halfway through the door she paused and looked back. "Too bad you never knew Daddy," she said hoarsely. "You'd have liked him. He never forgave me for being born without a dick, either."

The contents of the jug made a nice gurgling sound as she carried it into the cabin and set it down, very very carefully, on the floor beside the demolished bed. God bless Fat Bob, she thought as she struggled clumsily out of her coat and the cartridge bandoleer and stretched out atop the ripped blankets. He knew what a lady needed to get her through the night; and oh, but this was definitely going to be a long one.

chapter four

Dr. Peters said, "I'm really glad you changed your mind, Ann. I think you're going to be glad you did."

Ann sat down on the edge of the bed and shrugged. "If you say so."

"Hey," he said, smiling, "it's worth a try, isn't it? If nothing else—" He made a gesture that took in the little room and everything in it. "Change of quarters, anyway. For a little while."

Actually the little room wasn't all that different from her regular room back in the women's unit. Newer-looking, but not by a great margin; one thing about Spanish Hills Psychiatric Hospital, everything was kept clean and properly maintained. Nothing but the best private care for well-covered nutcases— and government scientists were very well-covered indeed.

"You know," Peters said, "I think you may be the first patient to occupy this particular room. We only opened this new wing last month, and it's still only about half filled."

They had brought Ann here just after lunch. Her clothes had been taken from her, except for her underwear, and exchanged for a light-blue hospital gown. Various forms had been brought in for her to sign, affirming that she had been informed of any possible risks of Lomazine therapy, that she had voluntarily consented to take it, and that she promised not to sue the hospital no matter how bad an idea this turned out to be.

She had signed without argument, not caring one way or another. She had peed in the little cup for a cheerful-faced aide, and held still while a young black technician shoved an enormous needle in her left arm and extracted what felt like a couple of gallons of blood. Now here was Peters again, being optimistic and supportive and irritating as hell. The madness was down for the time being, and she no longer wanted to kill him, but she wished he would leave so she could stretch out on the bed. Her head hurt.

"You'll only be in Special Care for five to ten days," he told her. "We just want you where we can keep a close eye on you, until we make sure there aren't going to be any complications from the Lomazine."

"I thought you said this stuff was safe."

"Theoretically it should be. But one of my mentors in med school used to tell us that a man has nipples because theoretically he might have a baby. Humor me," Peters said. "I'm just being careful, Ann. I don't seriously expect any problems. All the same, Lomazine *is* a new drug, barely out of the experimental stage. There's a lot we don't know about it. I'll feel better if you're here in the Special Care unit."

And of course the taxpayers would wind up paying through the gazookus for all this. Not that that was any big deal. Compared to what it was going to cost to put those three splendid bores on the surface of Mars next month, this was very small change.

"You'll have your meals in here," Peters went on, "instead of in the dining hall. You'll have a chance to use the exercise facilities every morning, and I hope you'll take advantage of it. We need to know how your system is responding to the Lomazine, and we'll know more if your body is in reasonably good condition. Hence the temporary semi-isolation," he said. "We've had a few cases of a minor virus infection in the women's wing, in the last week or so. I don't want you contracting anything that might create confusing symptoms."

"Is that why they took my clothes?"

"Just institutional nonsense, I'm afraid. This unit is supposed to be for patients needing special medical attention, which in most cases means some sort of physical trauma—suicide attempts, drug reactions, serious illness, whatever. So," he said, "they run Special Care more like a regular hospital. And that means the patients wear hospital gowns."

He moved toward the door. "I'll see if I can get them to make an exception in your case. Meanwhile, for what it's worth, that gown looks rather nice on you."

Good God. Was it possible—no. He was just being sweet, in his slightly goofy way. She knew she should thank him but she didn't have the energy.

"You'll get your first dose tonight at bedtime," he said. "I'm starting you on two milligrams. That doesn't sound like much, but trust me, this is a powerful drug. You could say a little of it goes a long way."

He raised a hand. "Take it easy, Ann. I'll look in on you tomorrow. Have a good one."

A good what? she wondered, and started to say, but he was out the door. She sat for a moment looking after him; then she laughed, a very soft short laugh that carried no mirth whatever, and lay back on the bed and closed her eyes. At least in here you could do that. . . .

◀ ▲ ▼ ▶

She spent the rest of the day lying on the bed, occasionally sleeping. Now and then the violent visions came into her mind, but without much strength, and not for long; right now she was too burned out to get seriously wild. If the usual cycle held, it would be anywhere from a couple of days to a week before she started losing it again. Mostly, now, she felt depressed and listless, and very tired.

From time to time a nurse or an orderly stopped at the open door and looked in at her, but no one spoke beyond an occasional diffident, "Hi." She made no response to any of them.

An aide brought her dinner on a tray. She picked unenthusiastically at the food—it wasn't bad, in fact it was quite good, she just wasn't interested—and tried to watch a news program on the television set above the foot of her bed. One of her old NASA bosses appeared briefly on the screen, announcing proudly that all was in readiness for the manned Mars mission. She thought she recognized her ex-husband among the crowd of scientists in the background.

A former Vice President of the United States had been indicted for tax fraud; the camera picked him up exiting a Federal courthouse, all shifty eyes and hunched shoulders and ratty little grin, giving a two-hand wave to the reporters. The Dow Jones was down. Another incomprehensible war had broken out somewhere in Africa. It was going to be a rainy night, but tomorrow would be clear. An auto dealer in Albuquerque claimed to have the lowest prices in the Southwest. The British royal family was having another scandal.

Ann watched it all with incurious eyes, letting the monotonous voices wash over her but rarely listening to what they said. None of it had anything to do with her; she had checked out of that world a long time ago and nothing was as unreal as reality. This was just something to pass the time. Or rather to maintain some awareness that time was passing, which in here was not always easy to do.

Later, she took a hot shower, standing for a long time under the stinging spray, letting the little needles of water relax the tension-braided muscles in her neck, feeling something close to genuine pleasure. It was, she had to admit, damned nice to have her own bathroom, plenty of hot water and nobody waiting to use it after her. She toweled off and pulled on clean panties and re-donned the cotton hospital gown. She was brushing her hair when the nurse came in with the Lomazine.

"Good evening, Jacqueline," Nurse Gopal said in her plummy Bombay accent. "I am bringing you your medication. Please to be putting down thee brush, now."

Having dealt with Nurse Gopal before, Ann knew better than to waste time or breath explaining yet again that she didn't use her first name and hadn't since she was a child. The chart said that the patient's name was Jacqueline Ann Lucas and that, to Nurse Gopal, was that. It didn't do, in any case, to suggest that she might have made a mistake, however trivial. Nurse Gopal did not react at all well to anything that might be interpreted as criticism—which, since she tended to interpret almost everything as criticism, meant that she spent much of her time in what could only be called a sulk.

Tonight, though, she seemed in a fairly good mood; she actually smiled as she held out the little paper cup with the two white tablets. "Take these, please," she said.

Ann dumped the pills into her own palm and studied them for a second. They were pretty ordinary-looking, for such high-powered stuff; in fact they could easily have been mistaken for large aspirins. One milligram each? They looked pretty big for that.

"Is there a problem?" Nurse Gopal's voice had gone up slightly in pitch; umbrage lurked behind her large brown eyes, waiting to be taken.

Ann shook her head. One thing she didn't need right now was a confrontation with Nurse Gopal in her attitudinous aspect. She popped the tablets into her mouth and washed them down with water from the plastic cup that Nurse Gopal handed her. "Thanks," she said automatically.

Nurse Gopal said, "Good night, Jacqueline. I will be turning out thee lights now."

Doing so, she departed, closing the door behind her. In the soft glow of the indirect all-night lighting—it was never really dark anywhere in this place—Ann stretched out on the bed and closed her eyes. If this stuff could buy her just one good night's sleep without the God-damned dreams, she thought, she'd gladly kiss the ass of whoever invented it.

◄ ▲ ▼ ►

When she awoke it was with a brutal headache and a churning stomach, and a sense that something was profoundly wrong. She sat up in bed and swung her feet to the floor and, after a couple of tries, stood up.

The room wheeled and tilted, but she steadied herself with a hand against the wall and, when she had her balance, shuffled into the bathroom. Letting herself down on the toilet, she urinated copiously. Done, she sat there for a time, holding her head in her hands, fighting down surges of nausea. For a few minutes she thought she was surely going to vomit on the bathroom floor, but finally her stomach settled down after a fashion and she raised her head and opened her eyes.

The night lights were still on. Not yet morning, then; other than that she had no idea what time it was. She felt disoriented and dizzy; when she looked down, her hands and feet seemed far away and grotesquely misshapen, and the floor did not appear quite solid. Her skin felt much too tight.

Her mouth was incredibly dry, as if she'd been wandering in the desert; her tongue felt thick. She got to her feet, pulling up her panties, and lurched over to the sink and turned on the cold water.

The sink was too small to let her get her mouth under the tap, but she managed to scoop up a little water in both hands, enough to relieve the worst of the thirst. It didn't help that much, though; she couldn't get a decent mouthful, and the tap water had an unpleasant metallic taste that did her nausea no good. She went back into the room and pushed the button to call the nurse.

Some time later, when it became obvious that the nurse wasn't coming, Ann went to the door and opened it—she thought it might be locked, but it wasn't—and peered down the corridor, which was deserted. The bright hallway lights hurt her eyes and she had to squint, but she could see a drinking fountain only a couple of doors away.

The tile floor was chilly beneath her bare feet as she padded down to the fountain and bent to drink. The water tasted wonderfully sweet and cool in her parched mouth, though it hurt her stomach when she swallowed. She dipped her fingers in the cold water and splashed a little on her face, thinking it might clear her head. It didn't, but it felt good anyway.

She was straightening up, about to turn and go back to her room, when a raspy voice behind her said, "Well, well. What are we doing out of our room at two in the morning?"

Muddled as she was, she still recognized that voice. She had just enough time to think *shit!* before a large powerful hand gripped her left arm and spun her around.

"Hey," Duncan Brady said. "If it isn't Annie. Haven't seen you since they put me over here in the bedpan ward. How's tricks?"

Ann closed her eyes for a moment, hoping this was a dream. When she opened them again, though, he was still there. She wanted to scream, or groan, but her throat was too constricted to do either.

"Heard about last night," he was saying. "Just don't ever quit, do you? Old Flipout Annie, in and out of here year after year, still as crazy as a shithouse snake."

Duncan Brady was an anomaly among the staff at Spanish Hills. Most of the nurses and orderlies here were humane, sympathetic types; even the few irritating assholes, like Nurse Gopal, basically meant well. This was, after all, a very expensive private institution, one of the most exclusive in the Southwest, and many of the patients had well-off and well-connected families. There was no place at Spanish Hills for the brutality and negligence that gave other mental hospitals, particularly the public-sector ones, their snake-pit reputation.

Brady, however, represented a rare but serious breakdown in the screening process. It wasn't just that he was crude and insolent; the big bastard was an authentic sadist with an evil genius for subtle humiliation, delighting in tormenting the patients—whom he openly hated, though he could put on a convincing show when senior staffers were around—in ways that could not be detected or proved. Ann had never actually seen him hit anyone, though there were credible rumors, but she had seen him do things at least as cruel. Most of the patients were afraid of him, and even the nurses made sure never to be alone with the hulking orderly, whose flat pale eyes had a way of sliding over a woman like violating hands.

Ann felt a shiver run through her body. "Please," she said. "I was just getting a drink of water. Let go my arm."

Brady's response was to tighten his grip. Her arm was still sore from the afternoon's blood-drawing; she winced and clenched her teeth against the pain. "Don't tell me what to do, baby." He grinned and gave her arm a jerk. "*I* tell *you*. That's how it works around here. You ought to know that by now."

There was an odd high-tuned note in his voice, something strange even for Brady. Looking into his eyes, seeing the dilated pupils, Ann suddenly realized what it was. Good Christ, the man was flying so high he was practically in orbit. She wondered what he was on. Working in this place, he wouldn't have much trouble getting his hands on drugs. The control system would be a trivial problem for a man like Duncan Brady.

"Come on," he said. "Back to your God-damned room, and I don't want any lip."

He began pulling her back along the corridor, taking long fast strides and yanking viciously at her arm. "Cold-ass bitch," he muttered, not looking at her, "walk around here with your nose in the air, think you're big shit, got that little wuss Peters all pussy-whipped—"

Almost running to keep up, trying to keep from falling on her face, Ann wondered dully what God had against her tonight. First Nurse Gopal, now Brady. How had the new section wound up with those two? But of course she knew the answer; she'd had enough experience of institutional politics. The new units always inherited the ones nobody wanted, while the long-entrenched department heads made sure to hang onto their best people. She'd played that game a time or two herself.

At the door to her room Brady released her and gave her a shove. "In there," he growled, "and I better not see your skinny ass out of that room tonight, understand?"

"All right." Clearly it was no time to cross him now; he was right at the edge—as much time as she'd spent there, she ought to know the signs—and anything was possible. "I'm sorry," she said placatingly, backing into the room, away from him. "I'm going to bed now."

"Yeah." With growing horror she realized he was following her into the room, putting out a big beefy hand and catching the door as she tried to close it. "Bed, that's right. Just the place for you."

She felt very afraid. Amazing; she'd all but forgotten what fear felt like. She wouldn't have thought she cared that much. But the prospect of being raped by Duncan Brady would have sickened a marble statue. "Get out," she said in a near-whisper. "Please."

Brady stepped into the room and closed the door behind him,

pushing it shut with his massive shoulders. He flipped on the overhead light. "Let's have a better look . . . no, can't have you running around like that." A long tongue came out and licked his lips as he looked her up and down, eyes lingering on the usual areas. "Not bad for an old broad."

Ann was all too conscious of the thinness of the cotton gown, and the fact that she wore almost nothing underneath. She started to cross her arms in front of her breasts but then she realized that would only excite Brady more. "Get out," she said again, and reached for the emergency button. "I mean it."

Brady laughed. "Go ahead, push that thing. It don't work," he said. "Nothing works worth a shit in this wing. They got in a hurry to open it and everything's still all fucked up."

With a sudden quick movement he crossed the room, crowding her back against the edge of the bed. His hand came up and grabbed her by the throat, squeezing not quite hard enough to choke her. "And don't try yelling for help," he said almost gently. "Everybody in this place has heard you scream at night. Just Ann having another of her crazy dreams—and then if you keep it up I'll have to hurt you, and tell them you got wild and came at me. Who do you think they're gonna believe?"

His breath was hot and rank on her face. His great weight pressed her back and down; his thick-muscled thigh pushed hard between her legs, grinding into her crotch. Through layers of fabric she felt his erection against her belly. "Get off me," she said desperately. "You son of a bitch."

She was trying hard now to summon up the rage, use it to help her fight back, but of course it wasn't there, the beast sound asleep just when she really needed it, nothing now but empty despair. In another minute this loathsome man was going to shove himself inside her and use her for a receptacle to empty himself, and there was nothing to be done about it and maybe it was better to get it over with, after all what was the big deal. . . .

He put his hands on her shoulders and whirled her about. "I got what you need," he said, his voice higher and hoarser, "what you been needing all along," shoving, bending her forward over the bed, "and I know where you need it—"

Feeling his hands up under the gown, his fingers scrabbling against her skin as he worked her panties down over her straining hips, she realized what he meant to do. Her mouth opened to scream and never mind his threats, but he snatched up the pillow from the bed and pressed it over her face. "Hold still," he ordered. "Just gonna hurt worse if you fight me. Better relax and enjoy it, baby."

Face down, pinned, Ann squirmed and fought for breath against the smothering pillow, while behind her Brady grunted loudly as he jabbed at her exposed bottom. "Hold still," he repeated, struggling to force himself between her clenched buttocks. "God damn it, I swear I'll break your fucking neck."

The fury was building now, the beast stirring at last but much too late. Wanting to kill and dismember, she could only struggle helplessly; and not even that for much longer, because she was starting to black out from lack of air. She felt her body begin to relax as the darkness gathered in her head, and through the roar of blood in her ears she heard Brady's triumphant, "Ah!" as his probing penis found her anus.

In a last lucid instant, as the pain of his penetration ripped through her body, she knew that by the time this was over she would have gone entirely and irrevocably mad. If Brady didn't kill her—

A woman's voice said, "Hey. Hey, motherfucker, let her go."

Brady stopped moving. His hands relaxed their grip; the pillow fell away from Ann's face. As he stepped back she fell forward onto the bed, gasping for air, unable for a moment to think about anything but filling her lungs. Which was why she didn't see what happened next.

She heard Brady say, "What the fuck?" and then, *"Uhhhh!,"* the last an agonized rising-pitch exclamation that sounded like a groan trying to become a scream. A moment later there was a crash that shook the little room. A framed picture fell from the wall, passing before Ann's dazed eyes on its way to the floor. In the bathroom something fell with a clatter into the sink.

Still gulping air, she pushed herself up off the bed and turned around. Her hands were raised, ready to fight off a new assault, but she saw right away that that wasn't going to be necessary.

Duncan Brady lay on his back in the middle of the room, arms outflung, staring upward with astonished eyes. A great spreading red stain had appeared on the front of his uniform jacket, centered just below his sternum, where blood continued to well thickly from a three-finger-wide rip in the once-white fabric. His mouth was open. So was the fly of his pants. His still-erect penis pointed straight up. Ann felt a hysterical urge to giggle. Really, it wasn't all that big, was it?

A tall black-haired woman stood beside Brady's body. She wore some sort of dark sleeveless shirt and military-style camouflage pants tucked into black knee-high boots. A black patch covered her left eye. On her right hip hung a heavy-looking pistol in a belt holster.

Ann registered these and other details without much immediate interest. At the moment her attention was focused on the big knife in the woman's right hand. The blade was very long and right now it was covered with blood.

The woman said, "You all right, there?"

Well, Ann thought crazily, it's finally happened. My first full-fledged hallucination. What next? Messages from God?

The hallucination said, "Say, what the fuck's going on? What *is* this place, anyway?"

chapter five

The woman staggered slightly and put out a hand to steady herself against the nearest wall. "Woo," she murmured. "Fucking Fat Bob and his wine, I swear—"

She looked around the room, her face registering utter confusion. Her left hand rose to her face and one fingertip disappeared for a moment beneath the black eyepatch. "Son of a bitch . . . hey," she said to Ann, "I'm kind of fucked up right now, you know? Got really shitfaced, feels like I still am." She ran her fingers through her short black hair. "See, my girlfriend ran off—"

She stopped and shook her head. "Never mind that. What I'm saying, I can't seem to remember shit since right after sundown." She gave Ann an odd, almost shy look. "And if I'm supposed to know who you are, well, hell, baby, I'm sorry."

Ann could only stare. She'd seen it all clearly for a moment: madwoman kills a man and then creates an imaginary figure, some sort of fantastic alter ego, on whom to blame the slaying. Who hadn't heard of such cases? True, she had no memory of stabbing Brady, but then she wouldn't, would she?

But it didn't work. She might be crazy enough for the rest of it—God knew she'd wanted to kill Brady; she still felt a powerful desire to go over and kick the body—but there was simply no way she'd have hallucinated a drunken one-eyed lesbian.

An *armed* one-eyed lesbian, she corrected herself. Which undercut the obvious alternative explanation: if the one-eyed woman was a fellow patient, where did she get a knife? To say nothing of that gun on her belt, which even to Ann's inexpert eye was obviously the real thing.

"Who are you?" she asked faintly. "How did you get in here?"

"Jesus Christ," the woman said irritably, "I told you, I don't fucking *know* how I got here. I don't even know where 'here' *is.*"

She bent down and wiped the knife blade on Brady's jacket sleeve. Ann watched, fascinated, as she stowed the weapon in a boot-top holster. "Oh, boy," she said then. "Did I just fuck up big? Was this guy your old man or something?"

It took a moment for Ann to realize what the woman was asking. "No," she said, and shuddered violently. "God, no. Thank you, whoever you are."

"No sweat." The woman kicked Brady's leg with a blood-spattered boot toe. "It looked like he was forcing you, but you can't always tell. Some people go in for funny shit, you know?"

She tilted her head, studying Ann. "You a slave?"

"Slave?" Ann said blankly, and the woman snorted.

"Okay," she said, "I know a lot of people don't like the word. Captive, then. Hell, it's nothing to be ashamed of. It could happen to anybody."

She glanced down at Brady's body. "I mean, just look at this asshole, the way he's dressed, not even armed—anybody can see he was no jacker. Had to be from around here, and he knew you were somebody he could grab and buttfuck without anybody doing anything about it. I may be drunk and I may be crazy, but I'm not stupid."

Then, as Ann started to speak, she raised both hands. "Whatever, whatever. This is no time to stand around shooting the shit." She jerked her thumb toward the doorway. "I don't know about you, baby, but I'm getting my ass out of here."

She raised an eyebrow. "You want to come along? Or wait for whoever shows up next? I guess you know this scene better than I do, maybe you'll be okay—but if this big sack of shit had any buddies, I guarantee you they're going to figure you were the one who did him."

And that, Ann realized, was absolutely right. The one-eyed woman might have a bizarre view of the situation—it was obvious that she was delusional—but her last words made perfect sense. If Ann stayed here and the stranger managed to escape, would anyone even believe she had existed? More likely the next stop would be the New Mexico Institution for the Criminally Insane.

"Make up your mind," the woman added. "Time's running out."

Ann nodded jerkily. "Yes. All right." Wrong answer, she knew, the wrong choice, but what were the alternatives? Anyway, her life had been in free fall for a long time now; decisions only mattered to people with at least the illusion of control. "I'll go with you," she said.

The woman said, "You got any other clothes?"

Ann shook her head. "Christ," the woman said, "no shoes either? Yeah, that's how they made sure you wouldn't run away. Got to get you something to wear, then."

She looked at Brady again. "Can't use his clothes, that's for sure. Better roll him, though, see if he's got anything on him we can use."

She squatted down beside the body, her boot soles squishing in the still-spreading pool of blood, and matter-of-factly began searching the dead man, seemingly oblivious to the red mess that quickly covered her hands and wrists. "Sure enough, no gun. Not even a knife—what was he, a slave too?" She held up a large leather wallet. "Have a look, will you?"

The wallet was the trucker's kind, with heavy snaps and a metal chain and belt loop. A ring of keys hung from the end of the chain. Ann opened the wallet, trying not to get too much blood on her hands. Inside she found only a set of credit cards, a New Mexico driver's license, a foil-wrapped condom, and eighty-three dollars in cash. She took the keys and the money and threw the rest on the floor and went into the bathroom to clean her hands.

A moment later, behind her, the strange woman said, "What the fuck? Running water? What a fancy setup."

She moved up beside Ann to wash her own hands, shaking her head and looking more confused than ever. "Holy shit," she muttered, turning her fingers this way and that under the stream of hot water, as if amazed by the sensation. "And aren't these lights electric? Man, nobody's going to believe this."

She dried her hands on the towel Ann handed her and then used it to wipe the worst of the blood from her boot soles. "Clean your feet," she advised Ann. "We don't want to leave a line of bloody tracks on our way out, do we?"

As they moved toward the hallway door the woman drew her pistol, a practiced fluid movement that was almost too fast to follow. "Okay, stay close to me but leave me a clear field of fire if we step in any shit." She paused, pointing a boot toe at the dead Brady. "Speaking of shit, any more like him around?"

Ann thought it over. Graveyard shift, in a half-empty ward? "Probably not," she said. "I mean, he was probably the only orderly on duty in this wing. There'll be a couple of nurses down at the station. And of course plenty of people in the rest of the complex, and the guard at the front desk—"

"Yeah, yeah." The woman tossed her head impatiently. "One problem at a time. Come on."

She moved to the door and opened it with her left hand, holding the long-nosed revolver muzzle-up and ready. After a quick look up and down the corridor she said, "All clear. Which way?"

"Right," Ann said. "I think."

"Think?" The woman scowled. "Damn well better *know*—"

She led the way down the corridor, moving with silent grace in her clumsy-looking boots. The room doors they passed were all closed and no sounds came from within. That was as Ann had expected; any other patients in the wing would be so sedated they wouldn't have heard an artillery barrage, or else off in their private worlds.

The corridor made a sharp turn to the left. The one-eyed woman paused, peered around the corner, and moved on, making a follow-me motion with the barrel of her pistol. Beyond the turn, the patient rooms gave way to closed and windowless doors with cryptic number codes. A little farther along, a door on the right bore a rectangular sign, red with white intaglio lettering:

```
┌─────────────────────────────────────────┐
│   PHARMACEUTICAL SUPPLIES                 │
│   NO UNAUTHORIZED ENTRY                    │
└─────────────────────────────────────────┘
```

"Wait," Ann said.

"What?" The woman looked back, her face angry. "There's no time to screw around, damn it."

"Then go on without me." Ann was examining Brady's key ring. "I'm not leaving without some meds. Trust me, you don't want me getting crazy on you."

"Shit." The woman put her back to the wall, glancing up and down the corridor, pistol at the ready. "Well, all right, make it fast."

The ring contained at least a dozen keys, but one, of shiny new-looking brass, caught Ann's eye. She ran a fingertip over its wards and felt rough edges, as if made with hand tools. Sure enough, it went into the lock—a little stiffly, but it fit—and a moment later the knob turned in her hand.

"Had himself a private key," Ann said, mostly to herself. "That's how he maintained his habit. Probably made some money on the side, too."

The storeroom held tiers of metal shelves, on which stood row on row of bottles and boxes. For a moment Ann despaired, but then she saw that everything was alphabetized, and after that it didn't take long to find the items she wanted. Zoloft, that would help when the depression came back, and a big bottle of Xanax tablets just for general peace of mind; she'd taken them both for so long, off and on, that she had a reasonably good idea how to use them.

The curious thing, she realized suddenly, was that right now she didn't feel the need of anything at all. In fact she felt pretty good, considering. Scared, sure, who wouldn't be, and excited, maybe a little manic, but nothing she couldn't handle. Still a little dizzy, too, from the Lomazine—

That reminded her. Might as well take some of that too; maybe it was working, maybe that was why she felt better than she had in years. There it was, several nice new bottles, labeled according to dosages: Lomazine 1 mg, Lomazine 2.5 mg, Lomazine 5 mg. Struck by a sudden suspicion, she unscrewed the cap of the last bottle and shook a few five-milligram tablets into her palm.

There was no mistaking the size of the things. She'd swallowed two of them only a few hours ago. She opened the one-milligram bottle and had a look at the contents, making sure, but there was no doubt about it. Somebody had screwed up.

"Wrong pills," she said aloud. "I was supposed to get two milligrams and I got ten. No wonder I'm so spaced out."

She looked around, then, and saw that she was alone. Clutching an armful of plastic bottles, she rushed back out into the corridor, but there was no sign of the one-eyed woman.

Panicking, all her new-found confidence instantly gone, she rushed back into the storeroom. Her shoulder slammed painfully into a metal shelf, knocking bottles of pills to the floor in a clattering cascade, but she kept going all the way to the rear of the storeroom, where she sagged against the wall and fought down a scream. Her heart thumped violently; she couldn't seem to get enough air into her lungs.

She had no idea how much time went by—it couldn't have been long, but it felt like several forevers—before the voice came from the storeroom doorway: "Hey! You ready to go?"

The one-eyed woman stood there, holding out a loose white bundle. "See if any of this fits you," she said. "Probably won't, but anything's better than what you've got on."

The bundle consisted of a couple of white uniform pantsuits, complete with underwear and white nurses' shoes. "Where were you?" Ann asked, feeling close to tears—that was strange, she never cried any more—as she unbuttoned the hospital gown.

"Scouting," the woman said, grinning. "Found these two women sitting at this big desk, just a little way down the hall there. They were shooting the shit, not paying any attention, didn't hear me coming till it was too late. Once they got a look at my baby here," she patted the holstered revolver, "they just got cooperative as all hell. Didn't argue or yell or anything."

Ann looked at the uniforms. "You took their clothes?"

"Yeah." The single eye fairly danced. "Left them locked in this kind of a closet, absolutely pussy-naked except for the tape I used to tie them and gag them. Good tape, too," she said, "found it in back of the desk, I should have looked around for more . . . man, they made a kinky picture, you know? One was kind of fat but the other was damn cute. Wouldn't have minded getting acquainted with her."

Down to the last button, Ann found her hands were shaking too hard to undo it. She gave a hard yank and the button popped off. "Please," she said, shrugging out of the blue gown. "Don't do that again. Leave me like that."

"Sorry. What'd you, freak out when you found me gone? I guess I should have said something. I don't blame you," the woman said. "This place is starting to get to me too. Creepy."

Ann examined the nurses' uniforms. One of the outfits was far too big—evidently "kind of fat" was an accurate description—but the other looked at least wearable. She bent and pulled on the ugly loose-cut polyester pants, conscious of the woman watching her. The pants were several inches too short, but otherwise the fit wasn't too bad. Ann slipped into the white jacket, not bothering with anything underneath, and struggled to do up the buttons.

"Let me give you a hand," the woman said.

Ann didn't object. She stood quietly, trying to control her trembling, as the woman buttoned the jacket for her with quick sure fingers. She felt a sudden urge to grab one of those strong tanned hands and hold it very tightly.

"There you go," the woman said. "No bra?"

Ann shook her head. "One's too big, the other's too small."

"Yeah?" The woman stepped back and picked up the two bras from the floor, looking at them. She held the smaller one up to her chest and sighed. "You're right. I was kind of hoping one would fit me—hell, I haven't had anything like this in years, look, the elastic's still good and everything. But my knockers would never go into those little cups . . . looks like we're about the same size, huh?" She tossed the bras on the floor. "Try the shoes."

Ann sat down on a stack of boxes and experimented with the nurses' shoes. Again, one pair was impossibly big but the other was close enough. "You'd never guess," the woman said, "but the fat one had the smallest feet. Okay?" she asked as Ann stood up.

"I wouldn't want to run a marathon in them," Ann said, taking a couple of experimental steps, "but they'll do. Shall we go?"

But out in the corridor, spotting a drinking fountain, she said, "Wait a minute," and dug out her drug supply from the capacious pockets of the nurse's jacket. Finding the Xanax bottle, she twisted off the cap and popped a tablet into her mouth, and then, after a moment's struggle between judgment and need, she added another. Not really a good idea, but she felt herself on the verge of disintegration. That moment of panic, when she had found herself alone, had made a shambles of her nervous system.

She bowed her head over the fountain, washing down the pills and trying again to relieve the dryness in her mouth. That was when it all came back: the other fountain, and Brady finding her, and what had happened after that. She choked and strangled for a second, feeling a rush of nausea. The one-eyed woman put an arm across her shoulders. "Take it easy, now—"

Ann nodded. "I'm all right." She wasn't, but she would be soon; she imagined she could already feel the tranquilizers starting to work. And the touch of that steadying arm . . .

They walked on down the corridor, side by side. The woman kept looking about her, a strange expression on her face. "Christ," she said at last, "I just realized something. Why this place feels so weird."

"This place *is* weird." The drugs were definitely starting to hit; the Xanax on top of the Lomazine had done the job. Ann was feeling much, much better. Her feet didn't quite seem to be contacting the floor. "Trust me on this," she said.

"Yeah, but—" The woman stopped and looked at Ann. "Believe it or not, I've been having these dreams." Her left hand came up and her forefinger dug briefly beneath the eyepatch. "I mean, I've had them for years now. And I'm in a place, I swear, it looks just like this. And people are doing horrible shit to me, and I can't get out."

She gave Ann a crooked half-grin. "Is that what's going on now? Am I just having another dream, and you're part of it?"

"Funny," Ann said, "I was wondering pretty much the same thing."

"Maybe we're both dreaming. Two people in different places having the same dream, hey, it could happen. I read about something like that in a book. I can read," she told Ann proudly. "And write, too."

"How wonderful for you," Ann said seriously. "Here we are."

The nurses' station seemed to be laid out much like the one in the women's unit. Ann went behind the deserted desk—wondering briefly which of the nearby doors hid the bound and nude and, no doubt, terrified nurses—and studied the building chart, marked with red arrows and labeled FIRE EVACUATION PLAN, that was taped to the back wall. She was fairly sure she knew the way out, but it wouldn't hurt to make sure.

Satisfied, she searched for and found the big black button mounted beneath the desk top. "Pull," she called to the other woman, who was shoving against the heavy main door.

She pushed the button and held it down. A buzzer sounded and the door came open, throwing the woman temporarily off balance. "How about that," the woman said in obvious surprise.

"Hold it till I get there," Ann told her.

A moment later they were out in the big central passageway that connected the various wards and units of the sprawling hospital complex. "There's one more door we have to get through,"

Ann said. "Way down at the end of this passage, then to the right. There'll be a guard at the front desk."

"Yeah?" The big revolver appeared in the woman's hand. "Armed?"

"I don't think so." Ann hoped not; Brady had deserved what he'd gotten, but she didn't want to be party to the death of some minimum-wage security guard. And there was no doubt in her mind that this woman would unhesitatingly kill anyone who got in her way.

An idea popped into Ann's mind; a genuinely crazy idea, even by the standards of this demented night, and one that undoubtedly owed more to the hell-brew of chemicals in her bloodstream than to any real thought processes—but still, now she thought about it, it could very well work.

As they approached the final turn she said, "Give me your gun."

"Say *what?*" The black eyebrows went up so high and fast even the eyepatch twitched. "No way in hell, baby—"

Ann explained. The woman looked very dubious. "Might work," she admitted, "but can you do it? No offense, but you look kind of wasted right now."

"I can do it," Ann said, trying to sound more confident than she felt, "and anyway, there's no other choice. The guard's desk sits in the middle of the lobby, a good fifty feet from that corner, so even you couldn't sneak up on him without being spotted. And he's almost certainly got some alarm he can trigger. Please, give me the gun."

The woman pursed her lips and blew out air in a near-whistle. "Okay. If you—" She shrugged and handed over the pistol.

"Don't drop it," she said, "or shoot your foot off."

Ann hefted the pistol, which was much heavier than she'd expected. "Is the safety on?"

"Oh, my God." The woman rolled her eye. "This is a *revolver*, all right? Revolvers don't *have* safeties. If you need to shoot anybody, which you fucking well better not, just pull back on the trigger until it goes bang. Otherwise keep your finger off the trigger." She grimaced. "I got to leave that wine alone. The shit I let myself get talked into when I'm juiced—"

Ann shoved the pistol under the waistband of the uniform pants. The elastic wasn't up to the job of supporting that much weight, but after a little experimentation she found she could hold the gun in place with the pressure of her left arm. It made her stance and walk grotesquely stiff and unnatural, but maybe the guard wouldn't notice. It was, after all, going on four in the morning—Ann checked the clock on a nearby wall and then did a double take; things couldn't possibly have happened that fast—and with any luck he'd be half asleep, registering nothing but a nurse leaving early.

She stepped around the corner and walked as briskly as possible in the direction of the lobby. As she'd anticipated, the guard looked up before she had covered half the distance. "Going home?" he asked, a bit drowsily.

He was a middle-aged black man with rimless glasses and almost no hair. He rose from his chair and picked up a clipboard and held it out as Ann approached. "Be sure you sign out," he said. "Say, did you know you forgot your badge?" He was looking at the empty lapel of the uniform jacket. "I'm not supposed to let you out without it."

Bodges, Ann thought goofily, I don't got to show you no stinking bodges. She said, "Sorry, got it right here," and reached inside the jacket and hauled out the revolver and pointed it at the guard. The range was about four feet.

"Please," she said anxiously and very fast, "just stand still and don't make any noise or try anything, all right?"

His hands were up over his head before she had finished speaking. "Sure," he said soothingly. "Take it easy, now."

Ann felt the gun wobbling in her hand. She reached up with her left and got it in a two-hand grip, like the cops on television. "Turn around," she said, "and no funny stuff. Don't make me blow you away. Dust you off. Turn your lights out. Whatever."

The guard turned obediently, hands still raised. "Now just stand there," Ann said. "I mean freeze."

The one-eyed woman appeared at Ann's side, holding out a hand. Ann gave her the revolver. She motioned with its barrel and Ann remembered the next part. The guard's handcuffs were in a neat little leather case on his belt, above the left hip. After a couple of awkward tries she managed to get them locked around one of his wrists. Before she could figure out how to proceed from there, he had obligingly crossed his wrists behind his back. She snapped the other handcuff in place. "Got a car here?" she asked.

He nodded. "Keys in my pocket. Right front."

She dug them out, feeling a little embarrassed; he seemed to be developing an erection. Probably a fear reaction, though for all she knew this was turning him on. "Make and model, and where's it parked?"

"Ninety-seven Ford Antares," he said. "Red, parked right out front. And I hope you either drive it to Mexico or total it, because I got more insurance on that turkey than it's worth."

"Lie down," she told him. "On your face."

That part gave him some trouble; lacking the use of his hands, he almost fell. "Just don't shoot me," he said when he was finally prone. "I got a family."

Ann examined the telephone hookup on the desk—evidently the guard also doubled as night switchboard operator—and found the main cord. A hard yank ripped it loose from its floor connection. She picked up the phone console in both hands and threw it across the lobby. It hit the tiled floor in a satisfactory smash of flimsy plastic.

"Have a good one," she said to the guard, and trotted around the desk toward the big glass front doors, where the one-eyed woman was already waiting.

Outside, she was surprised to find that it was raining; not hard, but a steady chill drizzle that soaked quickly through the thin uniform. The overhead lights cast yellow reflections on the wet pavement. Shivering, Ann looked around and saw the red Antares a stone's throw away. "There," she said to the woman, who was staring about her in all directions, looking confused again. "Come on."

Unlocking the driver's door, she paused. "Who drives? I mean, I'm stoned and you're drunk. What do you think?"

The woman shook her head. "I haven't driven a car in years. If you can drive this thing, do it." She gestured toward the rear of the Antares. "Want me to push?"

What an odd question, Ann thought. What an odd *person.* "Just get in," she said, and slid behind the wheel and stuck the key in the ignition switch.

As she started the engine the right door opened and the woman got in beside her. "I guess you know the way out of here?"

Ann thought of several possible replies, but all she said was, "I can get us to the main highway. Any ideas where we ought to go from there?"

"No. I keep telling you, I don't even know where we are."

"Of course. I forgot." Ann sighed and put the Antares into reverse. "Hang on, then. I don't know how good I'm going to be at this."

"You did fine so far tonight," the woman said.

Startled, Ann glanced at her and saw a flash of white teeth in the dim light. "By the way," the woman said, "my name's Jack."

She laughed self-consciously. "Or sometimes they call me Mad Jack, or Jack the Ripper."

Somehow Ann didn't find this particularly hard to believe.

"Just don't call me One-Eyed Jack," the woman added. "Man, I really *hate* that, you know?"

"I wouldn't dream of it," Ann assured her. And after a moment, "My name's Ann."

chapter
six

Watching the mountain road peel away under the car's headlights, Jack considered that she must finally have lost what was left of her marbles. She hadn't been this confused since the war. And even the war had made a kind of nightmare sense, once you accepted the fact that it had happened at all. But this was way to hell over the line between could-be and couldn't. Fucking Fat Bob and his wine, she thought for probably the thirtieth time tonight. Never again.

She'd had blackouts before—a couple of times when drunk and once, a long time ago, when a drifter had persuaded her to try some bad-tasting mushrooms—and lately, since the dreams had gotten so intense, she'd had occasional episodes of sleep-walking. Only a few nights back, Jennifer had found her wandering around in the dark, out on the hillside, and had had hell's own time getting her back to bed. Or so the girl had said; Jack had no memory whatever of the incident.

And she still assumed something like that must have happened tonight. The last thing she remembered was flopping down on the bed in the empty cabin—Christ, she hadn't even bothered to take off her boots or her gunbelt, that was pretty bad even for her, though a good thing as it had turned out—and guzzling wine on an empty stomach and feeling sorry for herself. Obviously she must have wandered off at some point after that.

Nothing so incredible, then, about finding herself in a strange place with no recollection of how she'd gotten there. But the *there*, that was what was unbelievable and in fact, any way she looked at it, simply impossible.

After all, she knew the area around Fat Bob's settlement; she'd lived there, off and on, for years, and hunted and foraged and generally bushwhacked around that part of the country, girl and woman, with Daddy and then alone, for over a quarter-century since the war. There was hardly a rock or tree or patch of dirt that she hadn't seen.

And she knew her own physical capacities, and had a good idea how far she could have traveled, on foot and in the dark, in a single night—and there was, she knew with absolute certainty, no place like this anywhere within that distance of her cabin. Not even if she'd been sober, not even in the daylight, and, by God, not even if she'd been on horseback. There was nothing like that building anywhere within a hundred miles of Fat Bob's village; she'd swear to it.

But then, up until tonight, she'd have sworn there was no place like that left anywhere in the world. . . .

All those electric lights! She remembered a lot about how it used to be, back before the war—after all, she'd been ten when it went down, old enough to have plenty of memories of what life had once been like—but she'd forgotten how bright those lights had been. The power systems had, of course, been among the first things to go. Daddy had often quoted something some old guy had said, a long time ago at the start of another war, about the lights going off all over the world.

Afterward, for several years, a few technical types had managed to produce a little electricity, running simple generators off windmills or water wheels or even old car engines modified to run on home-distilled alcohol. But the best anyone had been able to do was burn a couple of small light bulbs—the weak current usually producing no more than a yellowish glow, not much better than a candle—and maybe run an old refrigerator, or a fan in hot weather. And she hadn't even heard of anything like that in a long time.

As for that building, with all those long rows of brilliant white lights overhead—no. It just wasn't possible. For one thing, where the hell did they get so many bulbs?

The woman beside her said, "Ah—are you in some sort of gang?"

"What?" Off in her own thoughts, Jack had all but forgotten—what was her name? Ann, that was it. "No," she said, and laughed. "No, I'm no jacker. Well, okay, maybe I've done a little now and then, but strictly free-lance. Solo, you know?" Mad Jack hunts alone, Fat Bob often said, but she didn't repeat that.

Ann didn't ask any more questions, though Jack had the feeling she wanted to. A strange one for sure; she'd gone all to pieces for no good reason, but then she'd pulled it together at the end. That had been a really slick piece of work with the guard.

And that was another thing that didn't add up. A place like that, full of God knew what treasures—the medicines alone would be literally priceless—guarded by one unarmed man? No perimeter defenses, either, not so much as a fence, that was crazy.

Why hadn't some boss jacker taken the place and set himself up as warlord?

More lights appeared now, up ahead, not many but incredibly bright; they were coming into a small town. "Well," Ann said, "here we are."

They rolled slowly down the single street. Nothing was moving, nobody else seemed to be up and about, all the windows were dark, yet lights—electric lights—burned in front of several buildings. Jack stared, amazed. *Now* where the hell were they? There was something familiar about this place, and yet there was no way—

"Decision time." Ann stopped the car and gestured. Through the rain-blurred windshield Jack saw that they had come to an intersection, the blacktop road disappearing under an overpass. "Which way?"

She seemed to expect an answer, but Jack had no idea what to say. After a minute Ann said, "All right, then, south," and swung the car sharply up a curved ramp. Jack got an indistinct glimpse of a sign that seemed to say SANTA FE and a number she didn't catch, but that had to be wrong; her eyesight must be as confused as the rest of her head. No wonder, either, since she had so little practice seeing by this sort of light.

"Maybe we'll have a better chance in town," Ann said as the car picked up speed. "Less conspicuous," she added, and by now they were rolling along a wide multilane slab and even in the rain and the darkness Jack could see that they were going incredibly fast. It was a scary sensation but it was also a hell of a rush; she'd forgotten how fast these things could move.

Which brought up yet another impossibility. Not that a

working car was all that rare a sight; quite a few still putted along the crumbling highways and dirt roads, though they tended to stick to the valleys and the desert flatlands. The crude alcohol fuel didn't have enough power for the steep grades and thin air of the hill country, and passengers had to expect to get out and push now and then. Fat Bob had operated an old pickup truck for a time—he had even let Jack drive it once—and had finally given up and let the damned thing rust. A horse was less trouble, and just as fast except on a downhill, and if it had an accident you could at least eat it.

But this one was streaking along like a buggered roadrunner, and not even slowing when the four-lane—another miracle there, this fantastic smooth road with no breaks or potholes, no brush or even grass growing anywhere on it that Jack could see, and not a single wrecked car in sight either—climbed a rise. And still Jack had the feeling that the little car wasn't going all-out, that it could run a lot faster if Ann decided to go for it. She could feel the power waiting to be released.

Which meant it had to be running on gasoline; and that, of course, was just about the rarest item of all in these parts and probably in the whole world. In fact it was so rare that anybody who did somehow get hold of a supply would play hell finding a car capable of burning it; almost all the working engines had long ago been altered to run on alcohol.

None of which was completely out of the question; there might yet be untouched stashes of gasoline, storage tanks hidden in the ruins of the cities or at remote ranch sites. But what about the effortless way Ann had started the engine, with no downhill grade and no pushing? Whatever the fuel situation, one thing was certain: live batteries were as extinct as dinosaurs and had been for a very long time. Even while Daddy was still alive, the surviving batteries had begun to sulfate—that had been his word, whatever it meant—and lose their capacity to hold a charge. That was how she'd first learned to drive, holding the wheel and feeding gas carefully to the engine, while Daddy pushed the Jeep because she wasn't yet strong enough—

She shook her head against the memories and stared out through the windshield. Now she could see more lights coming from up ahead, over on the other side of the highway, moving in pairs—*more* cars, for God's sake! She said involuntarily, "Jesus!" but her words were drowned out by a sudden monstrous blare, like a giant trumpet, from behind. A moment later a huge truck roared past them in a spectacular dazzle of colored lights and vanished on up the road.

"Assholes," Ann said, a little thickly. "I don't care, fifty-five's plenty fast enough at night and in the rain. Anyway, I'm too doped to drive any faster. Shouldn't be driving at all."

Shaken, Jack leaned back in the seat and rubbed her bad eye. Everything was crazy and it just kept getting crazier.

Well, there were stories, rumors that kept turning up, told by passing travelers and passed on at swap meets or markets or around evening fires. Everybody had heard them: somewhere, it was said, there was a place where people had finally gotten it all together again, all the good life and the good stuff like before the war, electricity and cars and toilet paper and the rest of it, a place where you didn't have to pack a gun and there was plenty to eat. "Back East" was the usual vague alleged location, though occasionally the teller would drop some legendary name from prewar times, New York or Chicago or Boston, and never mind that everybody knew those places had been thoroughly vaporized in the first hours of the war.

Or the magic city might be in Canada, or even Europe or somewhere across the Pacific. Up in Taos last fall, a tall red-bearded drifter had held a big audience spellbound with a really detailed yarn about seeing an Australian submarine off the coast of California, and meeting and talking with its landing party. He had claimed the sailors had told him that space aliens had landed near Melbourne and would soon be coming to help the Americans too; and quite a few people had believed him—including, apparently, a couple of local women, both married, who had disappeared with him into the mountains that night.

That was maybe an extreme example; still, Jack had always regarded such tales as bullshit invented by hustlers and repeated by wishful fools. Pretty much like religions, when you thought about it, and maybe believed in for the same reasons.

And yet that was the only possible explanation. Somehow, she'd wandered off drunk and made her way to such a place; and, since nothing of the sort could possibly exist anywhere in northern New Mexico, she must have traveled for a long time, weeks or more. Which meant she'd had some kind of memory lapse—amnesia, that was the word, she'd read stories about people who couldn't even remember their names. Maybe she'd fallen and hit her head, or been knocked out in a fight. Now there was a comforting thought. You knew you were in trouble when it made you feel better to think you might have brain damage.

"I hate to say this," Ann said, "but I don't know if I can do this much longer. Those pills are really kicking in. I'm starting to fall asleep."

"Pull over to the side of the road and rest," Jack suggested. "I'll stand watch."

"And have some cops show up, wanting to know if we're all right? Please," Ann said, "can't you drive for a little while?"

"Huh uh." Jack didn't even have to think about it. She'd been a fairly good driver at one time—Daddy might have been a bastard, but his teaching methods had been effective in their way—but strictly low-speed stuff, dirt-road and no-road driving, at the wheel of a half-shot Jeep running on bad fuel. In the daylight, with enough time to practice, she felt sure she could master this car and this kind of driving; in fact she itched to try it. But tonight, in the rain? "No way," she said. "I'd just kill us both."

"Shit," Ann said. "Well, then—"

That was when the highway crested a rise and suddenly there it was, up ahead, spread out over what looked to be half the world: a great city of lights, so many and so bright that the glow rose against the sky and reflected off the low clouds. Jack felt her mouth drop open. "Wah," she said, or something like that.

"Santa Fe," Ann observed.

Bullshit, Jack thought and almost said. Santa Fe hell, she knew what Santa Fe looked like, she'd been there enough times. Well, to the outskirts anyway, she'd never worked herself up to actually enter that rat-warren of burned-out ruins, where nothing lived but packs of wild dogs and wilder humans—and not-so-human humans—and enormous, fearless rats. And the only lights that burned there at night were a few scattered fires tended by Christ knew who or what—

But just then the headlights picked up a large sign by the highway, its letters so big and bold there could be no possible mistake:

> ## WELCOME TO
> ## SANTA FE

"I'm sorry," Ann said. "I just can't go on. We'll have to find a place to spend the night."

Jack barely heard her. Reality was slipping through her grasp like a handful of sand. Maybe this was a dream after all. Or maybe Fat Bob had doctored that wine with locoweed. It was like something in one of those science fiction books Daddy used to read, where the hero found himself transported to the future or the past. Come to think of it—no, that was just flat-ass *too* crazy.

Jack decided to give up. After all, she'd seen the end of the world when she was ten years old. Why should anything else shake her?

"I'm going to take the next turnoff," Ann said. "I've got an idea."

◁ △ ▽ ▷

A little while later they were moving slowly down a two-lane road that gradually became a broad street lined with houses and small businesses. Ann seemed to be looking for something. "Ah, there," she said at last, and turned into the entrance of a small parking lot, where an ugly little building bore the mysterious title KWIK-MART. "Time to lose this car. If they don't already have a bulletin out on it, they will any time now."

The parking lot was deserted but brightly lit. Ann tucked the car into the shadowed area near the rear of the building. "Wait here," she told Jack. "You'll cause a panic if you go in looking like that."

She got out and disappeared around the corner of the building, running awkwardly, holding her hands uselessly above her head against the rain. Jack sat and waited, feeling very alone. A car pulled in off the street and stopped beside the row of gas pumps. A woman in a plastic raincoat got out and began pumping gas into the car's tank, evidently helping herself to as much as she wanted. Jack watched with interest but no great surprise. She would have had the same reaction, or lack of it, if a herd of giant purple armadillos had come dancing up the street. Her disbelief circuits seemed to be burned out for the night.

Finally Ann came back, carrying a good-sized plastic bag. "Come on," she said, opening the door on Jack's side. "I've already called a cab."

But then, as Jack started to swing her legs out of the car, "No, wait. Leave the gun, for God's sake, and the knife."

"The hell." Jack put a protective hand on the Smith & Wesson's butt. What was this woman, crazy? This was bad enough without having to go unarmed. "No way," she said. "Don't even say it again."

Ann sighed. "I should have known. . . ." She reached in past Jack and took the keys from the ignition lock. "Let me see, then—"

She went around behind the car and opened the trunk. A moment later she returned, holding up a bright-orange bundle. "You're in luck," she said. "Our friend was the careful type. Had himself a poncho in the trunk, in case he had to change a tire or something in the rain." She shoved the poncho at Jack. "I think it'll come down far enough to hide that cannon. Wish I had one too. This rain's really cold."

Jack climbed out of the car and pulled the poncho over her head, disliking the plastic smell but glad of its protection. It had little snaps along the sides and Ann helped her do them up, arranging the orange folds carefully to conceal the pistol. Jack noticed that her hair was dripping wet and the white uniform had plastered itself against her.

"It won't be long," she assured Jack. "Not at this hour."

Just as she finished speaking, a yellow taxicab turned into the lot. "There we are," Ann said, and picked up the sack from the fender of the red car. "Let me do the talking, all right?"

The driver was a dark-faced little man with sharp features and a small neat mustache. Jack listened without comprehension as he and Ann talked briefly in a language she didn't understand. Spanish, it sounded like; she'd heard it often enough, probably should have taken the trouble to learn to speak it. She leaned against the side of the taxi, feeling suddenly very tired and more than a little woozy, until the driver nodded and stepped back to open the door. She climbed in and slid over and Ann got in beside her.

"I told him to take us to a really cheap motel," Ann said as the driver went around to his own door. "One where no questions are asked. He thinks we're whores, but that's okay."

◄ ▲ ▼ ►

The motel was a row of dingy fake-adobe cabins set back off a narrow potholed side street. Jack waited in the cab while Ann went to the door where a neon OFFICE sign flickered. The driver turned and looked back at Jack. "Joo wanta buy some blow?" he inquired. "Good cheet, baby."

Having no idea what he was saying, Jack didn't reply. After a minute he shrugged and turned back around and lit a cigarette. By now Ann had disappeared inside the motel office. Jack waited, trying not to fall asleep. Just as the driver opened his window to toss out the butt of his cigarette, Ann reappeared, splashing across the puddled driveway. She yanked the taxi door open—the driver showed no interest in opening it for her—and said, "All right, I've got us a room."

As Jack got out the driver said something in Spanish. Ann replied in the same language, and handed him a couple of crumpled bills. There was a quick angry-sounding exchange; the driver seemed to be getting difficult. Ann said in English, "Look, that's more than enough, even if you did wait—"

Fuck this, Jack thought irritably. Time to get in out of the rain. She stepped past Ann and flipped the poncho back and pulled the Magnum and pointed at the driver's face. "Fuck off," she said, not raising her voice. "Now."

The driver said something under his breath, but he didn't argue; he put the cab in reverse and backed rapidly out of the drive, spraying gravel and water from under the cab's tires, not even pausing to roll up his window. Several shouted Spanish words, probably uncomplimentary, drifted back on the rainy breeze as he roared away.

"Jesus," Ann said. "You're a menace, you know? Well, let's get inside before you start a massacre."

The room was small and not very clean, and when Jack stretched out on the bed she could feel lumps and depressions in the wornout mattress, but right now she didn't care. It took a real effort to make herself sit up again and haul off her boots.

"Damn," she said, yawning, "I'm going to crash for a couple of weeks. Maybe when I wake up things will make more sense."

Ann was sitting in the single chair beside the bed, rummaging inside the bag she had brought from the Kwik-Mart. "Do you want to eat something first?" she asked. "I bought a few things— just junk food, not very nutritious, but better than nothing."

Jack thought about it. "Yeah," she said, "now you mention it, I'm about half starved. What have you got?"

"Microwaved burritos," Ann said, handing over a small oblong packet. "And a bag of chips, and a six-pack. Want a beer? I probably shouldn't have alcohol, with all these drugs in my system, but it's a little late to start being prudent."

Jack nodded, her mouth too full to speak. She hadn't realized how famished she was; the first bite of the burrito—which actually tasted pretty good, though it needed spicing up—had awakened a raging hunger. She held out her free hand and Ann passed her a can of beer.

The beer was something of a disappointment. She'd heard her father and other older men reminisce fondly about the cold beer of the old days and how they missed it; and she'd expected something really fantastic, but this stuff was so thin and watery she wouldn't have recognized it as beer at all if Ann hadn't told her. Not like the beer of Taos . . . but still, it was nice and cold and made a good drink to wash down the burrito.

And the potato chips, when Ann passed them over, were enough to make this whole insane adventure worthwhile. "MmmHMM," she mumbled, savoring the long-forgotten salty-greasy crispness. "Haven't had these since I was a kid. Got another of those burritos?"

For a short time there was no sound in the room but crunchings and munchings and the crackle of paper and plastic bags, punctuated a couple of times by the pop and hiss of opening beer cans. At last Jack dropped the empty potato-chip sack, tossed an empty beer can across the room without aiming at any particular target, and stood up.

She had already removed her gunbelt and draped it over the scarred little nightstand, the holster strap unsnapped and tucked out of the way and the revolver's butt ready to hand. Now she undid her camo pants and pulled them down and kicked them off, and shucked the sleeveless sweatshirt up over her head and dropped it on top of the pants. She wore nothing underneath. She knew the other woman was watching her but that was all right, in fact it might have been a turnon if she hadn't been so tired. She took off her eyepatch and laid it on the nightstand beside the pistol. "Me for bed," she said, pulling back the sheet and the thin worn blanket. "Coming?"

Ann had taken off the nurse's shoes but still wore the white uniform. She fingered the damp fabric of the top and made a face. "I was hoping this would dry. Oh, well—"

She took off the top and the baggy-assed pants and hung them over the back of the chair. She had a nice body, Jack observed, with really fine legs, but she looked as if she needed to get out more. Maybe she'd been sick. She hesitated for a moment, looking at Jack and then down at herself, and then she shrugged and hooked her thumbs under the elastic of her panties and slid them down too. Jack admired the curve of her haunches as she bent to pick them up. She'd even shaved her legs, it looked like; that was something you didn't see much any more. She turned and started toward the bed and then stopped, looking Jack square in the face.

"I just want to sleep," she said. "You understand?"

"Sure," Jack told her. "Me too. Hell, I'm too wiped out to jump anybody."

Ann nodded and switched off the light. Jack felt the bed creak and dip as she climbed in. "I hope you don't snore," she said as she pulled up the covers and rolled over, turning her back to Jack. "But then I'll never hear it if you do, not tonight. Good night, then."

Jack lay still for a couple of minutes, enjoying the smooth clean feel of the sheets against her naked skin. Then, with a quick movement and without pausing to think about it, she slid over against Ann, breasts to back and belly to bottom, putting an arm over her and snuggling close. For a second Ann's body went stiff and Jack thought she was going to object; but then she heard a sigh, and felt the other woman relax, and a moment later a hand closed tightly over her own.

And that was how they fell asleep at last, pressed together like tired children, while the rain continued to rattle against the window and the early-morning traffic began to hiss and rumble down the wet street outside.

chapter seven

Ann awoke to a confused awareness that the light was wrong, too dim even for nighttime in the ward and surely it had to be morning by now, there couldn't be more of this night left, more of these dreams. . . . Then her vision and her mind cleared simultaneously and she said, *"God!"* and sat up and swung her legs over the side of the bed and sat for a moment staring around her at the grubby little room, while beside her Jack rolled over and made drowsy complaining noises into her pillow.

She didn't sit there long; powerful and urgent internal pressures were asserting priority. She got up, swayed a little, and went lurching into the bathroom. As she seated herself on the toilet a sudden stab of pain shot up from her anus, dispelling any lingering uncertainty: whatever was going on, this wasn't a dream. Dreams didn't leave you with a sore butthole.

Back in the bedroom, standing beside the chair, she found and pulled on her panties, grimacing to herself as she did so; by now they were none too fresh. The white uniform pants still felt damp so she left them off for now and settled for the top alone. As she buttoned the jacket she felt something shift in the pockets and remembered her little collection of stolen medications.

She took the plastic bottles out and looked at them, wondering if she shouldn't take something. Surprisingly, she felt no great need. Her head hurt a bit, and her stomach was a trifle uneasy; there was a loathsome taste in her mouth, and when she held her hands up before her face she could see a slight tremor. But she'd had worse with ordinary hangovers, and her mind was clearer than it had been in a long time.

Still, she went back into the bathroom and washed a Xanax down with tap water, just on general principles. After a moment's hesitation she took one of the Lomazine tablets as well; something seemed to be making her feel better and she didn't want it to stop. She repocketed the bottles and returned to the bedroom, wishing for a shower but unwilling to risk waking the other woman with the sound.

She found herself looking in the direction of the bed, where Jack had turned to face the wall, dragging the covers with her in an untidy heap, exposing a smooth expanse of back and hip. The light that filtered past the badly hung blinds made soft highlights on her skin. Ann felt her cheeks flush as memory returned. Which was silly, of course, nothing to be embarrassed about; but then she realized that the prickly sensation wasn't caused by embarrassment. Not entirely, at least, and the warm rush of blood was not confined to her face. . . .

Well, she told herself a little defensively, and what's the big deal? You got into bed with another woman, both of you naked, and it turned you on a little bit; okay, maybe more than a little bit, and maybe you wouldn't mind climbing back into that bed with her right now, and why the hell not?

It wasn't a way she'd ever felt before, barring a couple of the usual early-puberty girl-girl crushes, but she didn't find it particularly disturbing. Not compared with some of the feelings she'd had to deal with in the last few years—

Abruptly she turned away from the bed and went to the window and pried open a crack between two blind slats and peered out. The rain had stopped, but the sky had not yet cleared; the light outside was gray and chilly looking. Another day in warm, sunny New Mexico, but what time was it? She wished Jack had gotten the nurses' watches, or that she had thought to take Brady's.

The television. She could get the time from that.

The set was small and old—it must, she thought, go back at least to Glenn's administration—and cheap even when it was new. When she switched it on it made a nasty crackling sound. She glanced over her shoulder at the sleeping woman on the bed, and turned the sound down as a man in a suit appeared on the screen, waving one arm at a lot full of cars.

There was no remote; Ann stood in front of the set and clicked the plastic knob from channel to channel, looking for something that would give her the time. The color was off register, too much red, making everyone look badly sunburned.

She recognized some of the shows, more or less—the women in the ward had been compulsive TV-watchers—but she didn't know their time slots. She knobbed on, ignoring the glowing faces and the faux-sincere voices, till she found the weather channel. At the bottom of the screen, below the columns of city names and temperatures, she read: WED MAY 13 10:38:26 A.M.

That was about what she'd guessed, but she wasn't happy to be proved right. "Checkout time twelve o'clock," the night clerk had said, and this was the sort of place that didn't cut the guests any slack. Time was definitely running out.

She reached up to turn the set off, somehow got hold of the wrong knob, and instead flipped to the next channel, where a middle-aged man with wavy hair and a shrill thin woman were shouting at each other. She said, "Shit!" under her breath and started to switch off the set, but then behind her Jack's voice said, "Oh, hey, wow, TV!"

She turned and saw the other woman sitting up in bed, staring wide-eyed and open-mouthed at the television set. The covers lay loosely about her waist, exposing firm pink-tipped breasts. Ann found herself momentarily unable to breathe properly.

"Damn," Jack said in a soft wondering voice, "I'd nearly forgotten about TV. Haven't seen it since I was a kid."

"No?" Ann glanced back at the screen, mainly in order to hide her own expression. "Well, I don't suppose you've missed much. I hardly ever watch it myself—"

"No," Jack said, so sharply that Ann turned again to look at her. "That's not what I mean, God damn it, that's not it at all."

She gestured at the screen, where the disagreeable hosts were still pretending to argue over some unidentifiable question. "Look, where I'm from—*when* I'm from, Christ, I don't know the words, maybe there *aren't* any words for this—"

Her hand came up to rub at the cruel mass of scar tissue where her left eye should have been. "I haven't watched TV since I was ten," she said, speaking more slowly now, "because that's how old I was when they had this big fucking war that blew everything to shit. The world I live in, we haven't had television or much else since seventy-three."

She looked about the dingy room. "And I still don't know what's going on, but it's obvious as hell that in your world—I figure this must be your world, you get around okay in it and nothing seems to surprise you—it didn't go down that way."

Ann opened her mouth, reconsidered, and closed it. Let the woman talk; interrupting her might not be safe.

"You know," Jack went on, "my father used to read a lot of these science fiction books. Even after the war, he'd find them in old stores and libraries and drag them home. And I read them too, sometimes, even though I didn't always understand them and he didn't like to explain, he was a pretty impatient—"

She paused, her face darkening for a moment; but then she shrugged. "Anyway," she said, "some of these stories, they had this idea of parallel universes. Or time tracks, they called it sometimes, or alternate realities. Like somewhere in another dimension or something, there's this world where the South won the Civil War, or Hitler died when he was a baby, or whatever. You know what I'm talking about?"

"More or less." Ann kept her face and voice carefully neutral; she even managed not to wince at 'dimension'—really, if these people had to write that stuff, couldn't they at least learn to use terms correctly? "I've read very little science fiction," she said, "but I'm familiar with the concept you mean."

"Okay, then." Jack spread her hands. "I think that's what we've got here. Somehow, and I'm fucked if I can figure how, I crossed over from my world into yours."

"Ah." Ann took a deep breath. "Well, um—"

"Hey," Jack said, "I know what you're thinking. Crazy old one-eyed broad, she's lost it, right? Out of her skull. Huh." She snorted. "Listen, I may be wrong about what's going on—but what I'm telling you about the world I'm from, it's *real*."

She touched a fingertip to the scarred ruin of her left eye. "I got this when I was sixteen years old, in a fire fight with a bunch of jackers—you don't even know what that means, do you? Looters, bandits, outlaws you could say except that doesn't mean much when there's no law—"

She stared at Ann with her good eye. "It happened just a few miles from where we are now. Right outside of Santa Fe," she said, "but not this one, nothing like this one at all. The Santa Fe I know, we wouldn't have gotten to spend the night in a nice clean room with lights and TV. We'd have had our hands full just staying alive till sunrise. Been to Albuquerque lately?"

The question caught Ann by surprise. "Last winter," she said blankly. "For a week, last winter, visiting friends. Why?"

"Where I come from," Jack said grimly, "if you'd spent a week in Albuquerque last winter, you might not be feeling too good by now. Oh, it's nothing like Santa Fe, in fact it's down-right peaceful. Just a little on the radioactive side, is all. They say the level's lower now, but I don't know anybody who wants to find out. Wouldn't even be anything there," she added, "only the Russians were lousy shots or their missiles weren't very good or something, and they missed Albuquerque—I guess they were trying to take out the airbase—and nuked the hills northwest of town instead."

She tossed the covers back and clambered out of bed, rubbing her bad eye. "And that's just a couple of details, I could go on and on. Maybe you've got some problems here—well, Christ, obviously something's wrong or they wouldn't have had you locked up in that place—but, baby, you don't have a clue how bad it can get. . . . Is that the can, in there? My teeth are floating."

Ann watched as she crossed the room, bare haunches switching, and disappeared into the bathroom. "Boy," she called through the open doorway, "now this is something I could get used to—"

Mad as the proverbial hatter; Ann had guessed as much since last night—there was, after all, no other possible explanation for the one-eyed woman's presence inside the locked and guarded complex at Spanish Hills. Clearly Jack, if that was really her name, was locked into an advanced and elaborate delusional system. Ann had heard many such fantasies, invariably related with the same absolute seriousness, during her various stays at the hospital; she had learned to smile and nod and tune them out, and above all never to challenge their reality.

Probably this one had been brought in by the police—unusual at a fancy private institution like Spanish Hills, but it did happen now and then; the scruffiest characters sometimes turned out to have important family connections—and somehow got free.

Ann looked across the room, at the big revolver lying on the nightstand, and thought unwillingly of the questions it raised. Just how had Jack gotten her hands on that gun? Was Duncan Brady the only person she'd killed last night?

"All *right*," Jack said, emerging from the bathroom. "Never mind the other fancy stuff, just give me a warm place to pee."

Watching her move naked about the room, bending to retrieve her scattered clothing from the floor, Ann felt her own knees go weak. And it wasn't, she realized, just physical attraction; what she was feeling toward the other woman—even knowing what she was, what she had to be—went far beyond any simple sexual urge.

Which was too damned bad, her own life being in more than enough of a mess without falling for a madwoman. But then it didn't really matter, not any more, things had gone past any possibility of recovery and what the hell? Free fall might be kind of fun, even if that final sudden stop was going to be a bitch—

Voices penetrated her consciousness, a steady babble just behind her head. The television set; she still hadn't turned it off. Irritably she turned and reached for the volume knob, but then the unpleasant man on the screen said, "And now let's go to our local affiliates for the latest news in your area."

Fancy spinning graphics appeared, to a brief fanfare of theme music, and resolved themselves into a program logo. Ann stepped back; after a moment's hesitation she went and sat down on the bed. She had a feeling there was going to be at least one local news item of great interest.

Sure enough, the TV now showed a neatly coiffed young woman seated behind a white-topped desk and gazing earnestly into the camera. "Good morning," she said. "Our top story: a man is dead, apparently slain in the course of an escape from Spanish Hills Psychiatric Hospital during the early hours of this morning. According to the sheriff's office, Duncan Brady, an orderly on night duty, was the victim of what is described as a brutal knife attack. Exact time of death has not yet been determined."

Behind the woman's head appeared a not very distinct face-on photo of Brady, probably from hospital files. He looked even uglier than in real life. Coming around the end of the bed, adjusting her eyepatch, Jack said, "Hey, isn't that—"

"Brady's death is believed to be connected with the escape of a patient with a history of violent behavior." The photo gave place to a head-and-shoulders of a skinny, staring-eyed woman with long wild black hair. It took Ann a moment to recognize herself. "Police are now searching for Jacqueline Ann Lucas, a patient at Spanish Hills, who allegedly escaped at about the same time that Brady is thought to have been slain."

"Jesus." Jack sat down beside Ann and whistled softly. "It's you, all right. How about that?"

The young woman said, "Roger Phillips is on the scene now. Roger, is there any new information?"

The picture cut to a waist-up shot of a pale, thin, bespectacled man in a dark suit—Ann thought he looked like an underweight Clark Kent—standing in the parking lot in front of the Spanish Hills complex. His right hand clutched a phallic-looking microphone.

"Well, Liz," he said gravely, "some questions still remain as to just what happened here this morning. According to the sheriff's department, Brady was stabbed to death. But three witnesses say the escaping patient definitely had a gun." His brow furrowed theatrically. "Two nurses were allegedly made to disrobe at gunpoint, then locked in a storage closet. The security guard at the front desk was also allegedly threatened with a handgun."

He paused for a dramatic half-beat. "Also, there seems to be some uncertainty as to just how many people were involved in the escape. A hospital spokesperson states that only one patient, Jacqueline Ann Lucas, is missing. The security guard, however, claims he is certain there was a second woman with the escapee. Also, the nurses' descriptions apparently do not quite match that of the missing patient. So it appears possible there may have been outside help involved."

The young woman with the pricey hair reappeared. Ann's picture still loomed behind her. "Thank you, Roger," she said. "Police are asking that everyone be on the lookout for the alleged escapee. Jacqueline Ann Lucas is described as a Caucasian female, thirty-seven years old, five feet nine inches tall, slender in build, with black hair and hazel eyes. She may be dressed in a nurse's uniform—"

She stopped suddenly, her eyes flicking downward at something on the desk. "This just in," she said then. "The vehicle used in the escape, a red Ford Antares belonging to the security guard, has been found abandoned beside a Santa Fe convenience store."

She paused and cleared her throat. "We'll keep you posted on any further developments in this case. Meanwhile, police advise that the alleged escapee is armed and should be considered extremely dangerous. If you have any information, please call the sheriff's office immediately. Do not try to apprehend this person yourself."

"You got that right, bitch," Jack muttered.

"Coming up next," the newswoman went on, "a quick look at this morning's weather. But first this message."

Another young woman replaced her on the screen, smiling

prettily and holding up a small white container. "Troubled by vaginal dryness? Now there's help—"

"Wow," Jack said as Ann strode across the room to switch the set off. "You're famous. Sounds like they're kind of confused, though."

"Let's hope they stay that way," Ann told her. "But I don't think we'd better count on it."

"No shit," Jack agreed. "Never assume the other bastards are stupid. Daddy used to say that."

She looked Ann over. "One thing for sure, you can't go out now dressed like that. Maybe I should go get you something," she said. "Doesn't sound like they're looking for me yet. But, well, fuck." She made a helpless gesture. "I'm not even sure I remember how to handle money."

"No," Ann said immediately. God knew what might happen if Jack went out on her own. If she didn't come back—"No," Ann repeated. "Don't leave me alone here. Please."

"All right," Jack said reassuringly. "Like I said, I wouldn't know what I was doing anyway."

She rubbed her bad eye. "But what *do* we do? Hole up for the rest of the day, I guess? Then after dark we can slip out and, I dunno, steal a car, make a run for it."

Ann found herself nodding. Well, it was as sound an agenda as any she could come up with. "I'd better go down and pay for another night," she said. "It's not very long till noon. I don't want the management taking an interest in us."

Jack looked dubious. "I guess you have to, but—" Her face brightened suddenly. "Hey, look, you can change clothes with me. Just till you get back, right?"

Ann started to protest, but Jack was already crossing her arms and skinning off the sleeveless sweatshirt. "Here," she said. "Let me get these boots off—"

"No," Ann said, "really, that's all right." She hoped Jack wouldn't push it any farther. She didn't want to have to explain that she didn't trust herself right now, that she didn't know what might happen if they both got naked again.

But all Jack said was, "Well, okay. At least take the shirt, though. That white top's a dead giveaway."

"All right." Ann turned her back, mostly to hide her face, and unbuttoned the uniform jacket with none-too-steady fingers. Tossing it onto the chair, she pulled the sleeveless sweatshirt over her head and tugged it down. It fit almost perfectly.

The white pants still felt damp when she pulled them on, but it didn't matter now. She started toward the door, stopped, and turned back to retrieve the nurse's jacket. "Almost forgot," she said, digging Brady's money out of the pocket.

At the door she paused again and looked at Jack. "Stay put," she said. "I'll be right back."

◄　▲　▼　►

The motel manager was dark and very fat, with glossy black hair and an unidentifiable accent. His expression, as Ann explained they would be staying another night, was so inscrutable as to constitute no expression at all. He took the bills she handed him, stowed them in a metal box, and said, "Room will be cleaned at two o'clock."

"No," Ann said quickly. "We don't want to be disturbed."

"So?" He shrugged microscopically. "As you wish."

Leaving the office, she spotted a couple of vending machines. She fed in dollar bills and, after a series of annoying MAKE ANOTHER SELECTION messages, succeeded in purchasing an assortment of canned soft drinks and several ridiculously small bags of salty snacks. Bending to take a Pepsi out of the slot, she caught a glimpse of her pants legs and felt momentarily sick; last night's rain had washed away most of the bloodstains, but several good-sized rust-brown spots still marked the white material. She wondered if the manager had noticed. Too late now to worry about it; too late, she thought almost cheerfully, stepping along the broken concrete walk, to worry about anything.

◄   ▲   ▼   ►

Jack opened the door in response to her clumsy hands-full knock. She had her gun in her hand. Stepping inside, kicking the door shut with her heel, Ann said, "Do you mind?"

"Just being careful." Jack sat down on the bed and laid the pistol on a pillow beside her. "Oh, great, you got some food."

"I'm not sure I'd call it that," Ann told her, dumping her armload of cans and packets on the bed, "but help yourself."

She peeled off the sweatshirt and held it out. Jack said, "Hell, I wasn't in any hurry. Looked good on you," she added, her voice muffled as she pulled the shirt over her head. "We must be the same size. In fact we look a good deal alike, don't we? No wonder those nurses thought I was you."

Ann considered it. There was some resemblance at that; at least they seemed roughly similar in height and build. But she studied their reflections in the mirror over the dilapidated dresser, comparing Jack's strong tanned features with her own pallid hollow-eyed face, and shook her head. "I can't see it," she admitted. "But thanks."

She re-donned the white jacket and dropped into the chair. "Hand me one of those sodas," she requested. "And a bag of chips."

They sat for a time without talking, munching chips and washing them down with fizzy pop. At least the drinks contained a good deal of caffeine; Ann had been yearning for a cup of coffee. The Xanax she had taken was starting to make her drowsy.

At last Jack lobbed an empty Pepsi can at the wastebasket, missed, and fired off an unself-conscious belch. "Shit, that's good, I was so dry . . . hey," she said, "I just remembered. Didn't those TV assholes say your name was Jacqueline Ann?"

Ann nodded. "Damn," Jack said happily. "Mine too."

"Really?"

"No shit," Jack assured her. "Jacqueline Ann Younger—"

That was when the door crashed open and a voice bellowed, *"Police! Everybody freeze!"*

A uniformed policeman burst into the room, holding a pistol in a two-hand grip. There were others behind him, quite a few it looked like, but Ann didn't get more than a glance before Jack shot him.

The bang was enormous, trapped and amplified by the small room; Ann felt the blast against the skin of her face. The cop stumbled backwards and fell, the gun falling from his hands and skittering across the floor. Jack fired again through the open doorway but the others had already jumped back out of sight.

Through the ringing in her ears Ann heard herself screaming.

Jack said, "Shut up," and, when she did, "Get his gun."

The pistol lay a few feet away, next to the dresser. Ann got to her feet and went to pick it up. Jack said, "Careful. Don't give them a clear shot at you through that door."

The gun was big and gray and blocky; it felt different from Jack's revolver. Ann stepped back, holding it carefully, wondering numbly what she was supposed to do with it.

"Check his belt," Jack said. "He ought to be carrying more ammo—no, wait!" The cop's head had moved slightly. "Stay back. He's still alive."

The cop's eyes blinked a couple of times. He raised his head and stared at Jack, or rather at the gun in her hand. "Easy," she told him. "Don't move. I swear I'll blow your head off."

He was a tall, well-built young man with freckles and curly red hair; not bad-looking, except that he seemed a bit thick about the upper body. Jack grinned at him. "Vest?"

He nodded, wide-eyed. He seemed to be trying to speak, but no sound came out. Ann guessed the bullet must have knocked the wind out of him.

"Take it off," Jack said. "Throw it to her. The belt, too."

He sat up, moving very cautiously and keeping his hands in sight. Without taking his eyes off Jack's gun, he undid the bulletproof vest and slid it across the floor toward Ann. While he was unbuckling his gunbelt Jack said, "Put it on."

It took Ann a moment to realize she was talking to her. She started to refuse, but this was obviously no time to argue with Jack. She laid the pistol on the dresser and struggled into the vest. It wasn't as heavy as it looked. She picked up the gunbelt, started to put it on, decided the hell with that, and slung it over her left shoulder. "What now?" she asked Jack.

"If you're smart," the cop interjected, "you'll put those weapons down before you make things any worse."

His voice was hoarse and not very strong; he still seemed to be having trouble breathing. He tried a phony smile. "Come on, nobody wants to hurt you. We just want to get you some help—"

Jack's gun went off again. Ann jumped and cringed. The cop said, "Jesus!" A fresh raw gouge had appeared in the floor next to his feet. Jack said, "Quiet, asshole. I'm trying to think."

Ann said, "Please don't kill him."

Before Jack could reply there was a great roar outside: "YOU IN THERE! THIS IS THE POLICE!"

The amplification—a powerhorn, Ann guessed—was so bad the words were barely distinguishable. Actually it sounded more like, "YVH IXH XHEHH! XHIX IX XHE VHLEEX!" Jack cursed and went to the window, as the voice continued: "THROW OUT YOUR WEAPONS AND COME OUT WITH YOUR HANDS ON TOP OF YOUR HEAD!"

"You're surrounded," the cop on the floor said. "You don't have—okay, okay." He raised his hands hastily. "Forget it."

Jack aimed her revolver at him. "Go stand in the doorway. Try to run and I'll drop you."

Reluctantly, looking unhappy, he got up and went to the open door. "Hey," he shouted. "It's me, Hoban. Don't shoot."

Someone outside called out, the words unclear. "I can't," Hoban answered. "They've got me covered."

Ann looked down at the phone on the dresser. Any minute,

she thought, it would start ringing. That was what always happened next in the movies; somebody got on the phone and tried to talk the bad guys into giving up, or at least releasing their hostages. Was Hoban a hostage? For that matter, was she now officially a bad guy? She wanted to take another Xanax—maybe more, in fact she could do with a handful of pills right now—but the jacket pockets were covered by the bulletproof vest.

"Regular fucking army out there," Jack said, peering out the window.

The phone did ring, then. Ann looked down at it a moment and then picked it up. "Yes?" she said politely.

"Dr. Lucas?" The voice in her ear was male, smooth and reassuring. "Is everyone all right in there?"

She didn't answer. After a moment the man went on: "I know who you are, Dr. Lucas. You're an intelligent, educated woman, a scientist. I know you don't want anyone else to get hurt." He modulated down to a slightly lower register, warm and concerned as a burial-insurance salesman. "Why don't we—"

The phone cord came loose from the wall with only a modest pull. Ann looked down at the dangling end. She hadn't known she was going to do that. She dropped the phone into the wastebasket.

Hoban looked back over his shoulder. "Bad move." His face was beaded with sweat. "You ladies—uh, women—better give it up. I'm telling you, the lieutenant out there, he's liable to do anything. Real fucking cowboy, excuse my language."

Outside the bullhorn sputtered into life again: "RELEASE

THE OFFICER IMMEDIATELY. COME OUT WITH YOUR HANDS UP."

Hoban made his move then, a big wild dive outward and to one side. Jack's shot chewed splinters from the door facing but he was already out of sight. There was an immediate blast of gunfire from outside, the other cops covering his escape. Bullets snapped and popped through the door and Jack cried, "Shit!" as the window beside her shattered into a million fragments.

When the shooting died away Jack looked at Ann. "Okay," she said. "Straight up: we're fucked."

She gestured with the barrel of her revolver. "They got us outnumbered, outgunned, out-everything. So—you want out of this now, go ahead. I'll hold off while you walk out the door."

"What about you?" Ann asked.

"Huh uh." Jack shook her head decisively. "Nobody's locking me up, baby. Might even wind up in a place like where they had you. I couldn't stand it a week . . . but hell," she said, "that's no reason for you to go down too. Adios, and all that."

Ann picked up the cop's pistol from the dresser. "How do you use this thing?"

Jack's eyebrows went up. "You're staying? Hey, you don't have to do this—"

"Yes I do. I'm not going back."

The pistol felt very heavy in her hand. She wondered if she could hit anything with it. It didn't matter; there was only one target she intended to shoot and it was one she could hardly miss. As she had told Jack, she wasn't going back.

She felt no fear, only a profound relief. No cure? I got your cure right here, Dr. Peters. . . .

"COME OUT NOW," the bullhorn blared. "THIS IS YOUR LAST WARNING."

Ann took a step toward Jack. "Listen," she said, "we don't have much time, and there's something I want to tell you—"

Something small and black flew through the door and rolled across the floor, trailing bluish-white smoke. Ann said, "What," and then Jack's arm swept her off her feet, and then there was a huge red and black noise and everything went away.

chapter eight

Jack regained consciousness with warm sunlight on her face. She opened her eye and found herself staring straight up into bright empty blue framed by ragged-edged darkness. "Wha," she said, blinking, realizing now that she was looking at a patch of sky through a hole in a roof.

She sat up fast and instantly regretted it; her head protested by exploding and showering pieces of skull everywhere. Or at least that was how it felt. She fought down a brief wrenching surge of nausea. Jesus, what a *hangover* . . . but then memory kicked in and she looked around in amazement at the wreckage that surrounded her. Boy, she thought dazedly, they sure blew this place to shit.

Then the jumbled pieces of memory finished interlocking and she saw that wasn't right, no little pissant stun grenade could have done that much damage and besides, this place had been wrecked a long, long time. Dust covered the rubble and the air smelled of rot and bird shit; weedy vines crept up one wall.

What in the name of Christ—?

She sat for a moment trying to collect herself, rubbing her bad eye with dusty knuckles. Her eyepatch had slipped up onto her forehead and she pulled it down into place. She hurt all over, as if she'd lost a fight or fallen down a rocky hillside.

"Ann," she said suddenly, and scrambled to her feet, heedless now of the pains in her head and elsewhere.

She saw the other woman almost immediately, lying only a few feet away; a pile of fallen roof fragments had blocked her view. "Ann?" she said again as she picked her way over the wreckage. "Hey, are you okay?"

Ann lay on her side in a near-fetal curl, knees almost to her chest. One outflung hand still clutched Hoban's pistol. Her face was streaked with dust and grime. Her eyes were open and blank. For an instant Jack's heart stumbled but then Ann's head turned and the large hazel eyes met hers. "Hello," Ann said after a moment. "Are we still alive?"

"Seems like it," Jack replied, feeling relief wash through her in a warm flood. "Either that or Hell's a lot more run-down place than I always heard."

Ann sat up and immediately grabbed her head. "*Ooohhh,*" she groaned. "My God, look at this mess! Were they crazy?" She stopped and stared at Jack. "And where are they now? Don't tell me they just went away—"

"Back up," Jack told her. "It wasn't the cops did this. Did you get a look at that thing they threw in?"

Ann nodded, and winced. "Concussion grenade," Jack said. "Small one at that, really not much more than a big firecracker. Just enough bang to stun somebody, long enough to let you move in and grab them, but no permanent damage. The military developed them for taking prisoners, and I guess the police copied the idea. Slavers like to use them, where I come from."

She waved a hand at the wreckage that surrounded them. "Anyway, take a closer look. This is the same room we were in—

at least it's the same size, same layout, that thing behind you looks like a piece of the same bed. But you can see it got wrecked a long time ago. I mean, we're talking years and *years.*"

Ann nodded again, more cautiously. "You're right. Of course." She was looking very confused. Jack didn't blame her. "But then," she said, "what happened? What's happening?"

Jack was studying the rubble on the floor. A gleam of metal caught her eye and she bent and retrieved her Magnum from between a couple of rot-grayed timbers, where it must have fallen from her hand. "Fuck if I know," she admitted, straightening, wiping the dust off the revolver, swinging the cylinder out and removing the three fired cartridge cases—two of them wasted, damn it, she couldn't afford that kind of stupid shooting—and replacing them with live rounds from her belt. "Only thing I can come up with—but hell, that's just too damn weird. Hang on a minute."

Moving carefully, trying not to dislodge anything—the rest of the derelict cabin looked ready to come down any minute—she clambered over the littered floor and peered out the wreckage-choked doorway, the heavy revolver ready in her hand. After a moment she said, "Oh, shit."

She didn't have much of a view from the doorway, but it was enough to confirm the hunch in her aching head. Just, she thought, when you think it can't possibly get any crazier . . .

Beyond the door was a scene of low-rent desolation. The row of little cabins lay in ruins, roofs collapsed, windows black and glassless, doors hanging half off their hinges or lying on the rubble-covered sidewalk. The walls still stood, their bogus-adobe surfaces pocked by what looked like bullet strikes. Graffiti had been painted or chalked here and there: NAVAJO BAD BOYS RULE. RAMON AMA CONSUELA. LUIS ES PUTO. FUCK THE RUSSIANS. FUCK NIXON. FUCK YOU. REPENT FOR THE END IS AT HAND. CHINGA TU MADRE. The crude lettering was faded almost to illegibility.

The gravel parking lot was holed and gullied, covered with litter and patches of straggly weeds. A couple of wrecked cars stood nearby, stripped of wheels and just about everything else.

From where she stood she couldn't see much of what lay beyond the motel grounds, but it didn't look a lot better. A big delivery truck lay on its side in the street, blocking both lanes. Past that, on the far side of the street, Jack could just make out a long one-story building, its big windows smashed and empty. The remains of a large sign still stood on its roof:

```
ACE AUTO PA
```

Behind her Ann said, "What is it? What do you see?"

"I got good news and bad news," Jack said without looking around. "The good news is, I think I just got back home."

She turned, then, and looked at Ann. "That's the bad news too."

"What?" Ann had gotten to her feet now; she stood amid the rubble, weaving very slightly, rubbing her left hand over her face. Her right hand still held the cop's pistol.

"Could be I'm wrong," Jack added. "I better have a look around."

Ann was looking more confused by the second. But she said, "That makes sense. I still don't understand, but looking around makes sense. I'll go with you."

She looked down at the gun in her hand, as if noticing it for the first time. "Do I need to bring this?"

"If I'm right," Jack said grimly, "and I bet I am, there's nothing you're going to need as much." She holstered the Magnum and held out her hand. "Give it here, let me have a closer look. *Careful*, God damn it!"

But a closer look wasn't much help; the big automatic was a new one to Jack. It was certainly the ugliest pistol she'd ever seen—it looked, in fact, like an overgrown toy—though the balance was nice, and it pointed well. It was lighter than it looked; it couldn't, she judged, weigh more than half as much as her .357. She didn't see any markings at first, but finally she spotted a discreet little inscription at the top of the handgrip: GLOCK AUSTRIA.

"Never saw one like this before," she admitted to Ann. "Must be one they developed later on—" She found the release and popped the clip out. It appeared to hold an amazing number of rounds. She thumbed the top cartridge free and studied the marks on its base. "Nine millimeter," she said. "Damn, look at that nice clean brass."

She replaced the cartridge and slapped the clip back home. "Far as I can tell, this thing doesn't have a safety—funny, autos usually do—so keep your finger clear of that trigger till you're ready to shoot."

She handed the pistol back to Ann. "What happened to that fool's gunbelt?"

"I don't know." Ann glanced around. "I must have lost it."

"Too bad. We could have used the ammo." She drew her revolver again. "Then if we do get into a fight, don't go apeshit and start throwing lead all over. Keep cool and pick your shots."

She paused, looking Ann up and down, considering. The woman definitely wasn't dressed for the occasion. The white pants were far too visible and didn't give enough protection; the jacket was nearly as bad, but at least it was partly covered by the bulletproof vest. That was the best thing she had going for her, that vest, though it also increased her value as a target. Plenty of people in Jack's situation would have killed her for it by now.

At any rate, the white uniform wasn't actually all that white anymore—mostly a dingy gray, streaked and spotted with dirt; in fact the material had begun to camouflage itself with the grime of its surroundings—and the nurse's shoes looked solid and comfortable. Better, Jack reflected, than her own boots, which were meant for riding rather than extended walking.

Not that this particular walk was likely to be all that lengthy. She'd be very damn lucky indeed if she survived long enough to get sore feet.

"Let's go, then," she said, and turned back and began climbing over the mound of loose debris that half-blocked the doorway, hoping Ann would at least remember to watch where she pointed that pistol. Just my luck, she thought, go through all this shit and then get shot in the ass by my new girlfriend.

She led the way across the parking lot, hearing Ann's crunching footfalls behind her, wincing a little at the noise, not from any concern about giving away their presence—anyone or anything that happened to be in the neighborhood must surely know by now that they were there—but because it interfered with her own hearing. Which wasn't all that great right now anyway; her ears still rang from the explosion of the stun grenade.

She didn't really think there was anything to worry about, not just yet; there was nothing here of any value even to the most desperate ruin-squatters, no shelter for anything bigger than birds and snakes and small animals. And she wasn't getting the prickly-neck feeling that usually warned her when she was being watched, or in somebody's sights. All the same, her pulse was galloping like a spooked horse as they neared the entrance to the motel grounds, and her mouth was drier than ever.

She made a palm-down stay-put gesture with her left hand and moved very fast out into the street, to crouch beside the cab of the wrecked truck. A backward glance showed Ann waiting beside the motel office, her back against the half-collapsed wall, holding the pistol muzzle-up in both hands. At least she'd had sense enough to take cover.

Drawing a deep and slightly uneven breath, Jack put her head out past the truck's crumpled fender and looked quickly up and down the street. Then she took a longer, more careful look; then she moved back to the rear of the overturned truck and did the same, and then she straightened up and stepped out into the street, beckoning to Ann.

"More of that good-and-bad-news stuff," she said as Ann joined her. "I was right, I do know where we are. But it's not a real great place to be."

Ann pushed back her long black hair, which the wind kept tugging across her face. "I'm sorry," she said blankly. "I still don't understand."

"Fucking hell." Jack snorted impatiently. "You mean you haven't figured it out yet? We're back in *my* world, baby. We're still in Santa Fe, but not yours, not the one we were just in. I don't know how we got here," she added, "but then I never got how I wound up *there*, either."

Ann was getting that look in her eyes once more, that puckered-ass pitying expression Jack was starting to get so tired of, that said loud as any shout *poor crazy thing, here she goes raving again*. "For God's sake," Jack said, "are you blind or what?"

She swung her gun arm, pointing. "This *is* Santa Fe, right? I mean, you'll admit that much? Christ, just look at those mountains."

Ann was already staring at the distant line of snow-topped peaks visible above the buildings on the far side of the street. Obviously she hadn't noticed them before; just as obviously she recognized them now. "Well, yes, but—"

"But, my butt. Look around you, look up the street, either direction. Does this look like the Santa Fe you remember? Is it the same Santa Fe we rolled into last night?"

Ann's face went paler than ever. The view wasn't an encouraging one. The neighborhood had looked seedy enough the previous night, but now it was a scene of utter desolation. The narrow street was silent and deserted, and there wasn't a whole building in sight. Windows gaped glassless from graffiti-painted or fire-blackened walls; doors were black empty rectangles. A wrecked and stripped car body lay on its back up at the next corner, its rusty bodywork riddled with bullet holes. Weeds and even sizable bushes, knee-high or bigger, grew through cracks in the pavement.

And nothing was moving, nothing at all. . . .

After a moment Ann said, "Riots?" Her voice was faint and hoarse, with no conviction at all. "Or some kind of natural disaster—that's why the police went away—"

"Ah, fuck." Jack grabbed her wrist and dragged her to the rear of the truck, ignoring her protests. "All right, then, what about this?"

She began rubbing at the license plate with the palm of her hand, wiping away the layers of accumulated dirt, exposing the peeling but still legible sticker. "God damn it, take a good look. What's it say?"

Ann stared; her mouth wasn't quite open but it wasn't quite closed either. "Yeah," Jack said. "Nineteen-seventy-fucking-three. And if you want to go around and look at the windshield, I bet you'll find a bunch more stickers, all with the same date."

"But," Ann said helplessly. "I mean—"

"Now," Jack said, "we could poke around in these buildings awhile and I imagine we'd find some more stuff—calendars, newspapers, magazines, it's pretty fucked up around here but we'd probably find something. And we could check some of these cars, if we could find one that wasn't burned and still had its plates. We could do all kinds of shit like that."

She put a hand on Ann's shoulder. "And if you want to do that, if you're still not convinced, then you go right ahead. Knock yourself out. Me," she said, "I haven't got the time. What I'm going to do now is get my ass out of here."

She turned and stepped away from the truck. "You can come along or not. Up to you."

And she started up the street, not looking back; and after a moment Ann called, "No, wait," and Jack heard the slapping of those damn silly nurse shoes on the pavement, not quite run-ning but close to it, as she rushed to catch up.

◀ ▲ ▼ ▶

When Ann reached the corner Jack was standing there rubbing her bad eye. "I don't guess," Jack said, "there's any chance you know your way around here?"

What a question, Ann thought, you're the local expert, how the hell should *I* know? "A little," she said. "Why, don't you?"

Jack shook her head. "People stay out of these ruined cities. At least regular people do." Before Ann could ask what that meant she went on: "If you know the shortest way to get clear of this place, you just might save both our cute butts."

Ann looked up and down the street. She'd never really known Santa Fe all that well; she'd driven in from Los Alamos often enough, of course, shopping or visiting friends or, later, seeing a series of therapists, but that was all. She was certain she'd never been on this street before last night.

Still, Santa Fe wasn't a very big city, and the mountains gave her some orientation. After a moment she said, "This way," and pointed up the street. "I think."

"You think?" Jack didn't look happy. "We need better than that, babe. Do you know where this street goes or don't you?"

"Not exactly. But it ought to intersect with one of the bigger streets," Ann said, "Cerrillos Road, maybe, or St. Francis Drive, and then we can get our bearings."

"Sounds reasonable." Jack was looking slightly embarrassed. "You got to remember, I don't have a lot of experience getting around in cities. Okay, then."

She shoved her revolver into its holster and stepped out into the street. "May as well walk where the going's easy," she said. She began walking, moving with an easy long-legged stride, her right hand staying close to her gun.

No doubt about it, Ann thought, following her; this woman may or may not be crazy, but I am, or else the world is. It's not as if I haven't been heading that way for a long time.

Besides, there was the indisputably real physical discomfort. Her anus still hurt when she walked, her feet were starting to hurt too—the nurse's shoes weren't a very good fit—her skin itched from its growing accumulation of dust and sweat salts, and her hair kept blowing into her eyes in dirty strands. Dreams and hallucinations didn't have grubby specifics like that.

Yet if this wasn't all in her head, if this was indeed reality, then something was seriously wrong with reality itself. Mad Jack's lurid apocalyptic visions might seem farfetched, and her alternate-reality notions might be something out of a comic book, but what else was there? Something was happening that flatly *couldn't* happen, not in the logical universe which she had lived in and studied all her life.

Of course, the theoretical quantum cowboys—like her ex-husband, and what a time to keep thinking of *him*—would tell you that things like reality and possibility were only consensual illusions; that in fact anything was possible, there were only probabilities. But they were just theorizing, they didn't really believe a word of it; put the whole lot of them on this street right now and they'd run screaming in all directions. . . .

Ann gave up. If she was crazy, she wasn't going to make logical sense of anything; and if she wasn't, then there were no possible explanations and Jack's impossible one was as likely as any. At least it was consistent with the visible evidence—and if the one-eyed woman was right about that, then she was also undoubtedly right about the dangers of their situation, and this was no time for mental drifting.

She switched the pistol to her left hand, wiped her sweaty right palm against the seat of her pants, and took a fresh grip on the blocky weapon. Armed and dangerous, she thought, that's me all right—

"I wasn't here when it happened," Jack remarked over her shoulder, "but I heard it got pretty wild. Of course the big cities mostly got nuked, but in the smaller ones, like Santa Fe, things just went to hell. People started looting, fighting over food and stuff, and others were trying to get out of town—that must have been a real cluster-fuck—and a good many just freaked out and started smashing things and setting fires, for no reason at all."

"The authorities couldn't maintain order?"

"Hah. Most of the 'authorities' hauled ass themselves, soon as the deal went down. And the soldiers and the cops took off too, or went into business for themselves, till after a few years you couldn't tell them from the rest of the jackers."

"It seems so quiet now," Ann mused. "Even peaceful."

"Peaceful?" Jack snorted as Ann moved up beside her. "Like a graveyard, maybe. And you better hope it stays that way. Have we got much farther to go? To get out of this town?"

"I don't think so." Ann didn't really know, but maybe she should encourage Jack, who clearly was very uneasy in these surroundings. Santa Fe had never been a very big city, and its haphazard streets, lined mostly with low, loosely spaced structures, were hardly the stuff of urban nightmare. But Jack seemed to find the place downright claustrophobic.

"Yeah, well, maybe we'll be all right. Long as we don't run into any—oh, fuck. *Oh,* fuck."

She stopped so suddenly that Ann almost bumped into her. The big revolver appeared in her hand again. Ann started to speak, to ask what was wrong, but Jack held up her free hand for silence, and Ann followed her gaze and then she saw the dogs.

Even then she didn't get it, not at first. Just a bunch of scruffy curs, maybe a dozen or so, standing in front of an abandoned gas station on the far side of the street. Some of them were pretty good-sized, and none of them looked like anything you'd want in your living room; but still, what was the big deal?

"Don't shoot yet," Jack said in a low urgent voice. "We don't want to do any shooting if we can help it. Nothing like gunfire to attract all kinds of company."

The dogs were moving now, fanning out unhurriedly in a kind of open formation, muzzles pointed at the two women across the street. They weren't barking but Ann heard a few snarls and growls. They really were a nasty-looking lot, she thought uneasily, and bigger than she'd realized. One heavy-set, big-headed black beast—Rottweiler blood in there somewhere, she guessed, though all the dogs were obvious hopeless mongrels—seemed to be staring straight at her.

"If they do come at us, though," Jack went on, "then shoot as soon as you hear me open up, and don't screw around, because they sure as hell won't. Try to hit—"

The dogs didn't let her finish. They came charging across the street all at once, teeth bared and tongues lolling, barking and yipping and snarling in a mad chorus, moving incredibly fast. They were past the centerline before Ann grasped what was happening; and still she stood, mind gone blank, unable to act.

Then Jack's revolver boomed twice and the big black dog

jerked convulsively in mid-leap and flopped to the pavement, no more than twenty feet away. Freed now, Ann raised the pistol in both hands and pointed it at the nearest dog and pulled the trigger. The gun went off with a loud sharp bang and bucked violently in her grasp, but she held on tight and fired again and was amazed to see a big-eared, vaguely Alsatian-looking animal go down in a sprawl of rangy legs.

The pack was nearly on top of them now, and Ann heard herself screaming, but she kept firing, no longer trying to aim, until suddenly the hairy wave broke, almost at their feet, and a moment later Jack was grabbing her arm and saying, "Okay, that's enough."

The dogs were scattering, galloping frantically back up the street, disappearing into the tangle of weeds and rubble between two houses. Three remained behind, lying still on the pavement.

Jack said, "Holy shit!" and spat. "Hey," she exclaimed, "you got one, huh?"

"It wasn't the one I was aiming at," Ann confessed.

"What the fuck? You got one, that's all that matters. Big bastard, too." She was busy reloading her revolver, her hands moving with quick practiced motions, thumbing fresh cartridges into the chambers. "Man," she said, "that was just too close."

"It was terrifying." Ann realized her voice was shaking. So were her hands; so was her whole body. "I'm sorry," she said helplessly, and, to her own utter disgust, began to cry.

"No, no." Jack holstered her gun and put an arm around Ann's shoulders. "You got nothing to be sorry for. You did just fine."

She raised her hand to stroke Ann's hair. "I was scared too.

Anybody that's not scared of a dog pack, they're too stupid to live. That wasn't some bunch of poor little stray doggies, you know. That was a pack of wild animals, the most dangerous kind you'll ever meet. They're smart, they're not afraid of people, and they know how to work in a group."

She jerked a thumb in the direction the dogs had gone. "The only reason they quit, we killed their leaders. Right now they'll be sorting things out, maybe even having a fight to see who's going to be the new boss dog. Once they get that settled, chances are they'll be back."

"You really think so?" The thought made Ann's bones go cold.

"Sure. Dogs are damn persistent. And, you know, they're *dogs*, they can follow our scent for miles." Jack shrugged. "It'll probably come down to how hungry they happen to be."

She looked at Ann's face, then, and laughed out loud. "Jesus, you mean you didn't know? We're food, baby, and lots of it. Especially here in town, where they hardly ever get a look at an animal bigger than a rat—and even the humans who live here probably don't have a lot of meat on their bones. What did you think they wanted? To hump our legs?"

Ann didn't answer; she didn't dare open her mouth just then, not with the contents of her stomach trying to come up. Jack patted her on the back. "That's why we need to get a move on, all right? Before they come back for another try."

Ann nodded weakly. She looked down at the gun in her hand. "I don't know how many shots I fired," she managed to say.

Jack holstered her revolver and took the pistol from Ann's

trembling fingers. "Looks like you got a few left," she said after a quick inspection. "Not enough for anything heavy, but then I'm kind of short myself. We'll just have to stay out of—"

Her voice trailed off; her single eye had gone very wide, staring over Ann's shoulder. "Oh, boy," she said softly. "Turn around real slow, keep quiet, and don't do anything sudden."

Ann turned—thinking in God's name what *now?*—and saw, coming down the street toward them, a group of the strangest-looking people she'd ever seen. There might have been ten or fifteen of them; it was hard to tell, because they moved in an odd shifting way, now in a close milling group, now strung out in a ragged file along the side of the street, as if unable to make up their minds how to proceed.

They were so small she thought at first they must be children; but as they came nearer she saw that most of them were simply badly stunted adults, some almost qualifying as dwarfs. Only one man appeared to be as tall as herself, and he was grotesquely proportioned, with huge shoulders and a tiny head.

All, in fact, were dreadfully disfigured in various ways: heads too big or too small, arms and legs too short or too long or missing altogether, faces so misshapen as to be almost unrecognizable as human. And that was only what she could see; what other deformities might lie hidden under the flapping tatters they wore, she didn't want to imagine.

"Muties," Jack whispered.

Ann wondered where they had come from. Then she saw that a second, larger group was forming up in front of a big sprawling building, or set of buildings—it appeared to have been some sort of school—a little way up the street. Doors were opening all along the rows of rooms, and more small figures emerged. High-pitched cries and chatterings drifted down on the wind; she couldn't recognize any words.

The first group had stopped by now, bunched closely together, a short stone's toss away. Ann noticed uncomfortably that all of them were carrying weapons, or things that could be used as weapons; she saw only a couple with guns, but the others clutched knives and sticks and even rocks.

And yet they didn't look hostile, not really. It wasn't easy to read emotions on those malformed faces, but her impression was that they were simply frightened half to death.

A man stepped forward from the group. He was perhaps a bit less than five feet tall; his head, however, was that of a much larger man. His arms were unnaturally short, but they ended in huge hands, one of which held a rusty machete.

He looked at the two women for a moment without speaking. His eyes were large and dark; they might have been called beautiful, except that one was set a good inch higher than the other. His face held a keen intelligence, unlike the rather bewildered expressions of the others.

He raised the machete, then, not in a threatening way, only to gesture. Ann realized suddenly that he was pointing at the dead dogs. His bushy black eyebrows went up.

"Sure," Jack said, and nodded vigorously. "You can have them. We don't want them."

A low excited mutter ran through the ranks. The man with the machete smiled, revealing even white teeth. "Thanks." His voice was that of a small child. "Just passing through?"

"Right," Jack told him. "Not looking for any trouble."

"Good." He gave a high-pitched laugh. "Be careful, then. The dogs have been really bad this spring. That pack you just fought, they took one of our women a couple of days ago."

Swinging his machete, he trotted to join the others, who were arguing noisily over the dog carcasses. *"Basta, muchachos,"* he called. "We'll carry them back to the school and butcher them there. Everybody'll get a fair share."

"Let's go," Jack said. "Before they invite us to the banquet."

chapter
nine

M uties," Jack said again, half to herself, as they walked
quickly on up the street. "You know, that's the first time
I ever saw that many at once. Close up, anyway."

They were passing the school grounds, where bizarre figures
in fantastic rags dashed here and there, carrying pots and pans,
bits of firewood and assorted cutting tools. Several people were
getting a fire started in the middle of the playground; smoke
curled upward and fanned out on the wind, obscuring the faded
sign: ST. JOHN'S ELEMENTARY SCHOOL. There was a great deal of
shouting in English and Spanish and what might have been an
Indian language or two, together with wordless gobbles and
hoots. Ann shuddered. "Muties?" she asked. "You mean mutants?
Birth defects caused by radiation?"

"Yeah." Jack's face was closed up very tight. "Seems like we're
getting more of them, too, the last few years. Of course not all
that many live, in fact most are born dead, which is probably a
mercy . . . but the ones that do make it, people sometimes bring
them down to the nearest city and dump them."

"The parents abandon them?" Ann asked incredulously. "Just
because they're—damaged?"

"It's not always the parents. Sometimes the community where

they live, the tribe they ride with, whatever," Jack said, "they'll take the kid away from the parents and get rid of it, one way or another."

She looked at Ann. "Understand, people aren't just being mean. Some of them are scared of breeding up a generation of monsters. I know, I know, but I'm just telling you how some people are. You need to remember," she said, "things have been pretty rough, ever since the war. It's made a lot of people crazy. And then, too, there's a good deal of plain-ass ignorance and superstition around. No schools any more, half the people can't even read, you know?"

"So they leave the deformed children in the cities, to fend for themselves? And they grow up," Ann canted her head in the direction of the school, "like this?"

"If they manage to grow up at all. And it's been going on for long enough, now, that they've got a whole new generation growing up, worse fucked up than the parents—Jesus, did you see some of those kids?"

Ann nodded jerkily. "And will for the rest of my life."

"It's not just radiation mutations," Jack said. "Lots of the small isolated communities are getting inbred as hell, brothers fucking sisters and fathers fucking daughters and the old insult's not just a joke any more, if you know what I'm saying. Sometimes they crank out strange-looking offspring without any help from those Russian warheads. But they're just as liable to get dumped. Hell of a thing, but that's how it is."

"It's horrible."

"Uh huh," Jack said. "Like a lot of other things. Welcome to my fucking world, lady."

◄ ▲ ▼ ►

A little while later they came to a broad four-lane street, running roughly northeast-southwest. "Cerrillos Road," Ann said.

She was in no doubt, now; there was no mistaking that once-busy, ever-tacky thoroughfare. It would take more than a mere holocaust to change Cerrillos Road: all those motels and auto dealerships and fast-food franchises, stretching away in either direction, and those magnificent mountains standing white-peaked against the cloudless sky beyond. The greatest view in Santa Fe, the locals said, and the ugliest street.

Now it was even uglier, its various hustling enterprises and tourist traps gone derelict long ago. Big fancy signs, that had once lit up the night in garish neon colors, hung crazily from buckled supports or lay fallen on the ground. Wrecked cars and trucks stood here and there, a couple on their backs. Right across the road, above a burned-out fried-chicken establishment, the huge face of a goateed old man smiled down at Ann and Jack, somehow untouched by the fire.

"Whatever you call it," Jack said, "I know where we are. Now I can see the mountains better, I'm okay. This is the northwest side of town, right? I've been as near as the river, plenty of times."

She was looking across the road. Between the buildings, beyond the developed strip, stretches of open country could be seen, brown and empty under the afternoon sun. Ann thought the built-up areas didn't seem to extend as far out into the desert as she remembered, but she couldn't be sure; the devastation was too great.

"We can just strike out that way," Jack mused, "cut straight toward the river—have to find a place to cross, but it's not too deep—" She frowned suddenly. "No, shit. See that smoke, off to the north?"

Ann looked. She didn't see anything, but she nodded.

"Might be nothing to worry about," Jack said. "Probably just locals living next to the river, or some tribe's fishing camp. Could be jackers, though. And even basically good guys might get tempted by a couple of women, on foot and practically unarmed."

She ran a finger over the handful of cartridges remaining on her gunbelt. "Christ, we don't have enough firepower to fight off a bunch of pissed-off old ladies. No, I think we better give whoever that is a wide pass. Let's head down this road a little way, and then swing north. We can cross the river at Agua Fria."

The sun was well past the zenith now, beginning its long descent toward the jagged horizon. The day had grown warm, and the air was dry and full of blowing dust. As they turned southwest along Cerrillos Ann said, "Isn't there anywhere we can get water? I'm not sure I can hold out till we reach the river."

Her voice was hoarse and thin; she licked her lips. She patted her pockets, making a rattling sound. "And I really would like a tranquilizer, and I don't think I can get one down dry."

"I could go for a taste myself," Jack agreed. "Don't know how much luck we'll have, though." She scratched her head. "Come to think of it, didn't it rain last night?"

"In the Santa Fe where we were," Ann pointed out. "Evidently not in this one."

She heard herself say it, and made a small wry face. But after all, there came a point where you had to accept the evidence of your own senses, no matter how incredible, or else give up completely and go into permanent catatonic withdrawal.

Jack said, "I guess the war might have changed the weather, huh? So it wouldn't be the same, both . . . places?"

"It's possible."

"How about that," Jack mused. "Still, I remember it did rain a few days ago. Might be some water still standing, if we knew where to look—" She glanced around. "Over there," she said, pointing across the road, at a landscaping contractor's yard. "Let's check it out, anyway."

The yard was full of bad-taste lawn ornaments, ugly fake-Oriental lanterns and corny statues, mostly lying broken on their sides—somebody had used a four-foot-tall praying-Madonna figure for target practice—but there was also a whole row of concrete birdbaths. Most of these were wrecked too, but a couple proved to hold a few inches of clear water. "All *right*," Jack said, and bent down and drank, making cheerful slurping noises. "Man," she said after a moment, raising her head, "I *needed* this."

Ann had the vest off and was digging in her blouse pocket, getting out the little bottles. A Xanax, she decided, that was all she really needed right now. Any tendencies to violence or rage had been more than adequately vented during the battle with the wild dogs. And she didn't, at the moment, feel particularly depressed.

Anxiety, though—yes, you could definitely say she was experiencing that. She popped one of the little white tablets into her mouth and cupped her hands and scooped up water to wash it down, then more, splashing and dripping heedlessly, wiping her wet hands over her dusty windburned cheeks.

"I don't suppose there's any moisturizer left in this world?" she remarked. "I could definitely use some now."

"Lot of things we could use," Jack said. "Going to be a good trick just surviving, you know, once we get out into the boonies."

She was studying the big flat-roofed building that occupied the next lot. "What's that, a hardware store? Wonder if there's anything we could use—"

She started off at a quick trot. "Be right back," she called over her shoulder. "Keep a lookout, will you?"

Left alone, Ann sipped a bit more water and then walked over and sat down on an ornamental imitation-marble bench, laying the pistol carefully beside her. She thought no particular thoughts; her mind was temporarily off duty, while the Xanax worked its way through her bloodstream, settling her screaming nerves, and her body considered which parts of it were merely uncomfortable and which ones actively hurt.

She looked at the bulletproof vest, thinking she ought to put it back on, but unable to make herself do so. It had been driving her crazy for some time now; it wasn't terribly heavy, but it was stiff and bulky and restricted her breathing, and her skin beneath had begun to sweat and itch. Getting it off had been like finally getting out of a girdle after a long night. She stood up and turned, intending to throw it away; Jack was going to raise hell, but screw her; let her wear the damn thing. Anyway, who could feel threatened while standing next to a waist-high cement cherub?

She was standing there, the vest dangling from her right hand, when the two men appeared in the middle of the road.

That was how it looked for a moment there: they just

appeared, materialized from nowhere, amid a brief shimmering of the air, exactly like Jeffrey Hunter and Leonard Nimoy beaming down on the old *Star Trek* show. But of course she must simply have missed their approach, distracted by the vest; there were, after all, limits to the possible even in impossible worlds.

They were about the same average-white-male appearance, nothing all that remarkable about them, except for the odd silvery-gray coverall outfits they wore—and, she noticed now, the even odder black angular devices that they held across their chests. They were facing in her direction; in fact they were looking straight at her.

Before she could react, before her mind could do more than register the bare fact of their arrival, the one on the right took a step forward. "Dr. Lucas," he called, his voice sharp and high. "Dr. Jacqueline Lucas."

She made no response, couldn't have; her mind had gone emptier than ever. The other man said, "Dr. Lucas, we've come to take you out of here."

Later, she was never able to say why she acted as she did. There was certainly no conscious thought process involved; she wasn't even unstuck enough, mentally, to feel real fear.

She turned and started to run. Behind her there was a soft rattling sound, like rain on leaves, and something popped past her head. She ran harder, toward the contractor's building. Her foot struck a fallen lawn-jockey figure and she fell sprawling on her face, gravel stinging her knees and elbows.

Half-dazed, she rolled onto her back and tried to sit up. The gray-suited men were coming across the street, moving at an unhurried walk, holding the strange gadgets—weapons, she felt sure, though she'd never seen anything like them—at the ready. "Dr. Lucas," the first man shouted. "Don't try to run away."

The bulletproof police vest lay beside her on the ground; she hadn't thought to throw it away as she ran. She grabbed it up and clutched it to her chest in a hopeless protective gesture. The pistol still lay on the bench, too far away.

"Stand up, Dr. Lucas," the second man called, and raised his weapon to point at her, as did his partner. "Come here—"

That was when the dog pack reappeared, tearing out of the nearest side street and sweeping across the road in a yapping, snarling, snapping rush. They must have been tracking the two women for hours, but now they went for the obvious prey: the gray-suited men, standing exposed in the street.

The two men turned, just as the pack charged in. One managed to fire his weapon briefly—Ann recognized that muffled pattering sound again—but too late. As Ann got to her feet first one gray-clad figure, then the other, went down and disappeared beneath the growling mass. If either man made any sound it was drowned out by the barking and growling of the dogs.

Jack appeared at her side, yanking at her arm. "Jesus, what's happening, come on, run—"

She followed Jack across the contractor's yard—pausing only to grab up the pistol from the bench—and through a gap in the half-fallen chain-link fence. A couple of angry barks sounded behind them, but a glance over her shoulder showed the dogs were still occupied with the men they had pulled down.

"Keep running," Jack panted as they pelted up the street. "Don't slow down. They'll probably forget about us, now they got something else to chew on, but you never know."

And, a moment later, "Who *were* those guys?"

◄ ▲ ▼ ►

"And you never saw these two before?" Jack asked, a bit later, as they walked on down Cerrillos Road. "You're sure?"

"Never." Ann shook her head. "But they knew my name, and they were looking for me."

"Huh," Jack said. "Listen, I'm sorry I didn't come quicker. I heard a voice and some funny sounds, but, well, tell the truth, I was having a quick pee. Caught with my pants down, you know?"

She looked over at Ann, studying the line of neat holes across the front of the bulletproof vest, which the other woman had grudgingly put back on. Damn good thing she hadn't had it on at the time; whatever had hit it had gone through the thick armor like shit through a duck. And this was the same vest that had stopped a .357 Magnum round at point-blank range. Whatever those strangers had been packing, she wanted one.

"They were going to kill me," Ann said wonderingly. She seemed to be having a lot of trouble with the idea. "I don't even know who they were, and they were going to kill me."

Privately Jack suspected Ann had imagined the part about the strangers calling her name—after all, she was obviously close to flipping out at the time, look at the way she'd whipped out her damn pill collection first chance she got—but it wasn't a priority matter. Right now Jack was more interested in the plume of dust moving across the open land off to the north, coming straight toward them.

"I think," she said, "we've got more company on the way."

Ann groaned. "Oh, God, no—"

"Don't freak out yet," Jack advised. "This may not be so bad."

By now it was possible to make out what was raising the dust: a group of figures on horseback, strung out loosely line-abreast, moving at a brisk gallop. Jack counted eight and thought there might be a few more horses following, though the dust made it hard to tell if they all carried riders.

"Keep your gun ready," she said, drawing her own weapon but holding it down beside her thigh. "And let me do the talking."

A few minutes later they were surrounded—she didn't like that part, but there was nothing to be done about it short of starting a shootout—by a gang of laughing, dark-tanned men on shaggy-maned horses. All held automatic weapons pointed skyward or resting across their saddlebows.

A tall young man with his hair in chest-length braids said, "Well, well, what we got here?" and a shaven-headed rider beside him said, "Looks like pussy to me," and they all cackled and guffawed, and some comedian made a loud *meow.*

But then somebody else said, "Hey, wait, you guys know who this is?" and after a moment's general silence there was a sudden chorus of, "Mad Jack! It's Mad Jack!"

One of the riders heeled his horse forward a couple of steps. "Jack," he said. "Long time no see. Now what the hell are you doing here?"

He was a big husky-looking man, older than the others; gray streaked his neatly trimmed beard and the dark hair that hung to his bare brown shoulders. He wore a black cowboy hat, the brim turned up on one side, Australian style, and pinned in place by a set of silver captain's bars.

Jack said, "Ernie," and deliberately reholstered the Magnum. "Long story, Ernie, and you wouldn't believe it if I told you.

How about you guys? Long way from home, aren't you?"

"Been taking care of some business." Ernie was looking at Ann. "Got us a camp up by the river . . . who's this? Your new girlfriend, or just trade goods?"

"She's not available." Jack's hand still rested pointedly on the .357's butt. "Tell these horny gorillas to forget it."

Ernie laughed. "You heard her, boys. Get your alleged brains out of your balls." To Jack he said, "Want to ride with us a few days? We could use another gun hand right now."

Jack shook her head. "We just need to get home. Can we get a couple of horses from you, and a little food and water?"

Ernie tilted his head to one side, making the sun wink brightly off the silver bars on his hat. "Got anything to trade?"

"This." Jack slapped lightly at Ann's back. "Bulletproof vest, cop issue. Stop anything short of armor-piercing."

"Shit." Ernie grinned. "Bulletproof my ass, I can see the holes from here. Who're you trying to con, Jack? Give old Captain Ernie a little respect."

His face went serious, the steel-wool eyebrows coming close together. "But you're still your daddy's girl, and I still owe him. So—" He gestured to the horsemen behind him. "Give them those two pack ponies, boys. Take the gear off, share the loads among yourselves till we get back to camp. Fix them up with a couple of blankets, and that sack of jerky. Ray, you always carry two canteens, give Jack one."

"Thanks," Jack said, as the riders hustled to obey. "I won't forget this."

"No sweat. You still staying at Fat Bob's? We'll be up that way in a few days, on the way north. Take care of those two animals till we can pick them up. I traded a pretty decent-looking Mex woman for them."

He studied the two women. "Sorry we don't have any extra rifles. Figuring to cross the river at Agua Fria?"

"If nobody's got the bridge staked."

All the riders laughed at that. "There was a guy," Ernie said, "had himself a little racket there, up till a couple of days ago. That was when he tried to charge us to cross."

"He's kind of out of business now," the rider with the braids added. "Permanent."

One of the men was riding toward them, leading a pair of barebacked horses. "Sorry we can't provide saddles," Ernie said.

"We'll be okay." To Ann, in an undertone, Jack said, "You can ride a horse, can't you?"

"I've done it," Ann murmured. "Not many times, not very well, but I've done it. Don't worry, I'll manage. I'll manage anything, if it means no more walking."

◁   ▲   ▼   ▷

"Those men really scared me," Ann said, a good long time after. "Good thing they were friends of yours."

They were well clear of the city now, riding across the open country north of the Santa Fe River, along the narrow strip of desert flats between the river and the foothills. The sun was halfway down the sky by now, and square at their backs; their shadows ran long and dark ahead of the horses' feet.

Jack said, "Friends? I don't make friends with jackers."

"That's what they are?"

"Oh, they do a little legit trading, now and then they shoot a few wild cows and sell the meat and hides. Mostly they just ride

around and rip things off and hurt people. More fun than bust-
ing your ass trying to scratch out a half-starved living, which is
all most people manage to do nowadays."

"They seemed to know you."

"Sure." Jack snorted. "Everybody knows Mad Jack. I'm a
fucking legend in my own time."

"The leader mentioned your father."

"Uh huh. He and Daddy served together in Nam. I think
Daddy saved his life once, but I never heard the story." She looked
at Ann. "I hope you didn't buy that good-old-boy act of his. If I
hadn't been along, he'd have let those bastards gang-fuck you
right there in the middle of the road, and then again back at
camp, and finally he'd have taken you up to Taos and sold you."

"But you accepted his help."

"Damn right. Like I said, welcome to my world. Where the
number one rule is, you do whatever it takes."

Ann considered this. "What's the number two rule?"

"Take it before it takes you." Jack grinned. "Hand me that
canteen, will you? I'm drier than a mummy's asshole."

◄ ▲ ▼ ▶

They spent the rest of the day working their way past Santa
Fe, picking up the main highway north of town, the horses'
hooves ringing sharply on the cracked and crumbling pavement.
They saw no more riders, or anyone else at all.

Late in the afternoon, as the sun at last began to set fire to the
sky above the mountains to the west, Jack said, "We need to
make camp for the night. Come on, I know a place."

She led the way off the highway and up into the foothills, following a narrow and barely visible trail that was barely wide

enough for the horses to walk single file. It wasn't far, no more than a couple of miles, but the climb was fairly steep and the horses were blowing and sweating by the time they reached the little canyon with the stream and the old rock cabin.

"Sheepherder's shack," Jack told Ann as they slid off the horses. "At least that's what somebody told me it was. Anyway, I've stayed here a few times before."

Ann was rubbing her bottom. "My God," she said. "How can anything stuffed with grass be so hard?"

"Let him have a drink," Jack said, leading her horse toward the stream. "Not too much, though, till he's cooled off—"

She showed Ann how to rub the horses down with handfuls of grass. From the crude rope halters she improvised hobbles for their forelegs; at least the poor beasts wouldn't have to spend the night tethered. There wasn't much for them to eat here, only a little grass poking through the carpet of brown needles beneath the big pines, but they wouldn't starve in a single night.

The rock house consisted of a single windowless, dirt-floored room with a ring of blackened rocks in the center. The roof was long vanished, its beams pulled down for firewood. Jack said, "Let's look around for wood. It'll be cold tonight."

Some time later, as darkness fell outside, Jack leaned back on her elbows and watched the orange teeth of the fire eat away at the wood. Fallen pine limbs, really piss-poor fuel—too smoky and stinky, and too fast-burning for an all-night fire—but still better than nothing. She yawned and reached for the canteen. Good water, anyway, nothing like spring snowmelt for a cold drink at the end of a long day, and hadn't *this* been a long one. . . .

Beside her, wrapped in one of the blankets, Ann said sleepily, "How did you start that fire? I was getting water, I didn't see."

"Flint and steel." Jack patted the little leather pouch on her gunbelt, which lay on the ground beside her hip. "I'll teach you how to do it, it's not hard."

"I'm so tired," Ann said in a thin voice. "I didn't know it was possible to be this tired."

Jack watched as she squirmed a little, trying to get comfortable and not succeeding. Her breathing changed, becoming deep and regular. One hand slipped out from under the blanket; the fingers twitched briefly and then were still.

Jack sighed and lay down beside her, pulling her own blanket up against the creeping cold. For God's sake, she thought, snuggling up close against the other woman and putting an arm over her. Two nights in a row and still no action. I must be losing it.

◄ ▲ ▼ ►

Next day they rode north again, still following the old highway. They didn't talk much. Ann appeared to be off somewhere within herself. In shock, Jack decided, and just starting to feel it. Well, who wouldn't be? Most people, in fact, would have gone clear babbling loony by now. Jack remembered her own bewilderment two nights ago—two nights? That couldn't be right, it felt like forever. Make that two women in shock, then.

Ann brightened up a little in the afternoon, looking around her at the scenery, even asking about the group of mounted Indians who appeared by the roadside and sat watching them until they had passed.

"Just making sure we keep going," Jack told her. "Some of the pueblos have really gone back to the old ways. No white people allowed, and you can't exactly blame them. I mean, they weren't the ones who blew up the fucking world."

Not long afterward Jack took them off the main highway again, following a washed-out gravel road, so as to miss the town where she'd had the shootout. She didn't really think those four jackers had any partners in the area, but it was possible and she wasn't taking any chances in their practically unarmed state. Finally they came to the blacktop road that wound up into the mountains. "Won't be long now," Jack said.

At last there was the turnoff and the familiar rutted dirt track; and soon they were riding up the hill toward Fat Bob's settlement. People came to their doors and windows, or paused in their work to look up, as the two women rode through the village; here and there a voice cried out that Mad Jack was back. Ignoring them, she led the way to her cabin. "Home," she announced. "Never thought I'd be so glad to see this dump."

When they had put the horses in the corral—the roan pricking up his ears, coming over and making little snuffling greeting noises at the new arrivals—Jack pushed the cabin door open and held it for Ann. "It's kind of a mess," she said apologetically. "I got drunk and tore the place up. Sorry."

"It's—very nice." Ann looked around the interior of the cabin, doing a pretty good job of pretending not to notice the junk on the floor and the wrecked bed. "Do you live here alone?"

"I do now," Jack said bleakly.

Or maybe not, she thought with a sudden leap of spirit, maybe not any more; but she didn't have the nerve to say it aloud.

"Want something to eat?" she asked instead. "There's not much here, the little bi—uh, somebody cleaned me out. Got some goat cheese, though, and some fry bread, maybe not too stale."

"That sounds wonderful." Ann sat down on the edge of the bed while Jack opened the latched wooden grub box—pack rats and raccoons would get into anything you didn't lock up—and got out the bread and the soft white cheese. "Thank you," she said when Jack passed them over. "Aren't you going to have any?"

"Later." Jack turned away with elaborate casualness, afraid to let Ann see her face. She wasn't interested in food just now; the sight of the other woman sitting on that bed had driven everything else from her mind. God damn it, she told herself, you're acting like a lovesick kid, get a *grip*—

She undid her gunbelt and hung it on its peg on the wall, glad to be free of its weight. The Magnum would need cleaning but later for that. She sat down on a wooden bench and pulled off her boots, wiggling her toes with pleasure.

"You want to hand me that piece?" she said. "Not likely you'll need it real soon."

"Piece?" Ann said indistinctly, her mouth full. "Oh, you mean this damned gun." She pulled the Glock from her waistband and passed it over. "I'm afraid I never did work out a good way to carry it. Almost lost it several times along the way."

"I'll find you a holster." Jack popped the clip out and cleared the chamber. "Or make one. How about the vest?"

"God, yes." Ann was already undoing the Velcro tabs. "I hate this thing—" She shucked it off over her head and tossed it aside. "Tell me, is there any place to, ah, clean up?"

"If you mean you need to go," Jack said, "the outhouse is around back. If you really mean clean up, I've got plenty of water. Or Fat Bob's got a shower down the hill—"

"That's all right. I'd just like a washup, for now."

"No problem." Jack took the lid off the big steel water barrel and reached for a gourd dipper. "Uh, it's just cold water. I could get a fire going, heat some up for you—"

"This will be fine." Ann watched as Jack dipped water into a white enameled basin. "You've been so kind."

"Sort of a rule in this country," Jack mumbled. "You take care of your guests. Let me get you a towel."

When she turned around with the towel—a real towel, loot from a deserted guest ranch down near Belen; it was something she saved for special occasions—Ann was sitting on the bed again, removing the nurse's shoes. She stood up and unbuttoned the filthy uniform top and slipped it off her shoulders, her breasts dangling free for a moment, like bells, as she turned and laid the garment on the bed. She hooked her thumbs under both elastic waistbands and slid pants and panties down at once, stepping out of them with a delicate graceful motion like a dancer.

Jack's heart was pounding like a wild-horse stampede. She couldn't believe the other woman couldn't hear it.

"I don't have any washcloths," she said with difficulty, as Ann walked naked across the little room toward her. "That box of rags there, though, they're real clean." Oh, Christ, that was going to gross her out for sure—

"That's fine." Ann took one of the rags and dipped it in the basin and squeezed it to her face. "Oh, that feels so *good.*" Little rivulets ran down her neck and breasts and dripped off the tips of her hardening nipples. She lowered the rag and said, "Aren't you going to wash up too?"

"Company first," Jack managed to say. Her voice seemed to belong to somebody else.

"Nonsense. Come on, it feels glorious." She gestured with the rag. "Out of those clothes. You're making me feel silly, being the only one naked."

Pulse thundering, throat constricted, Jack hastened to peel off her own dusty clothing. Kicking everything aside in a heap, she croaked, "Let me get your back."

"Thanks." Ann passed her the rag and turned around. "Aahhh," she sighed as Jack ran the rag over her shoulders and downward to the flare of her buttocks. "That's lovely—"

"You've got such beautiful skin," Jack said hoarsely. "So soft and white."

"Why, thank you. I always wished for a tan like yours."

Then, after a minute or so, "Let me do you, now."

She turned to face Jack, taking the rag; but before Jack could turn her back Ann moved closer and began sponging her face and then her breasts and down over her belly. Their eyes were exactly at a level. "We match," Ann said softly, moving slightly closer, and their stiff wet nipples bumped and fenced for an electric moment.

Jack cleared her throat. "I want to make love to you," she got out. "Can I make love to you?"

Ann smiled. "Well," she said, stepping back and dropping the rag, "what the fuck took you so long?"

chapter
ten

Quite some time later, Jack said, "Wow. Now this bed is *really* in a mess."

They lay in a close embrace, Ann on her back, Jack half-curled against her, their legs still intertwined. Jack's face rested against Ann's shoulder. She still wore her eyepatch. That was all either of them wore; the light from the single window gleamed softly on their damp naked bodies.

"Oh, I don't know." Ann ran a hand over the back of Jack's head, remembering how that short-cropped hair had felt a little while ago under her digging fingertips, how it had felt against the inner surfaces of her thighs as she thrashed beneath Jack's probing tongue. "It's not so bad," she said.

"Yes it is." Jack raised her head and looked around. "I can just hear Daddy yelling, 'All right, let's get that rack squared away!'"

Ann laughed softly, not because she understood the line but just because she felt good. Everything felt good, right now. Especially Jack's body touching hers. She closed her eyes for a moment, savoring the various sensations: the still-hard nipples poking at her ribs, the strong-muscled leg trapped between her own, the moist woolly pressure of that dark pubic bush against her thigh.

But then Jack said, "I'm sorry, but my arm's about to go to sleep," and Ann reluctantly sat up and Jack rolled onto her back and stretched luxuriously. "Yeah," she said, adjusting her eyepatch, "Daddy'd just about shit bricks if he could see me now."

"You talk a lot about your father," Ann remarked. "Was he the one who brought you up?"

"Well, that's sort of a yes and no. See, my mother died when I was little—"

"I'm sorry."

"No, no, it's okay. I mean, it's not *okay*, but I never even knew her." Jack turned her face away and stared at the wall. "From what they told me, she had a lot of trouble with depression, and it got worse right after she had me. And then Kennedy was assassinated, not long after I was born, and for some reason that really got to her. So," Jack said, "she killed herself."

"God!"

"Yeah. Dropped me off at her sister's, checked into a motel room and did a number on her wrists with a razor blade. Damnedest thing," Jack said, "but they said there were these burnt matches lying around, and it looked like she'd sterilized the blade first. Weird, huh?"

"God," Ann repeated numbly. Then, "Wait, wait. Kennedy was assassinated, in this world?"

"Sure." Jack rolled onto her back, staring at Ann. "You mean he wasn't, in yours?"

"No." Ann rubbed her face with both hands. "Hard to imagine—which one?"

"Which Kennedy? Well, *President* Kennedy, of course—"

"Yes," Ann said, "but which one?"

Before Jack could reply there was a loud knock on the cabin door. A male voice called, "Yo, in there!"

Jack sat up. "Hang on," she cried, and got out of bed and trotted, barefoot and bare everything else, to the door. "Fat Bob," she said, and flung the door wide open, standing nude in the bright rectangle of light, making no effort to conceal anything from the stocky black man who waited outside. "What do you need?"

"Bad time?" The man looked past her and grinned at Ann, who had grabbed a blanket and was clutching it up under her chin. "Sorry if I interrupted anything," he said, "but I saw you ride in, looked like you'd had a rough time. So I brought some stuff."

He held out a long wooden box, covered with a white cloth. Jack said, "Oh, hey, man, thanks," and took the box from him. "I was going to come down and see you—"

"No hurry. I'll be there." Fat Bob started to turn to go, then paused. "You guys think you might want a shower, later on? I'll save some water for you if you do."

"That'd be great."

"All right, then. Oh," Fat Bob said, "and I'll send a couple of the boys up, have them look after those horses. *Bon appetit,* children."

He swung around on his heel and walked away. Jack kicked the door shut with her heel and walked back toward the bed, carrying the long box, which Ann now saw had once been a drawer from a dresser or bureau; brass handles still dangled in front.

"Good old Fat Bob," Jack said, setting the box on the floor and pulling back the cloth. "Look what he brought us. Fresh bread, couple of big bowls of stew—wonder what's in it, it'll be good anyway, you can bet on that—even a bottle of wine. If he wasn't a man I'd marry him. Well, and if he didn't already have three wives."

"You, ah." Ann fumbled for words. "You didn't mind, um, that is—"

"You mean didn't I mind him seeing me naked? Hell, Fat Bob's seen me bare-assed before. He's practically family."

Jack sat down on the bed and gave Ann a hard look. "Or maybe you didn't think I'd want *any* man eyeballing me? Girl, you don't quite get it, do you? Look," she said, "I'm not the kind of lesbian who hates men. I don't think I'm really a dyke at all, I mean like somebody who's born that way or whatever. I've seen plenty of men who looked good to me, known a few who really turned me on in fact. I did it a few times with guys when I was younger, and I don't mind telling you I enjoyed it."

She put out a hand and touched Ann's shoulder. "But—remember those poor damn muties, down in Santa Fe?"

Ann nodded. "Well, then," Jack said, "that's what did it for me, when those fucked-up babies started showing up and everybody figured out why. I don't know how much radiation I've picked up over the years—probably not as much as some people, I wasn't close to any of the nuke targets and I've been damn careful where I traveled—but *everybody's* had a dose, the fucking stuff's everywhere, in the ground, in the water, I think the whole world got dusted at least a little."

"And you're afraid of having a defective baby?"

"You got it. No way in hell am I going to take a chance, any chance at all, of bringing another mutie into the world."

"If everyone felt that way," Ann observed, "the human race would become extinct."

"Yeah," Jack said, "well, would that be so bad?"

Ann started to reply, and then realized she had nothing at all to say to that.

"Anyway," Jack went on, "that's something everybody has to decide for themselves, right? All I'm saying is *I* couldn't stand it, couldn't even stand nine months of not knowing what I've got growing inside my belly, what kind of nightmare's going to come out between my legs. And there's no pills or anything like that any more—sometimes guys use these condoms made from sheep guts, but they aren't really reliable and who wants something like that stuck inside you? So," she said, "I just swore off doing it with men, not long after I was old enough to start doing it at all."

"Which only leaves one alternative," Ann said dryly. "I see. Is that what I am? An alternative?"

"You know better than that." Jack's voice went suddenly soft. "At least I hope you do. I think if I'd never gone for a woman before, I'd still have fallen for you." She stroked Ann's cheek with the back of her hand. "Did you ever, you know, do this before?"

"No." Ann thought suddenly of her ex-husband, who had been fascinated by the subject, addicted to pseudo-lesbian videos, which he sometimes pressured her into watching with him. The garishly lit closeups of tongues and teeth and vulvas, the painful-looking fingerings and dildo-pokings, hadn't done a thing for her, to his obvious disappointment. Now and then—with increasing frequency, toward the end—he'd assured her that if she ever did find herself "attracted" to another woman, it wouldn't be a problem for him. . . .

"No," she said again, "and I'm glad you were first."

"Me too," Jack said. "Come on, let's get into this stuff. I don't know about you but I've got a real appetite now."

Jack's table was broken, a casualty of whatever drunken explosion had trashed the interior of the cabin. They sat on the bed and ate, balancing the bowls in their laps. Ann tackled the food with real enthusiasm; she had been hungry all day and, though she hadn't wanted to say so and hurt Jack's feelings, the soggy stale fry bread and the moldy goat cheese had been almost inedible.

Fat Bob's stew was excellent, seasoned with various herbs, though the chunks of meat—beef, Ann guessed after a taste— were rather tough. The bread was fresh and chewy. "Here," Ann said, "have some wine."

The wine was less of a success; in fact it was easily the worst wine Ann had ever tasted, heavily oxidized and thick with sediment. It seemed to be a kind of missing link between really bad wine and simple spoiled fruit juice. A hand-lettered label read OLD FEAR AND LOATHING. Ann managed to swallow a mouthful and then handed the bottle back. "Thanks," she said, "but I'd better stay with water. The medication I'm taking—"

"Sure." Jack took the bottle, put it to her lips and tilted it for a long pull. "Not bad," she said approvingly. "Fat Bob's getting better."

Ann said, "You were saying, before? About your father?"

"Oh, sure." Jack wiped her lips with the back of her hand. "Well, see, my old man was in the Corps—career officer, you know—and there was no way he could take care of a kid on his own. So I got raised by aunts and cousins and then later on he put me in this private girls' school in Albuquerque. Real expensive place, snobby as hell, I hated it . . . but anyway, he'd come to visit me now and then, and when I got older he took me for little trips, once or twice a year. You understand," she added, "we didn't go to Disney or anything like that. That wasn't Daddy's bag. We went hiking and fishing up in the mountains, or rode around the desert in that God-damned Jeep checking out ghost towns."

She shrugged. "I have to admit, though, some of it was fun. Or would have been, if Daddy hadn't been such a prick—everything had to be done just right and you couldn't do it fast enough to suit him. I got so fucking sick of hearing, 'Move like you've got a purpose!'"

She stopped, her face gone blank. Her left hand came up and rubbed her bad eye. Ann sat quietly, waiting.

"When the war started," Jack went on at last, "we were on a trip like that, camping up in the Sangre de Cristos. Didn't even have a radio with us, so the first we knew anything was happening was the night we heard the first explosion—that was Albuquerque getting it—and saw the light against the sky. By the time we got down out of the mountains it was all over."

"He didn't try to report for duty?"

"No. Daddy may have been a bastard but he wasn't stupid. He said there wasn't any United States any more, it was going to be every man for himself and the faster we accepted that and started thinking survival, the better chance we'd have. And so," Jack said, "for the next seven years it was just the two of us. And you don't want to get the wrong idea, he took good care of me in his way—taught me everything I know, really, about how to take care of myself, but he also made sure I read books and learned math and stuff like that. Shit." Jack grimaced. "I guess the son of a bitch loved me, as much as he knew how to love anybody. There were times he went hungry because there wasn't enough food for both of us, and he stayed up a lot of nights taking care of me when I was sick."

She fell silent again. Ann said, "You said seven years. What finally happened?"

"Some jackers ambushed him and killed him." Jack's voice was entirely without expression. "He made it home before he bled to death."

"And then?"

"I tracked the fuckers down and killed them." Jack looked at Ann. "And I've been on my own ever since. So much for the story of my life. What about you?"

The question caught Ann off balance. "Different from yours," she said after a moment. "I don't mean in the obvious way—I mean, it was my mother who raised me. She'd had some problems with depression, like yours, but she finally got some help and, among other things, decided her marriage was part of the problem. So she divorced my father and took me with her. I don't really remember him," she admitted. "He was killed in the Middle East, on some stupid special mission, while I was still a small child."

"Your old man was in the military too?" Jack asked. "Army?"

"Now I think of it, he was in the Marine Corps too." Ann hadn't thought about her father in years. "I don't know much beyond that."

"No shit?" Jack looked interested. "Maybe he and Daddy knew each other, wouldn't that be a kick? What outfit was he in?"

"I have no idea. All I know is that when I was born he was stationed at Camp Pendleton, where he was some sort of training officer—"

"I'll be God-damned. Mine too. Was he stationed there when he met your mama?"

Ann shook her head. "He met her in Hawaii, I do know that much." She remembered the photo she'd found one day in her mother's underwear drawer, the white-gowned bride and the husky young man in dress blues; she'd never told her mother she'd seen it. "That was just before they transferred him to Camp Pendleton."

"Holy shit . . . wait a minute." Jack's good eye had gone very wide. "No, wait, it can't be—"

Ann felt the blood drain from her face. A long-stuck circuit closed; a memory rose at last to consciousness. "Back at the motel," she said in a near-whisper, "just before the police arrived—what did you say your name was?"

Then they both said it, almost in unison: *"Jacqueline Ann Younger!"*

They sat for a moment staring at each other, mouths open. "Lucas was my husband's name," Ann murmured. "I kept it after the divorce, it was just so much trouble to change back—"

"Hold up your hands," Jack said suddenly.

Ann complied. Jack raised her own hands and placed them against Ann's, pattycake position. The match was exact, even to the slightly overlong ring fingers that had cost Ann so many jokes about werewolves. She felt a slight but definite tremor; Jack's hands were no steadier just now than her own.

"This," Jack said, "is just fucking nuts."

"You mean—" Ann had gotten there too; she just couldn't make herself say it.

"One way to find out." Jack hopped out of bed and crossed the room in a quick bound, to paw through the contents of a big wooden trunk that stood open against the far wall. "Little bimbo took my good mirror," she mumbled, "but I've got another one in here, I know. Right, there we go, now where's that glass I was going to use to start fires—"

She came back to the bed holding a small hand mirror, mounted in tacky-fancy plastic, in one hand. In the other she held a big magnifying glass. "Run your fingers over that bread," she instructed Ann. "So they pick up a little flour—right, now press them against the mirror. Leave room for mine."

A few minutes later, peering through the magnifying glass at the two lines of fingerprints on the silvered glass, she said, "Take a look for yourself. You're not going to believe me if I tell you."

Ann took the magnifier. Her hand was shaking so hard she had to brace her wrist across her left forearm before she could see anything. Once the fingerprints came into focus, though, it took very little time to see what Jack meant. She knew almost nothing about fingerprint identification, but it looked to her as if the patterns of loops and whorls were the same, finger for finger and thumb for thumb.

She looked up. "So—"

"You're me!" Jack tossed the mirror aside and grinned crazily at Ann. "Or I'm you. We're each other? How do you say it?"

Ann's mind made a last-ditch effort at denial and then surrendered. Well, why not? Once you accepted the concept of parallel realities—and she'd already worked her way through that, after yesterday there was no doubt left—it stood to reason that two alternate worlds could, indeed logically must, contain alternate versions of the same individual.

And if you somehow wound up in a parallel world, and met your parallel self face to face—

They began laughing, then, schoolgirl giggles that turned into barnyard cackles and then great helpless, belly-hurting howls, falling into each other's arms and rolling together on the bed, hooting and shrieking like demented apes. Till finally they fell back, side by side, and lay looking at the ceiling, still shaking with sporadic internal spasms.

"Jesus," Jack said, wiping tears. "I been told a few times to go fuck myself, but I never thought I'd *do* it."

"What about me?" Ann asked plaintively. "Here I was all excited about my first lesbian act. Now I find out it was just masturbation."

That set them off again, whooping idiotically, grabbing each other to keep from falling off the bed. "Man," Jack gurgled weakly. "*Hoo* boy."

She pushed herself up off the bed, still shaking. "Hey," she said, "let's go see Fat Bob about that shower. I'll fix you up with some clothes—we sure as hell ought to wear the same size."

"In a minute," Ann told her. "Where's that bottle of wine?"

◄ ▲ ▼ ►

That evening, lying once again together in the more or less rehabilitated bed—the old mattress still bore the knife rips, but at least they were covered by fresh bedding—Ann finally made herself say it aloud:

"Where does this leave us?" she asked Jack. "I mean, all right, you're me, I'm you, it's either a big joke or a cosmic paradox—"

"Or both," Jack suggested.

"All right. But what about *us?*"

Jack rolled up onto one elbow and looked down at Ann. The cabin was lit only by a single tallow candle; the flickering yellow light threw their faces into deep relief.

"You mean are we still . . . lovers?"

"Yes," Ann said, wanting to reach up and pull her down and kiss her (herself? stop it, this way lay madness) but afraid to move. "What do you think?"

"What do I think?" Jack lowered her head and began browsing at Ann's left breast, flicking the nipple lightly with her tongue. Ann shuddered and closed her eyes. "I think," Jack murmured, "you think too much."

Ann felt herself going liquid inside; her breath had gone short and ragged. But she made herself open her eyes again and push Jack's head away and say, "No, really, I'm serious. We do have to think about this, Jack. We have to talk."

"What for?" Jack's voice held an edge of impatience. "Baby, don't get your feelings hurt, but you *do* think too much. All this constant checking yourself out, worrying about every damn thing you do or feel, I swear I wonder if you're capable of taking a pee without stopping to analyze your motives."

She jabbed a finger at Ann's face. "And don't give me that line about how the unexamined life isn't worth living. Oh, yeah," she said, "I know you think I'm an ignoramus, maybe compared to you I am, but I did go to a pretty old-fashioned school till I was ten, and then Daddy made sure I read the important stuff. And

I know about the guy who said that, and he also did a hitch as a combat infantryman—and you can bet your pretty ass when some Persian soldier came at Socrates with a spear, he didn't wait to wonder about the philosophical angles. He just did his best to stick the son of a bitch before *he* got stuck."

"Yes, but—"

"No, just listen. This is something you need to understand. See," Jack said, "none of that shit means anything in this world. Nobody's got the time for it. Like I told you before, people do whatever it takes to survive—and most of the time that's all they get to do, that's a full-time job, you know? But if you do get lucky, get a chance to do something just because you want to do it, then why the fuck not? Long as you don't hurt anybody else, and a lot of people aren't even particular about that."

She picked up Ann's hand and held it in hers. "Right now there's only one question worth asking, and the rest is bullshit. Do you still want me?"

"Desperately." The word came out almost by itself.

"Then," Jack said flatly, "that's all there is."

Ann felt as if she'd just let fall a great heavy weight. "Yes," she said. "You're right."

"Damn straight," Jack affirmed. "Now can we for Christ sake get off this?"

Her free hand began roving over Ann's body, cupping one breast for a moment and rubbing her thumb over the almost painfully erect nipple, then sliding downward over the smooth belly flesh. "Too much thinking, too much talking, we've got better things to do . . . damn," she said, "if this is how good I feel no wonder men keep wanting to fuck me. . . ."

Her hand was lower now, moving over the nappy fur between Ann's involuntarily parting legs, coming to rest atop the pubic mound. "My, my," she murmured, beginning a gentle circular stroking motion, "what have we here—"

Her mouth came down on Ann's, open and greedy. A moment later they were making love again, tongues duelling, thighs straddling and clasping, hips bucking and pumping spasmodically as they tumbled across the bed in a tangle of long slender limbs. Feeling the first warm ripples of orgasm rising through her lower body, Ann heard herself call out without words, a long high cry of simple mindless joy.

◁ ▲ ▽ ▷

She woke once during the night; she had no idea of the time, but the cabin was absolutely dark and no light came through the little window. Beside her Jack slept on, snoring faintly into her pillow.

Moving carefully, trying not to awaken Jack, she got out of bed and moved toward the door. The floor was frigid under her bare feet, but she couldn't stand the thought of putting those shoes on again. She did pick up a blanket and wrap herself in it before going out; these people seemed very casual about nudity but she wasn't quite that acclimatized yet.

The night air struck her like a cold whip as she stepped outside; the blanket hardly checked the gelid breeze that poured down the hillside. Yet she paused, heedless of the chill, lost in the incredible display overhead. She didn't think she'd ever seen so many stars; they fairly crowded the sky, dazzling uncountable myriads, clustered and scattered from horizon to horizon, the largest ones so fat and bright that it seemed you might knock them down with a stone. For a moment she had a vertiginous sensation of starting to fall upward, into the depths of the night sky, and she grabbed involuntarily at the corral fence.

And hello there, she said silently to the stars. We were headed your way, working on it anyway, but we seem to have gotten sidetracked, at least in this particular part of the continuum or whatever it is. Not that you give a damn, of course, you never did, why should you, we're the ones who need you, you got along fine without us for thirteen billion years . . . and now I'll bid you good evening, or morning or whatever time it is, because my feet are freezing and so is my ass.

She went on around the cabin to the little outhouse. There was no proper seat, just a board with a rough hole in it; trust Jack to ignore little details like comfort. Rucking the blanket up around her waist, Ann sat and, after a moment, peed. A little tender down there? That's what you get, she thought, for playing with yourself so much.

When she was done she got up and left the outhouse, making sure to turn the little wooden latchpiece, as Jack had shown her, to keep the door from banging in the wind. An outhouse, good God, shades of Snuffy Smith—come to think of it, hadn't Jack also said that Fat Bob person had a still?

I am, she reflected, somehow trapped in a squalid and barbarous world, one in which the things to which I devoted my life have ceased to exist—or never happened at all—and in which life promises to be nasty, brutish, and short, not to mention devoid of toilet paper and let's not even ask yet what they use for tampons. And I can't even dream about finding a way back to my own world, because back there I'm wanted for murder.

Why, then, am I happier than I've been in years?

Smiling a little foolishly, she went back around the cabin and inside, hurrying now, to dive under the fur sleeping robes and wiggle down into the warmth their two bodies had made. Jack stirred and mumbled a few cryptic syllables, probably complaining about Ann's cold feet, but she didn't quite wake.

Just before sleep reclaimed her, a stray memory drifted through Ann's mind; she wondered fuzzily who the gray-suited men had been, and why they were after her. But the thought got away from her and she slid gratefully once more into the waiting dark.

Part Two

chapter
eleven

The Indian kid came in carrying the last of the bags. He set it down on the living-room floor next to the others and said, "That's it."

Jay reached for her purse but he grinned and raised a hand. "No, no. The Scotts are already paying me."

He was a husky young man—not really a kid, Jay realized now, he had to be in his middle twenties, of course that was practically infancy from where she stood—and very dark, with the classic big-shouldered, big-chested, lean-hipped build of his race; he was no more than medium height, maybe even a little shorter than Jay's own ridiculous five feet nine, but he stood so straight he looked taller. He had on a Miami Dolphins T-shirt and snug jeans faded almost white and serviceable-looking running shoes. His coarse black hair was done up in a kind of knot in back, secured by a purple bandanna headband. Not bad at all, Jay considered, and felt a brief stirring of a long-neglected sort, but that died away as quickly as it had come.

She said, "Well, uh—I'm sorry, um—"

"Danny," he said, still grinning. "Danny Santos."

"Oh, yes. Sorry." He'd told her when he met her at the Albuquerque airport, and for that matter Melanie had mentioned him by name in her last letter, but Jay's memory these days was only slightly less leaky than the *Titanic*. "Well," she gestured vaguely, "care for a drink?"

She didn't think for a minute that Melanie had left any booze in the house, but that was no problem, not yet; she'd come more than prepared.

But Danny Santos shook his head. "I better not. Gotta drive back down those roads, you know?"

And maybe there were some parting instructions from the Scotts? *Whatever you do, for God's sake don't give the old lush any excuse to start drinking*—but no, he sounded sincere enough.

"I can't risk getting stopped with liquor on my breath," he added apologetically. "Cops around these parts, they don't like Indians, you know? This one deputy, works the county roads sometimes, he'd really love an excuse to nail me."

He stopped, looked thoughtful, and began digging in his jeans pocket. "Almost forgot," he said, and pulled out a couple of keys on a little chain. "The shiny one goes to the house. The brass one opens the garage. Mr. Scott said you wouldn't be driving the car, but you might need to get in there for some reason."

She took the keys from his extended hand, her fingertips briefly brushing his. "Thanks." She dropped the keys into her purse, let her hand linger on her wallet. "Sure you won't let me give you a little something?" Christ, that sounded like hell. "A little money," she added hastily, "for your trouble. You had quite a drive, down to Albuquerque and back."

"No, that's okay." He flashed his teeth again. Nice teeth, Jay noticed. "Like I said, they're already paying me. Besides," he said, looking suddenly self-conscious, "it's kind of an honor for me, driving you around like that. See, you've always been one of my favorite writers."

Jay opened her mouth and closed it. She couldn't think of a thing to say.

"I've read everything you ever wrote, I think," Danny Santos went on. "In fact—well, I was wondering if you'd sign a couple of books I got at home. If I brought them out here some time."

"Why . . . certainly." She smiled at him, hoping it wasn't too idiotic a smile. "I'd be glad to," she told him.

"Great. That'd be great." He actually sounded as if he meant it. "Well," he said, "I better get going. Anything you need, my phone number's on the wall by the kitchen phone."

He turned and disappeared through the front door, closing it quietly behind him. A few minutes later Jay heard his pickup truck start up out front. She listened to the sound of gravel crunching beneath his tires and then the diminuendo rumble as he drove off down the mountain road.

She let out a long sigh and strode quickly across the living room, to the collection of luggage piled next to the couch, and squatted down and undid the snaps of a big brown-leather-covered suitcase. Laying it flat on the floor, flipping back the lid, she pushed aside a layer of miscellaneous folded clothing and sat back on her heels, gazing fondly at the double row of big long-necked bottles, reading the familiar labels: Jack, Jim, George, all the good old boys from Kentucky. . . .

"Hi, guys," she said softly. "Did you miss me?"

She trailed her fingers over their smooth cool surfaces for a moment: decisions, decisions, but what the hell. For no partic-ular reason she settled on a liter of Jim Beam—not the seven-year-old kind, but the cheaper undated variety; why not give youth a chance?—and stood up and headed back toward the kitchen, the bottle dangling from her right hand, leaving the suitcase open on the floor.

The house was a big rambling affair, everything on ground level—that was going to take some getting used to, after nine years in New York—and it had been over a year since her only previous visit, but she remembered the basic layout. The kitchen was clear in back, at the end of a long shiny-floored hallway. Much too far to walk without replenishing vital body fluids; Jay paused, halfway down the hall, and unscrewed the cap off the Jim Beam and took a quick pull, straight out of the bottle. She leaned against the wall for a moment, enjoying the first spreading warmth, letting the bourbon thaw the cold empty places inside her. "Oh, yes," she said aloud.

The kitchen was enormous, at least by the standards she was used to; it would have taken up a third of her New York apartment. It didn't take long, though, to determine that her guess had been right; there wasn't so much as a bottle of cooking wine in evidence. A glass-fronted cabinet beside the hallway door held an assortment of drinking glasses—everything from wine to shot—but its shelves were otherwise empty. Jay laughed sourly to herself as she selected a big glass and took it over to the refrigerator to get some ice.

A magnetic clip on the refrigerator door held a large yellow envelope marked JAY—READ, PLEASE. She ignored it until she had filled the glass with ice and splashed in a healthy slug of Jim Beam; then, after a quick satisfying sip, she took the envelope down and carried it back to the living room and sat down on the couch and leaned back and addressed herself to the drink in her hand, leaving the envelope unopened on her lap. You had to have your priorities, after all.

Not that this was one of those die-for-a-drink days; in fact she'd been feeling a good deal better than usual, maybe because the dreams had left her alone the last few nights. She didn't really think that would last, but it was damn nice while it did.

But flying anywhere in this country, she considered, would make a Mormon elder reach for a drink. The miserably uncomfortable terminals with everything spread out for maximum inconvenience—not to mention the prices in the airport bars, the drinks must be made with unicorn blood—the humiliating "security precautions," the insolent stupid people behind tickytacky desks, the endless delays and finally the airplane itself with its cramped spaces and the seats designed to fit no human ass ever known . . . when you thought about it, it was enough to make you despair for the future of democracy, because if the American people stood for this on a regular basis then they'd stand for anything.

And the awful dry air on board the plane had left her, as always, with a sore throat; in fact, she told herself, that was the main reason she needed the whiskey right now, to ease the pain of raw tissues. She took another drink and closed her eyes: damn, but it felt good going down.

At last she opened her eyes, set the drink very carefully on the glass-topped coffee table, stuck a finger under the envelope flap and ripped it open, and pulled out the letter within.

Dear Jay, she read. *I suppose by the time you read this we will be winging our way across the Pacific. Hope you had a good flight and nothing got lost or smashed by the baggage-handler gang.*

I want to tell you again how pleased we are that you will be staying in the house while we're away. Believe me, you're doing us a favor. Four months is a long time to leave a house standing empty. It will make me feel so much better to know you're keeping an eye on things.

I just hope you'll be happy there. I know it's a change from the city, but maybe that's what you've been needing—to get away from that New York scene and get back in touch with yourself. This is the country where you grew up, after all. Maybe here you can do some thinking about where you want to go with your life.

Translation: dry out and get your sorry shit together, Jay thought, sipping.

Of course the main thing is your work, and I think you'll find you're all fixed up in that regard. Richard's old computer is set up in your room—he says for you to feel free to make any changes you want, he never uses it any more.

Sorry the insurance company wouldn't let us give you the use of the car too

"Uh huh," Jay said aloud, sipping again. "Uh fucking huh."

but Danny will be happy to drive you anywhere you want to go, or get whatever you need from town. Just try to give him some advance notice—his pueblo is a couple of hours away, and he's also got his classes at the university in Santa Fe.

I'm just hoping I'll be able to adjust to life in Japan. From all I've heard it's very

Jay crumpled the letter and dropped it on the floor without bothering to read what Japan was supposed to be very. Melanie would be happy as long as Richard was happy—or she'd tell herself she was, which for Melanie amounted to the same thing—and Richard would be happy as long as he was doing whatever mysterious scientific things he did.

She drained the rest of her drink—the ice was starting to melt and she hated the taste of watery bourbon—and looked around for the bottle, before remembering she'd left it in the kitchen. She looked at the row of bottles in the still-open suitcase and considered opening another one rather than make the trip, but decided that would be silly and inefficient. Besides, she thought as she hoisted herself up off the couch—legs protesting, still stiff from the plane ride—that was a bad sign, when you started having part-full bottles lying around in different rooms. Only alcoholics did things like that.

◄ ▲ ▼ ►

Back in the kitchen, reaching for the bottle on the counter by the sink, she saw the clock above the stove and did a double take: six-thirty, how did it get so late? And she ought to do something about dinner; she had the typical New Yorker's horror of dining early, but she hadn't eaten anything all day and besides, her body, still running on EST, thought it was two hours later.

She opened the refrigerator door, stared briefly at the unpromising contents—a couple of boxes of yogurt, a package of cheese, a plastic jug of orange juice (she wished she'd brought a bottle of vodka; screwdrivers would be good for a little variety)—and then tried the freezer. That was better; Melanie had thoughtfully stocked the box with stacks of frozen dinners. She took one out at random, made a face at the brand name—Healthy Choice, for God's sake!—and studied the package for a moment. Country Herb Chicken. Good old Country Herb Chicken, Jay thought, crossing the room toward the microwave. Another sixties great. Whatever happened to him after his band broke up?

She ripped the box open and stuck the plastic tray into the microwave, remembering at the last minute to peel back the covering at the end to let steam escape. She checked the instructions, punched in six and a half minutes, and headed back toward the hallway, scooping up the Jim Beam on her way and feeling rather proud of herself. I can handle it, she thought, I can do this.

◄　▲　▼　►

But, standing in the middle of the living room, unscrewing the cap on the Jim Beam, she felt a sudden growing edginess, that the whiskey dulled but didn't fully relieve. She didn't belong here, in these fine tidy people's fine tidy home; and out in the middle of the God-damned wilderness at that, miles and miles from anywhere—if you could call Santa Fe anywhere, Christ, what a pretentious tourist trap.

There had, to be sure, been a time when she called this part of the country home, felt at ease in such surroundings, but that was long ago and mixed up with too many memories and associations of the kind best left unexhumed. . . .

She found herself looking across the room, at the fancy stereo setup over by the far wall. That was it, she decided; it was too fucking *quiet* around here. She wandered over to have a look. A neat wooden cabinet on the wall held rows of CD disks and tape cassettes; Richard and Melanie were big music lovers, though their tastes were far apart. She remembered her earlier visit, and the arguments on that very subject.

Swigging bourbon, she looked through their collection. Richard liked country music; it wasn't her own favorite sound by any means, but at least it was better than the New Age schlock Melanie went in for. She chose a CD and put it in the machine—after some difficulty figuring out the controls—and went back and sank down on the couch, while Waylon Jennings' dark brooding voice filled the room.

The ice in the glass, she discovered, was mostly melted by now. That was all right; she didn't know why she'd bothered. She sat back and closed her eyes and swigged from the bottle, thinking idly and then not quite so idly about the way Danny Santos' butt had looked in those faded jeans. Damn if she wasn't starting to get horny, lately. She'd thought all that was long behind her; for the last year or so she'd been as numb below the waist as everywhere else. She considered playing with herself, but she would have had to stand up to pull down her own jeans, and she was tired of bobbing up and down like a yo-yo. She hoisted the bottle instead; another drop or two and the itch would pass.

Waylon Jennings was singing that the devil made him do it the first time but the second time he done it on his own. "I'll drink to that," Jay announced, and did.

◀ ▲ ▼ ▶

She sat there, drinking, while the light began to fade outside; now and then she got up to change disks, or to stumble down the hall to the bathroom, but otherwise she remained on the couch. When it got dark she switched on the end-table lamp at her elbow. The level of bourbon in the bottle had dropped, she noticed with dull surprise, by quite a bit.

A couple of times it came to her that there was something she'd forgotten, something back in the kitchen that she was supposed to do something about; but it was much too far to go back there and it couldn't be very important anyway.

Finally, as the fog rose behind her eyes, she turned and pulled down the woolen Indian blanket that lay folded across the back of the couch. Stretching out, pillowing her head on the armrest, she covered herself with the blanket. She reached over and flipped the lamp off and turned over, her back to the room, cuddling the bottle like a baby. The blanket rode up, exposing most of her back, but the room was fairly warm and she didn't notice. A minute later she was asleep.

chapter twelve

Morning sunlight glinted softly off the worn blue metal of the revolver's long barrel. Ann steadied the piece on both hands, lined the blade sight up on the target, and squeezed the trigger. The hammer fell with a click and Ann said, "Bang."

The target glanced around, sat up, wiggled its ears, and hopped unhurriedly away up the rocky hillside. Ann lowered the pistol and was about to reach for the handful of cartridges in her pocket when a deep male voice behind her said, "Runs pretty good, doesn't he, with his head shot off?"

Ann jumped slightly, turned, and saw Fat Bob standing a couple of yards away, grinning at her. "Hi," she said, relaxing. "Damn rabbit ducked behind a tree just as I shot."

"Yeah, I hate it when that happens." He looked pointedly at the gun in her hand. "You know, it's not really a good idea to be walking around with an empty gun."

"Jack said to do a lot of dry firing," Ann said. "She said there wasn't enough ammunition for serious target practice and this would be the next best thing."

"And she's absolutely right. Especially for somebody like you," Fat Bob said. "I mean, it's pretty obvious you don't have much experience handling firearms, right? But," he added, "that's something you do close to home. Out here, out of sight of the settlement, you never know who might come along. Or what."

She nodded and thumbed the little sliding catch to release the cylinder. With her left hand she dug cartridges out of her jeans pocket and slipped them into the chambers one by one. She snapped the cylinder back into the frame and stuck the revolver back in her belt. Jack had promised to make her a holster but hadn't gotten around to it yet.

"Did that pretty well," Fat Bob said approvingly. "You're coming along just fine. Like that piece all right, do you?"

Ann shrugged. "It seems all right." Jack had made a swap with Fat Bob for the old .38, saying the Glock was too tricky for an inexperienced user. "I know almost nothing about guns," she said. "I'm not really qualified to have an opinion."

Fat Bob laughed. "Never knew that to stop very many people from having them. That's what democracy is all about."

"Was," she pointed out.

"You got that right," he admitted. "Not a hell of a lot of democracy left, is there? Anarchy with little pockets of dictatorship, would seem to be the general pattern nowadays."

He reached up and ran his hand over the gleaming dark-chocolate surface of his bare scalp. "Damn, I shouldn't go out in this sun bareheaded, specially at this altitude . . . you ever have to shoot anybody with that," he told her, "shoot him a couple of times, at least. A thirty-eight doesn't have a lot of hitting power. Even if he goes off somewhere and leaks to death, that's not going to do you much good if he's taken you out first."

"That's what Jack said."

"Yeah, well, you listen to Jack, you won't go wrong. She knows this stuff forwards, backwards and sideways."

"I've noticed."

"I bet you have. I bet you two have quite a story to tell, and I'd give a lot to hear it. Claims she found you living in the ruins down in Santa Fe, but you're awfully healthy and well fed for a ruin-squatter, and you sure don't look like any mutie I ever saw."

She started to speak but he added quickly, "I know, I know. Jack already told me not to ask questions. You hear me asking?"

He sat down on a big rock and gave Ann a long thoughtful look. "Whoever you are, however you hooked up with Jack, I'm glad you did. Anybody can see you're good for her."

"Thanks."

"Hey, I'm serious. She's been different, ever since you came along. You got no idea what she used to be like, they weren't kidding when they called her Mad Jack, she scared the shit out of people. Scared the shit out of *me*, sometimes," he admitted, "and I guess I was about as good friends with her as anybody. She used to scream at night, drank like you wouldn't believe—"

He snorted. "Maybe I shouldn't be happy about that particular development, she was one of my best customers. Couldn't make anything so bad she wouldn't drink it. But I like to see her happy."

"I'll be glad when she gets back," Ann said.

"Shouldn't be much longer," Fat Bob assured her. "Supposed to be back tomorrow or next day, but of course you never know."

Jack had ridden off with most of the settlement's men, a couple of days ago, on a wild-cattle hunt. There had been no question of Ann's coming along. "You can't keep up," Jack had said with her usual bluntness. "Not yet, anyway. This is pretty damn rough work."

With very little interest in spending days on horseback and nights on the bare ground—and even less in shooting and butchering the stringy undersized feral cattle that roamed the canyons and river valleys—Ann had cheerfully accepted her exclusion; she didn't think she was missing much. But she hadn't realized how much she was going to miss Jack.

She said, "She'll be all right, won't she? I mean, you know— one woman, out there alone with those men—"

Fat Bob threw back his head and guffawed. "Oh, babe, that's funny—" He laughed some more, wiping his eyes at the end. "Listen," he said, "you don't want to worry about Jack. Not in that department. Even if they were inclined—and basically that's a fairly decent bunch of guys—they know better than to try anything with her."

He looked off across the hillside, his shoulders still shaking with internal laughter. "A few years back," he said, "Jack went off on a hunt like this—elk, I think they were after, I don't know, she wasn't living here at the time, I heard the story second-hand. Anyway, these half a dozen characters she was with, seems they decided she ought to provide some entertainment. You know what I'm saying."

"What happened?"

"Nobody's ever heard the exact details," Fat Bob said. "All anybody knows, she came back home alone, leading a nice little string of horses. Had herself a collection of extra guns and ammo and equipment, too. In fact I think that's where she got that three-fifty-seven she packs."

"She killed them all?" Ann asked, fascinated. "Not all six of them. She couldn't have."

Fat Bob spread pink-palmed hands and shrugged. "Like I said, nobody really knows what happened. Could be she just got the drop on them some way, left them unarmed and on foot. Of course in this country that's practically a death sentence, but—well," he said, "if you're really curious, I imagine she'd tell you."

"I wonder if I want to know."

"You probably don't." He got up off the rock, paused to dust the seat of his khaki shorts with both hands, and jerked his head in the direction of the settlement. "Come on. Let's go back. It's not safe for you out here alone."

She followed him down the trail, past the rock outcrops and the clumps of brush and cactus, and then along the line of the sagging old fence. Beyond the rusty barbed-wire strands, scattered out over the hillside, horses and cattle grazed on the sparse bunchy grass. Mostly horses; as Jack had explained, it was too much trouble trying to keep cattle, too big a drain on the grass and water supply, when there were plenty of the wild kind available for easy killing. In fact there were more horses than usual just now, Fat Bob having made some sort of deal with a nearby settlement to pasture part of their horse herd for the spring. Ann looked but couldn't spot the two horses she and Jack had ridden up from Santa Fe. They were in there somewhere, though; Captain Ernie still hadn't shown up to reclaim them.

"Not that it's all that safe back there either," Fat Bob said as the settlement came into view, "with the men all gone hunting, and I'll be damn glad when they get back. But the jackers usually leave the village alone, because I trade with them. Out here, though, you'd be fair game by any rules they'd recognize."

At the edge of the little village he turned. "All right," he said, "no more wandering off like that, okay? Jack'll have my old black ass for dinner if I let anything happen to you."

Watching him walk away, Ann thought about his earlier words. Good for Jack, she thought, what a sweet thing to say. I only hope it's true, God knows she's been good for me.

It had been a little over a week—ten days? eleven? have to check, have to take better note of the passage of days, all too easy to lose track here—since their arrival at Fat Bob's settlement. During that time she had learned a great deal about this world, almost all of it bad and much of it very bad indeed.

But she had also slept soundly every night, and the terrible visions were gone; her mind was clearer than it had been in a long time, and on the whole she felt ridiculously happy. Love? Undoubtedly, but that was too easy a word and too simple a concept; being with Jack, the interaction between them, had changed her—had changed them both—in ways she still didn't fully understand.

Well, she thought, Doctor Peters always said I needed to improve my self-esteem. . . .

No; the obvious jokes aside, she had known for some time that her identity with Jack was not much more than a technicality. Whatever the scientific facts, they were not the same person and never could be, not in any real sense. Their genotypes might have given them the same hair and eyes and physical build and fingerprints and the other consequences of identical DNA; but different worlds had shaped them, forced the development of different potentials, till they were as they were.

Anyway, it was rather like studying advanced physics: you

learned that the apparently solid world around you was really
nothing but a swarm of tiny particles, whirling and whanging
around in a lot of empty space—but that didn't change the way
you dealt with that world; that oncoming truck might be mere
illusion but you got out of its way so you didn't become an illu-
sory corpse.

And it was impossible to think of Jack as anything but her
unique and magnificent self. . . .

"Maybe," Jack had said, the last time the subject came up,
"we're kind of two different pieces of the same person. Maybe
that's why we're less crazy when we're together."

"We do fit together nicely," Ann had responded, wiggling
closer in the bed, and that had ended the intellectual discussions
for the evening, and next day Jack had ridden off on her hunt;
but Ann had thought, later, that Jack's idea made as much sense
as any.

And none of that mattered either. She had been crazy and
now she wasn't; or else she'd gone *really* crazy and this whole
thing was an all-time championship-grade delusional system—
but either way, she'd take it.

Walking down the trail toward the cabin, she caught herself
humming softly: "Cindy Lou," the old Buddy Holly standard,
hadn't heard that one since school, whatever brought it up now?
Regressing, were we? Going to start giggling, next, and saying
"barf"?

She stuck her tongue out at herself and walked on, humming,
singing under her breath: *if you knew Cindy Lou, something something Cindy Lou,* her feet doing a little dance step on the rocky
trail.

◀ ▲ ▼ ▶

But that night she slept poorly, waking several times, troubled by strange dreams—not the real nightmares, thank God they still hadn't returned, just weird little scenes that made no sense and receded from memory as soon as she woke—and missing Jack more than ever. At last she got out the pills and reluctantly— she'd been trying to quit—took a couple of Xanax, and fell into a dull stupid oblivion.

Morning found her puffy-eyed and clumsy, head aching, wishing desperately for a cup of coffee. She burned a finger getting the fire started; she scorched Jack's best pan trying to make breakfast, and then couldn't make herself eat the lumpy coarse-cornmeal mush.

That was how it went all day; her nerves refused to settle down and she couldn't seem to do anything right. Chopping firewood, she missed a stroke completely and hit a rock and took a chip out of the axe's edge, that Jack had spent an hour sharpening just before she left. She let the fire go out and then took forever getting it going again, even though she had thought she finally had the hang of using flint and steel. And she didn't dare even touch any of the guns; life was dangerous enough around here as it was.

She dosed herself repeatedly from the dwindling supply of pills, refusing to let herself think what she was going to do when they were gone. The drugs didn't do all that much good; mostly they just made her even groggier. And that night, despite her fatigue, it took a really pushing-her-luck dose to bring sleep.

Next day was even worse, her nerves wound tight as the high strings of a piano. Her stomach revolted at even the thought of food, though she gulped water compulsively, seeking to relieve the dryness and the sour taste in her mouth. When the woman in the next cabin sent a small boy over to invite her to lunch, she snapped at the child so viciously that he ran away; then she put her head down on the table and cried for a long time.

Jack, Jack, she thought, where are you? but then she imagined Jack coming home and seeing her like this, and the thought was enough to send her groping for the Xanax again.

◁ ▲ ▼ ▷

Later, a little after midday, she decided to go and apologize to the woman in the next cabin, and to the child. Not their fault, after all, that she was being a neurotic idiot today.

The sunlight hurt her eyes when she stepped outside, making her squint. She went back inside and dug in the odds-and-ends basket; Jack had quite a collection of sunglasses, salvaged from various sources, and she took the first pair that came to hand— trashy-looking things with bright red rims and mirror lenses, but she didn't care how she looked today—and went back out, and that was when she saw the horsemen coming up the road.

For a heart-surging moment she thought it must be the hunting party returning; but then she saw that there were too many, at least a dozen and perhaps more, hard to count accurately through the trees and the cloud of dust their horses were raising. They were coming right up the middle of the old dirt road, across the open ground, headed toward the village with no attempt to use cover, and they stayed in a loose column without sending out flanking riders.

Peaceful visitors, then, no doubt come to trade with Fat Bob; she had been about to run back inside the cabin for a gun, but now she relaxed and watched the riders approach. There was something vaguely familiar about some of them, particularly the one in the lead, but the distance was too great for a clear view.

They stopped on the road, bunching up, some of them dismounting. The leading figure rode his horse up to Fat Bob's house and shouted something she didn't catch. After a minute or so Fat Bob came out. His hands were empty; that was another reassuring sign.

She saw Fat Bob walk up to the leader, who bent down in the saddle and held out a hand. They appeared to talk for a moment, and then they both turned and looked straight in Ann's direction. Fat Bob appeared to be pointing.

The horseman straightened and reined his horse around, making a gesture to the men behind him. A couple of them detached themselves from the group and fell in behind him as he rode slowly across the hillside, swinging well clear of the scatter of cabins and tents. By the time they had covered half the distance Ann's memory had kicked in, and she stood beside the cabin door and waited, half wishing she'd gotten that gun after all.

Captain Ernie pulled his horse to a stop in front of the cabin and said, "Yo, honey. We meet again, eh?"

"Come for your horses?" she asked, and jerked her head in the direction of the distant pasture. "There they are."

"Yeah, I saw them. Looks like they're in good shape. Appreciate it."

He swung down off his horse and stood for a moment, stretching and grinning, while the men behind him dismounted as well. "Man," he said, "been a long ride, you know?" He took off the black bush hat and ran his fingers through his long iron-streaked hair. "Think you could spare a drink of water?"

Ann didn't want to give him a drink or anything else; she wanted this smiling thug to take his damned horses and go away, as quickly as possible. But Jack had been at some pains to impress on her the local code of hospitality; among other rules, you never refused a stranger a drink of water. To do so was tantamount to a declaration of enmity.

"All right," she said, and turned back toward the cabin door.

She had meant to bring the water out, but Captain Ernie and then the other two men came pushing through the doorway right behind her, without so much as a may-I. She reached for the gourd dipper, trying to ignore the rudeness, but then a hand gripped her shoulder, not painfully but very firmly, and turned her around.

"Never mind," Captain Ernie said softly. "Seems like I'm not all that thirsty after all."

Her mouth opened and Captain Ernie put his other hand to her face. "Now, now. No hollering. We're not gonna hurt you, not gonna pull anything, don't worry. Just as long," he said, "as you don't give us any trouble."

He stared into her face for a few seconds. His eyes were a strange straw color, like a lion's. "All right," he said, releasing her. "I think you got it."

The other two were systematically ransacking the cabin, collecting all the guns and other weapons. One—a shaven-headed young man with dark Indian or Mexican features; she remembered him from the meeting outside Santa Fe—said, "Okay, all clean."

"Good," Captain Ernie said without turning around. Still looking at Ann, he waved a hand in the direction of the bed.

"Go sit down. Keep your hands where I can see them and don't make any sudden moves, and let me know if you have to pee or anything, and maybe I won't have to have Ray tie you up. He enjoys that a little too much."

"Shit," the skinhead said. "You never let me have any fun." All three men laughed.

"Jack will kill you for this," Ann said to Captain Ernie.

"Oh, she'll probably try," he agreed cheerfully. "If she gets a chance. But we're not planning to let her have a chance."

Ann sat down on the bed. "I thought you were her father's friend."

"Yeah, well—" Captain Ernie looked slightly uncomfortable for a moment. A very short moment. "Hey," he said, "business is business, all right? I mean, what can I say? Some people made me an offer."

He turned his head as the door curtain flapped inward. "In fact," he said, "here they are now."

Two more figures came into the room. This time Ann didn't have any trouble at all in recognizing them. Or rather the silvery-gray suits they wore.

chapter
thirteen

J ay stared at the computer screen, took a deep breath and let it slowly out, and typed:

> Sunlight glinted on the blade of the Saxon's sword as he raised it for a killing blow. With a sudden lunge Janet drove her own weapon FUCK

"Jesus *Christ*," she muttered, deleting hastily. She looked around for the current bottle, remembered the promise she'd made to herself this morning, and turned back to the keyboard.

> "Eat death, Welsh whore," the Saxon snarled, raising his sword for a killing stroke. "Stroke this, asshole," Janet reFUCK

Shuddering, Jay deleted again. Computers, she reflected, were great things, but this was the one time you really missed the old days; deleting onscreen just didn't provide the same vicious satisfaction as physically ripping a page from a typewriter and wadding it up and throwing it across the room. Though admittedly this was less wasteful of paper, and therefore kinder to the trees. But fuck the trees; how could you respect something that big that would let a dog piss on it?

She typed:

> **The Saxon swung his sword back for a killing stroke. "Oh, fuck this shit," Janet said suddenly, and pulled out her 9mm. Uzi and blew the silly son of a bitch to dogmeat FUCK FUCK FUCK FUCK FUCK**

She pushed herself back in Richard's old swivel chair, took her hands off the keyboard and raised them to her face, and sat for a long minute, trying really hard. God damn it, she told herself, *I can do this.*

She deleted again, typed again:

> **Tje Saxpm swimg jox FOCL**

"All right," she said aloud, "*all* right, *that's* it."

Standing up, she crossed the room and strode down the hall to the kitchen, where a half-emptied bottle of George Dickel stood on the counter next to the sink. The bottle which is half empty, she thought, picking it up and unscrewing the cap, contains the same amount as the one which is half full, but not for long, baby, not for long.

The bourbon hit her stomach with the usual first-drink-of-the-day impact, and for a moment it seemed to want to make a round trip, but she held it down and waited while it got comfortable. Then she took another one so it wouldn't be lonely down there, and that was a lot better.

So, she thought, I promised myself no booze today until I get some work done. So hey, self, sorry about that, okay? That was then, this is now. Sue me.

Carrying the bottle, she went back up the hallway to her room. The glowing computer screen still displayed the garbled line but she didn't feel like touching the keys again, even to delete. The hell with it. At least she'd tried.

God damn it, she said to herself, I *can't* do this, I don't even *want* to do this, why am I trying? Why the fuck did I ever tell Ruth I'd do a story for her silly anthology, anyway? I don't know how to write that sword-and-sorcery crap. Hell, I don't even read it.

There was, to be sure, the alternative. . . . She stared for a moment at the little plastic box beside the monitor, that held, among other things, a disk containing the half-finished novel that she hadn't touched since last winter. She hadn't even bothered to transfer it to this computer's hard drive, so far, even though finishing it was supposed to be the main reason she was here doing this Old Bitch of the Mountain routine.

And, if she wanted to get into self-analysis now, that was probably why she'd taken on the stupid story job, practically jumped at the chance when Ruth Raeder emailed her about it yesterday. Writing about flashing swords and armored sociopaths and babes in bronze Wonderbras—she'd watched part of a crypto-dyke TV show last night, hoping to get into the mood of the thing—might be an exercise in gormlessness, but it made a good excuse to avoid doing any *real* writing.

Speaking of time wasters, she hadn't checked the email today. Always good for burning another chunk of the day. . . .

She sat down and scooted the chair forward and set the bottle beside the computer tower, within easy reach of her left hand. Her right found the mouse. A few clicks later the unfinished manuscript page had been replaced on the screen by the unimaginative graphics and eye-straining print of the email inbox. That had been a pain in the ass, setting it up to have her email forwarded here from her New York account; and a total waste so far, since nothing of any real interest had come in in the week and a half she'd been here. Maybe today—

A Tarzan yell blasted from the speakers under the desk. The you-have-mail signal; she'd managed to waste a whole day customizing Richard's old Dell with silly-ass downloads. A string of message headings appeared in the inbox. "Ah," Jay said, reaching for the bottle. Not opening it yet, just holding it in her lap; you had to be ready, when you did this. That was something you learned very early in the wonderful world of cyberspace.

She clicked open the first message and read:

```
How would you like to receive red-hot
adult pictures in your email every
day, ABSOLUTELY FREE? Just
```

Snarling, she hit REPLY and typed rapidly FUCK OFF AND DIE. She started to hit SEND and then remembered what someone had told her: some of these outfits had it set up so that when you used the reply button you sent your email address out to another bunch of one-hander purveyors.

Instead she deleted and opened the next one, which proved to be an offer to show her how to use the power of the Internet to make big money with her own home business. The one after that was another porn spammer, and the one after that was a chain letter.

She sat back and opened the bottle. Definitely one of those days. She took a good stiff drink and told herself to go to hell.

The next one was at least from a human being: an old school acquaintance who liked to keep up the illusion of having lots of friends by forwarding an endless stream of ancient and never-funny jokes, fatuous Deep Thoughts, and anything else that came her way, in mass e-mailings to everyone she knew or thought she knew. She never wrote anything of her own, beyond the occasional "This is funny!!!" or "Something to think about!!!" or, lately, the idiotic "LOL!!!" This time, Jay saw, she had swallowed yet another virus-warning hoax. The heading read PLEASE READ—E-MAIL VIRUS ALERT!!!

Jay glanced over the remaining items and saw a familiar address. Wondering why she hadn't spotted it before, she opened it:

```
Jay--

Bad news, I'm afraid, and I really
hate to break it to you in this tacky
medium. But you'd already left for
New Mexico when I got back into town,
and I tried several times to call you
but there was no answer. I hope
you're all right?
```

Anyway--I managed to corner Hugh, after the Nebula Awards banquet, and finally he admitted that Swallow Street isn't going to push NORTH FROM NOWHERE. The decision was made a couple of weeks ago. They haven't even got an advertising budget for the title.

It's the numbers, he said. The bean counters looked at the sales figures on the last two books and that was that. They feel--please understand, Hugh was just quoting, don't blame him for this--that you represent an older generation of SF writers, and that your name no longer has the sales power it used to, especially among the younger bookbuyers they're going after now.

(Before you take that too hard, let me add that Hugh also told me, off the record, that the main reason is that Swallow Street's management has basically lost interest in the traditional SF novel; they think it's a dying genre. They're shifting more and more of the emphasis--and the money--to media-tie-in books, such as the new STAR WARRIORS series. So it's not just you. It's happening to everybody.)

And of course that's the real reason Hugh had to bounce CEREMONIES OF THE HORSEMEN last month. He said he didn't even bother taking it to committee because he knew there wouldn't be any point in it.

I don't know what to say, Jay. I feel terrible about this. I've been your agent for a long time. I was the one who hooked you up with Swallow Street to begin with. I feel somehow responsible. And yet there's nothing I can do.

Don't despair. I'm working on some ideas. Somehow, we'll get you past this.

Oh yes--Stephanie Rogers at Piper Press is reading CEREMONIES and so far she likes it, but she says she'd have a lot better chance of getting the bosses to go for it if you'd be

```
willing to consider using a pen name.
I know, I know, you've told me how
you feel on that point, but . . .
well, frankly, Jay, it may come to
that or nothing. Think about it at
least, won't you?

Best as always--

Nate
```

For a few minutes Jay sat immobile, staring at the words on the screen. Her mouth hung slightly open but she was not aware of this.

Finally, slowly and with very careful movements, she pushed herself and the chair back and got to her feet and turned and walked to the door. She left the bottle where it was.

She walked down the hallway, moving faster now but still with measured steps. She crossed the living room and went out the front door onto the long porch. And stood there with both hands resting on the railing, looking out over the rocky brush-dotted mountain slope below the house and the pine woods a mile or so below and beyond that the great valley and then the next snow-peaked range. Her eyes were wide and unfocused. Her face was dead-woman white and utterly blank.

After a while she turned and walked back through the house to her room and sat down once more at the computer table. Crisply and efficiently she minimized the email window, pulled up the Word page she had been working on, and began to write:

> Overconfident, the Saxon stepped in, swinging his broad-bladed sword in a stroke that would have taken Janet's head off if she had stayed put. Instead she ducked, lunged, and drove the point of her own weapon home two fingers' breadth below his breastbone. An odd look, half surprise and half embarrassment, came over his face; he dropped his sword and she felt his death shiver through her blade and up her sword arm.

She wrote fast, without hesitation or pause for thought. The page rolled away up the screen, finished, and another moved into its place, then another. She did not touch the bottle; her eyes never left the screen or her fingers the keyboard.

She was in the middle of the climactic scene, her fingers dancing on the keys and her face streaked with sweat, when Tarzan bellowed from beneath the desk.

She jerked upright in the chair, blinking. After a stunned second she said, *"Shit!,"* and started to kick at the speakers, but then she stopped; it wasn't the machine's fault she'd forgotten, like an asshole, to turn off the incoming-email alarm.

She put her hands to her face and rubbed, hard, pulling the skin down tight over her cheekbones. A shiver ran through her whole body. "Shit," she said again, more softly.

Scribus fucking interruptus.

She shook her head and reached toward the keyboard, then the mouse; she hesitated, her hand making small uncertain motions. But then she said, "Fuck it," and palmed the mouse. Whatever she'd had going was Rice Krispies now. Might as well see who or what had arrived. More good news, maybe. Like Ruth writing to tell her the anthology had been cancelled—

```
Hi there!!! Don't read this!!!

If you don't like romance, adventure,
and a GOOD READ to curl up with at
night!!!

Chances are you're already one of my
thousands of DEAR PERSONAL FRIENDS
out there in cyber-land!!! If so, you
already know that my latest novel,
FOREVER SWEET PASSION, has just
received an award from the Romance
Authors' League and is still climbing
in the sales ratings of all the major
bookstore chains!!!

If you haven't yet read FOREVER SWEET
PASSION, remember, your local
bookseller has it--or if she's out,
you can order from Amazon. I love
online ordering--tho it's not as much
fun as REAL SHOPPING, right, girls?
```

Just a quick note: I will be signing
at Romance Ink bookstore in
Evansville, Illinois, on May 15, from
2:00 to 4:00 o'clock p.m. Then I have
to jet on out to San Francisco for
the RAL convention to pick up that
nice award!!!

Thank you all for your support--lots
of love!!!

Leola Markens

Author of FOREVER SWEET PASSION (my
27th!!!), published by Pierrot Books,
paperback, $4.95

If you don't want to receive this
newsletter any more, just use the
little Reply thingy and tell me--but
I'll cry!!!

Jay said, "Son of a bitch. Son. Of. A. Particular. Fucking. BITCH."
She drew back her right hand and made a fist and punched
the screen, hard, dead center. Pain flared in her knuckles but she
struck again with her other fist, and then began slapping at the
screen, wild open-hand swings, screaming, *"God damn fucking
son of a fucking bitch God damn it—"*

The big monitor rocked slightly under the pounding but the glass was thick and strong; it took no damage. Her hands were less durable, and after a couple of minutes the pain forced her to stop. Then she rested her arms on the desk, pushing the keyboard back, and put her head down on her forearms and cried for a long time.

Eventually, though, she sat up and dried her eyes with sore swollen hands, and reached for the bottle. Good old George, always there when you needed a friend.

But the bottle felt wrong, and when she raised it up to the light she saw that good old George wasn't there after all, at least not nearly as much of him as there should have been. Must have spilled some, she couldn't possibly have drunk that much. Just had a few little sips. . . .

Swigging at what remained, she got up and opened the closet door and looked up at the top shelf. More bad news, maybe the worst of the day; the basic-food-groups supply had shrunk to an appalling degree. Another bottle of George Dickel, and a pint of Black Jack that she'd been saving to celebrate with when she finally finished the story—and there was a liter of Jim in the living room, maybe a quarter of that gone as best she could recall, and that was all. *All.*

Which wouldn't do at all. Not for present purposes. No way.

◀ ▲ ▼ ▶

The garage was dark and Jay had to fumble around a minute before she found the light switch. She flicked it on and smiled to see that Melanie still had the same little white Toyota. Typical; she made enough to afford something bigger and pricier, but that wouldn't have been environmentally responsible. The other half of the garage was empty; no doubt Richard's beloved BMW was stored somewhere in Santa Fe or Albuquerque.

It didn't take long to locate the little magnetic metal box up in the left front wheel well. Popping it open, jingling the keys, Jay laughed softly to herself; did they really think she wouldn't know to look for a spare-key stash? More likely Melanie had simply forgotten about it. The accumulation of dirt on the outside of the box indicated it hadn't been used in a long time, if ever.

She got the garage door open and, after a little experimenting with the keys, unlocked the car. She slid in behind the wheel and stuck the main key in the ignition. "Talk to mama," she whispered.

A few minutes later she was rolling down the steep gravel drive. The car swerved and slewed a good deal—living in New York, she hadn't driven a car in a couple of years, and she'd never before handled one with front-wheel drive—but she managed to keep it between the ditches, and the skills came back quickly enough. By the time she turned onto the blacktop road that wound away down the mountainside, she was doing pretty well, hardly weaving at all.

"All *right*," she said happily, and let go the wheel with one hand long enough to unscrew the cap off the bourbon bottle clasped between her thighs. The cap got away from her and rolled somewhere out of sight but that was all right, only one good swallow left anyway, so she tilted the bottle up to her lips, peering one-eyed past it as she drained it, and then she rolled down the window and tossed the empty out.

"Litterbug, litterbug," she sang, leaving the window down, enjoying the wind in her hair, "fly away home. . . ."

◄   ▲   ▼   ►

The liquor-store manager was impressed enough with the size of her purchase to have his young Mexican assistant carry it all out to the car for her. She unlocked the trunk and watched the kid's ass as he bent over and set the cardboard box down. "Any particular place?" he asked her in unaccented English, and she shook her head.

"Thanks," she said, and handed him a couple of bills without looking to see what they were. She started to slam the trunk lid down, reconsidered, and took out a bottle before shutting the trunk. She went around and got in behind the wheel and reached over and put the bottle in the glove compartment: emergency supplies for the journey. Better leave it alone if she could, though, or she might not make it back up that road.

She had expected to have to drive all the way to Santa Fe, but she had found this little town down in the valley, where the blacktop met the main highway. She pulled jerkily out and headed down the street, barely missing a woman coming out of a beauty shop—EDITH'S, the sign said—and running a stop sign, but no pursuing cop cars appeared in the mirror, and soon the whole place was lost to sight.

She forced herself to take it easy and drive slowly, when the road began climbing into the foothills and then snaking up the big mountainside; she might not give a damn about herself any more but the idea of all those lovely bottles getting smashed and all that lovely whiskey running out on the ground was horrible enough to make her cautious. She thought a couple of times about the bottle in the glove compartment but she managed to leave it alone, and finally there was the dirt turnoff and the house.

She started to leave the car in the yard but then reconsidered and ran it very carefully into the garage, at a gingerly crawl, and got out and locked the garage door. Then she went around and opened the trunk. She was about to pick up the box when something in the forward recesses of the trunk caught her eye. Curious, she reached in and pulled out a small zippered leather case. She undid the zipper and found herself holding a medium-sized nickel-plated revolver.

"Hah!" she said aloud, and then laughed. So they'd locked the gun in the car too, away from crazy old Jay. Well, that had probably been pretty good thinking on their part.

She turned the piece this way and that, studying it. She knew a bit about guns, having gotten spooked enough to take a shooting course a few years ago when a friend was raped, though she hadn't been able to get a permit and hadn't felt up to taking chances with New York's draconian firearms laws. This one was a Charter Arms .44 Special, for God's sake. She'd never have suspected Richard would own a gun—especially given Melanie's views—and certainly not a serious piece like this. Maybe he'd gotten nervous about living out here so far from everybody else.

She swung the cylinder out. Empty, of course, but the case turned out to hold a plastic box of cartridges. Well, well.

She thought for a minute, laughed again, and then replaced the gun in the case and the case back in the trunk. Nice to know your options, but no, she didn't think so. Not quite yet.

She carried the box up the steps and through the back door and through the kitchen, up the hallway and into the living room, where she set it carefully on the coffee table, the bottles inside making friendly little clinking and gurgling sounds. She began lifting out bottles and lining them up on the glass-topped table, well back from the edge for safety's sake. This time she'd kept it simple: nothing but Jim Beam, a case of it. Simplify, simplify, wasn't it Thoreau who said that? Or maybe it was Harlan Ellison. Who cared?

She picked a bottle at random, twisted the cap hard to break the seal, and held it up at arm's length. "Let the games begin," she said.

chapter
fourteen

Captain Ernie said, "Well, here she is. Just like I promised, right?"

The gray-suited men ignored him; they didn't even glance in his direction. One turned back and stood in the doorway, looking out, cradling his odd-looking weapon in front of his chest. The other came over and stood in front of Ann. "Dr. Lucas," he said in a voice neutral as distilled water.

He was, except for the strange shiny-gray garment, the most ordinary-looking man she had ever seen. Everything about him was medium: medium height, medium build. Even his medium-brown hair was cut to medium length. His features had the utter regularity of a clothing-store dummy.

She felt very afraid.

He said, "Please listen closely, Dr. Lucas. We are not here to harm you."

"You tried to kill me." Her voice came out hoarse and ragged; her mouth had gone painfully dry.

"This is true. Listen to me. Our orders are to bring you with us, living and uninjured, if at all possible. But understand this," he said, "you will not be allowed to remain alive in this plane. We are authorized to use any means necessary to prevent that."

He laid a hand on the odd-looking weapon slung across his chest. "I repeat, any means necessary. Do you understand?"

"You'll shoot me if I try to run."

"Precisely." He nodded again, a firm quick movement of his mannequin head. "So I advise—"

The other suit, over by the door, said something in a language Ann didn't recognize.

Captain Ernie said, "Charlie, go on and help the boys. Everything's cool here."

The third jacker nodded and left. "Won't be long," Captain Ernie said to the suits. "Just making sure we've got things under control around here."

The suits continued to ignore him. The second one was still looking out the door. After a few minutes he said something in that strange language. It wasn't anything Ann understood or even recognized, yet somehow it had an almost familiar sound.

The first suit replied in the same language. There was a brief exchange, and then the second one left his post by the door and came over and stood beside his partner, looking at Ann. He was, she saw now they were side by side, almost a foot taller than the first suit; otherwise they might have been constructed from interchangeable parts. Mr. Long and Mr. Short, she thought semi-hysterically.

Short said to Ann, "Keep quiet, now, unless we speak to you."

They both turned back to face the doorway. A moment later the blanket curtain was pushed aside and Duncan Brady came in.

The shock was so great that Ann made an involuntary low sound in her throat, causing Long to give her a brief warning glance. Brady, however, didn't even look at her. To Captain Ernie he said, "We got the nigger. Want us to bring him here, or what?"

Captain Ernie looked at the suits. Short said, "Yes. Do it quietly."

Brady nodded and went back outside. Ann watched, still dazed, as he disappeared through the doorway. It was him, all right. He'd lost some weight and acquired a deep tan, and generally appeared to be in better shape, and his hair was now almost shoulder length, but she'd know Brady anywhere. He wore nothing but boots and ragged khaki shorts, plus a leather cartridge belt around his waist. A rifle of some sort was slung across his broad bare back.

"Ugly fucker, ain't he?" Captain Ernie said, grinning at Ann. "Don't worry, he won't bother you."

Well, why not? Once you accepted the idea of alternative realities, it stood to reason at least some of the same people would be found in both. And Duncan Brady would be excellent survivor material; his physical strength and utter lack of scruples would stand him in good stead in this brutal world. Still, the fact remained that she had last seen him lying dead in a puddle of his own blood. Seeing him alive, now, was not an easy thing to accept.

Then she looked again at the men in the silvery-gray suits and Duncan Brady didn't seem particularly scary.

She tried to keep her voice steady, though, as she said, "I thought the dogs got you two. Too bad they didn't."

They did not react; at least nothing showed on their faces. Short said, "That was unexpected. This world has more animal life than we are accustomed to."

"I believe it," Captain Ernie said. "The way you ride a horse, like you never saw one before—"

The door flap bulged inward again and Fat Bob stumbled into the cabin. Behind him, Duncan Brady said, "Here he is, Captain Ernie. Had to bust him up a little, but he's alive."

Ann choked back a gasp. Fat Bob looked terrible. His face was bruised and battered, his left eye swollen shut; his nose was flattened and crooked. His left hand clutched his right arm, which hung at his side at an unnatural angle. His skin was an ashy gray.

Captain Ernie said, "Well, well. Gave the boys a little trouble, did you?"

"You son of a bitch." Fat Bob's voice was little more than a dry whisper. "You lousy son of a bitch."

Captain Ernie laughed. "Could be. I been told so, more than once. From what I remember about Mama, it sounds about right."

Fat Bob looked at Ann. "Are you all right?" he asked.

Ann nodded. Captain Ernie said, "She's okay. You would be too, if you hadn't decided to be a fucking hero. That's stupid, you know. I was a hero once myself, and it didn't pay worth shit."

"Didn't, huh?" Fat Bob said. "And being a backstabber does?"

"It's about to." Captain Ernie grinned and waved a hand in the direction of Short and Long. "These two gents are about to fix me up with the damnedest payoff you ever saw."

"Thirty pieces of silver?" Fat Bob managed to raise a blood-caked eyebrow.

"Better than that, my man." Captain Ernie dragged the last two words out in a mocking drawl. "You want to see? Check this out."

With a couple of quick strides he crossed the small room, to stand next to the gray-suited men. "You never saw anything like this," he promised, taking a long curving knife from a belt sheath. "Watch—"

Suddenly he swung the knife upward and around in a fast stabbing motion, straight at Long's midsection. Ann's mouth fell open in amazement, then stayed that way as she saw the knife glance off to one side without penetrating or even denting the silvery-gray material of Long's suit.

"See?" Captain Ernie stabbed again, and again, grunting with the effort, the big muscles of his arm bunching and jumping. The shiny fabric—or whatever it was—remained untouched. Perhaps literally; from where Ann sat, it almost seemed that the knife point skidded away without making actual contact.

On the third attempt, there was a twanging sound and the knife blade snapped off clean at the hilt. Captain Ernie looked down at the bladeless handle in his hand, grinned, said, "Shit!" and threw it carelessly into a corner.

"That's all right," he said. "I can get me another knife. I can get anything I want, when I got me one of these." He looked at Fat Bob. "And they'll stop a bullet, too, any kind. I bounced a couple of thirty-ought-six bullets off these guys at point-blank range, while we were getting acquainted. Didn't do anything but knock them back a little."

"That's right," the skinhead put in. "Saw it myself. God-damnedest thing."

"Protects you against other stuff, too," Captain Ernie added. "They took a couple of bad falls, learning to ride, and got kicked some by the horses, and never got a scratch. And it's not just what the suit covers, there's some kind of invisible what-do-you-call-it that comes up over your head and face, look—"

He started to swing his fist at Long's face, but Long caught his forearm in one hand. "Don't do that," Long said mildly.

Captain Ernie's eyes went wide for a moment. "Hey, okay," he said hastily. "Sorry—"

Long released him and he stood for a moment rubbing his arm and flexing his fingers. "Well, so anyway," he said after a moment, "these guys are going to fix me up with suits like that for me and all the boys. Along with some of those neat little buzzguns like you see there—you wouldn't believe it, damn things weigh practically nothing and I swear they got more fire-power than a sixteen on full auto—and all the ammo we need."

He laughed. "How's that for a payoff? I'm going to have me the strongest little military force in these parts, maybe the world. We're going to be unstoppable, man, I'm going to be Attila the fucking Hun. You bet your black ass I sold Jack out. I'd sell my own family, if any of the useless bastards were still alive, for a deal like that."

He glanced at the gray-suited men. "Uh, speaking of that, any chance we could get on with—"

"You will receive your payment," Short said, "when you complete your part of the bargain. Not before."

"When we have them both," Long added. "That was the agreement."

Both? It took a second for Ann's dazed mind to register the implications. "No," she said, and then much louder, "No. Not Jack. Please, I'll go with you, I'll do anything you say," voice going up through a couple of octaves, words starting to run together, she knew she was starting to babble but she couldn't stop, "you can do anything you want to me, just leave her—"

"Be quiet," Long told her.

"We already can do anything we want," Short pointed out. "We already have the power to make you do whatever we wish. Don't offer meaningless inducements."

"But please, listen—"

"Be quiet," Long repeated. "Or we will have these men bind and gag you."

"It's okay," Captain Ernie put in. "They already promised not to hurt Jack. They want her alive, same as you. They just want to find out some stuff."

He didn't sound very convinced; his eyes shifted away, not looking at Ann, and his shoulders hunched slightly. But he added, "Do like they tell you, now, or I'll have to have the boys tie you up. You won't like it."

It was unnecessary advice; Ann was already sinking into paralyzing despair, all energy and will draining away. She felt an almost irresistible urge to curl up on the bed with her back to them all and fall asleep.

Head down, staring at the floor, she heard one of the suits— it was impossible to tell their voices apart—say, "You. When are the others expected back?"

Fat Bob's voice mumbled something unintelligible. Then, louder and more clearly, "Fuck you."

"Watch your mouth, nigger," Brady growled. "Want me to hurt him some, boss?"

Ann raised her head and watched as Captain Ernie took a step toward Fat Bob. But then Short raised a hand and said, "No. That won't be necessary." He looked at Brady. "Go find a woman and a small child. No, two small children. Preferably a girl and a boy."

"Wait," Fat Bob said. "Okay . . . they're supposed to be back today. Any time, should have been here by now in fact."

"Good." Short made one of his tiny crisp nods. "What route are they taking?"

"They'll be coming by the northwest trail." Fat Bob tilted his head in Captain Ernie's direction. "He knows what I mean."

Short gave Captain Ernie an inquiring look. "Sure," Captain Ernie said. "We use that trail all the time. How many men we talking about?"

"Nine." Fat Bob's voice was low and dull. "Eight men plus Jack."

Captain Ernie stuck his hands in his back pockets and appeared to think for a moment. He looked at the gray-suited men. "I better get the boys out there, then. Might not have any time to waste."

"Yes," Short said. "Do that."

"You guys figure you can handle things here?" He gestured at Ann and then Fat Bob. "Or do I need to leave a man to help keep an eye on these two?"

"Of course not," Long said. "Why would we need help?"

"Right. Okay, Brady, go have the boys round up the rest of these people. Do it fast and don't put up with any shit, but no shooting, just club the fuck out of anybody who gets out of line, you never know how far the sound of a shot will carry. Find a place to keep them together—"

"That old bus," Brady suggested. "Where the nigger lives."

"Good, yeah," Captain Ernie said, "herd them in there and pick yourself a couple of men to stay with you and guard them. One man to stay outside and watch the road in case somebody shows up from that direction, you can take turns if you want. And God damn it, keep your dicks in your pants, I know that might be tough with a bunch of women in front of you but no fucking around till this is over with."

"Gotcha."

Brady made a thumbs-up motion and left, unslinging his rifle as he went. When he was gone Captain Ernie said to the skinhead, "Ray, I'm putting you in charge of the ambush. Soon as you've got the prisoners together, you take the rest of the boys and get out on the northwest trail. Move ass, we probably don't have any time to waste."

The skinhead nodded and started toward the door. Captain Ernie fell in beside him: "Now I think the best place would be right below that big rock outcrop, you know the one where we used to—"

Together they disappeared out the door, Captain Ernie talking and the skinhead nodding. Short and Long gazed after them with unreadable eyes.

Ann said very faintly, "Excuse me."

The suits looked at her and she raised a hand as if in school. "Excuse me," she said again, "but may I take my pills?"

"Pills?" Short almost looked surprised. "This is medication that you take?"

"Yes. I have to," she said, "please, if I don't get them I'll get wild and out of control, then maybe you'll have to shoot me, you don't want that, do you? Let me take them and I won't be any trouble at all. You'll see."

Short and Long exchanged glances. "Where are these—pills kept?" Short asked. "You have them here?"

"There." Ann pointed. "That white buckskin bag, hanging on the wall by the window."

Long went over and took the little bag down and brought it back. He undid the drawstring and began taking out pill bottles and handing them to Short, who held them up and studied the labels. He tried to open one, struggled for a moment with the childproof safety cap, and gave up. There was another exchange in that mysterious language. Then Short said, "Very well," and handed the bottles to her. "Do you require water?"

"Please."

Long looked around the little room and then went and dipped water out of the barrel and brought the dipper to her, waiting while she poured pills into her palm: a couple of Xanax and, why not, a Zoloft. She swallowed those, washed them down with water from the dipper Long handed her, and twisted the cap off the Lomazine. Three left. Without pausing to think about it she popped them all into her mouth at once and reached again for the dipper.

"You're not trying to commit suicide?" Short asked as she swallowed. "That would be useless. We have the means to resuscitate you."

Ann shook her head and handed the dipper back. "Why would I do that? I already have a better way out, if I want it. You said you'd shoot me if I tried to escape."

"This is true." Short took the pills from her. "Good that you understand."

Long was looking at Fat Bob, who was starting to sway on his feet. "You may lie down," he said, "if you wish."

Fat Bob lurched over to the bed and stretched out beside Ann, very carefully, wincing with pain and clutching his injured arm. As he lay back he said, "What happens now?"

"Now," Short said, "we wait."

◄ ⋀ ⋁ ►

The afternoon wore on. Captain Ernie came back and announced that "the boys" were on their way. After a little while he began wandering idly about the cabin, picking up various objects and looking at them; then he sat down on a wooden chest and started whistling, a tuneless monotonous sound, till Long told him to stop.

Except for that the gray-suited men did not speak, to anyone else or to each other. They didn't sit down or move around; they just stood there, over near the door where they could see everyone, and waited, their faces blank as ever.

Ann took only a peripheral interest in any of this. By now the drugs had taken hold and she was drifting on an internal chemical tide. She no longer felt any fear; she no longer felt much of anything. Now and then she tried to focus, but her mind kept slipping out of engagement like a worn-out clutch.

Finally, when internal pressures became impossible to ignore, she made a request. After a quick conference in that fast-sounding language, Long followed her outside and to the outhouse, keeping his weapon trained on her. He wouldn't let her close the door, and he watched while she pulled down her pants and peed, but that didn't really bother her, it was all too impersonal and even inhuman to be embarrassing and anyway what did it matter? They were going to kill her—whatever they said, she knew that was what they were going to do, they were just keeping her alive in case they needed her as bait to get Jack—and she didn't even care all that much about that either. . . .

But then, as they walked back to the cabin, Long said, "Wait," and she stopped and looked back and saw that he was looking off to the northwest. He seemed to be listening, though she heard nothing but the endless whine of the wind across the hillside.

"Quick," he said, and gave her a push with the muzzle of his weapon, hustling her the rest of the way down the footpath; but when they reached the cabin he said, "Stop. Stand still," and stepped over to the door and pushed the flap back and called something that sounded like, *"Livenni!"*

A moment later Short emerged, with Captain Ernie close behind him. By now Ann's ears had picked up the sound: a distant thudding rumble, coming from the northwest. Captain Ernie said, "All right! That'll be the boys. Didn't I tell you they could handle it?"

"Go back inside and get the other one," Short said, not looking at him. "You should not have left him alone."

The sound of hoofbeats was now growing clear and strong; they seemed to be moving fast. The suits were both looking off across the hillside now, seemingly paying no attention to Ann, though she knew they would cut her down instantly if she tried to run. She followed the direction of their gaze and saw only the usual rocks and brush and grazing animals. Then a dark mass appeared over a low ridge, moving fast toward them, and almost immediately resolved itself into individual shapes of men on horseback, trailing plumes of yellowish dust as they galloped down the slope.

Captain Ernie came through the cabin door, pushing Fat Bob ahead of him. "Keep still and keep fucking quiet," he told Fat

Bob, and turned and took off his black hat and waved it at the oncoming riders. "Yo!" he shouted.

But as the leading horsemen came nearer, he stopped waving, and his arm fell to his side; he almost dropped the hat, and had to grab hastily to keep it from falling to the ground. By now it was obvious that something was badly wrong. The riders didn't look triumphant or happy; they looked, in fact, very unhappy indeed.

Ann's eyes were fixed on the horse one of the riders was leading. Or rather on the dark object—the size and shape of a human body—slung across its back. Her pulse was so loud in her ears it all but drowned out the clatter of hoofbeats as the horsemen pulled up to a noisy, dust-swirling stop next to the cabin.

The skinhead heeled his horse a couple of paces forward and stopped in front of Captain Ernie. He said, "It went down. Didn't go down good."

"For Christ sake, Ray," Captain Ernie said. "What the fuck *happened?*"

Ray raised a hand and wiped sweat from his forehead. "We hit them just like you said, right where you said. They were coming slow up the trail, leading their pack horses. Didn't have a chance. We blew them right out of their saddles."

He hunched his shoulders. "All but one," he added. "The cunt. She got away."

Ann's eyes went wide; she put a hand over her mouth to keep herself from shouting aloud.

"She got away?" Captain Ernie echoed. His eyebrows had linked up to form a single thick gray line above his eyes. "You let Jack get away?"

"You said take her alive if we could." Ray's own face and voice registered anger, now. "Turned out we couldn't. She got Charlie, too." He made a thumb-jerk gesture at the body slung over the horse's back. "He broke cover and tried to jump her, drag her off her horse. She shot him before he even got close."

Short said, "But you were authorized to kill her if you couldn't capture her."

"Yeah, well," Ray said, "we tried that too. Threw enough lead at her, I don't know, she might have taken a hit or two. Sure as hell nothing to stop her, though. She rode off over the ridge and by the time we got mounted up she was long gone."

Short was staring at Captain Ernie. "This is not good," he said. "You said your men could do this. You said it would be simple."

"Simple," Ray said, before Captain Ernie could reply, "ain't the same as easy. Nothing's easy, when you go fucking with that crazy bitch. I could have told you that."

"Shut the fuck up, Ray," Captain Ernie growled, and set the black hat on his head and shoved it down hard. "Just shut up and let me do the talking, okay?"

"Don't tell me to shut up." Ray's hand was not quite resting on the butt of his holstered pistol, but it was very close. "God damn it, don't give me any shit. We did it the way you said and now Charlie's dead and Mad Jack's out there on the loose, fuck knows how many others she's going to take out just because you—"

"Stop this," Long said. "Fight among yourselves after this is finished. Now, you must post guards around this area. She may try to rescue Dr. Lucas."

"Right." Ray swung his horse around and began issuing

orders. The other horsemen began to scatter out, not very fast, taking it easy on their winded mounts. One man took the reins of the horse that bore the dead man, and led it away down the hill.

"No sweat," Captain Ernie said. "She'll come back for her girlfriend, just like you said, and then we'll nail her."

He didn't sound all that confident. His voice was a little higher than usual, and his grin was a bit too wide.

Long said, "Have your men shoot the other prisoners."

Captain Ernie blinked. "What—"

"You will need all available men," Long explained, "to guard this area, and to capture the woman if she comes. You're wasting personnel, guarding irrelevant prisoners. Shoot them."

"Hold on," Captain Ernie objected. "That's a lot of valuable merchandise down there. At any slave market—"

"He's right," Ray said. "If we'd had those three more guns on the ambush, we might have got her. I'll go tell Brady."

He rode away down the hill, not waiting for a reply. Captain Ernie's face had gone very white. "Son of a bitch," he said through his teeth.

Fat Bob said, "Losing control of the horde, Attila?"

Captain Ernie spun around. "Oh, yeah," he said. "You guys got any reason, you want to keep this old coon alive?"

"Coon? You mean this man?" Short considered it. "No," he said after a moment. "You may terminate him too."

"Or we will do so," Long offered, raising his weapon.

"No, no." Captain Ernie reached for his pistol. "It'll be a real pleasure—"

He stopped; everybody stopped moving, listening, as a sudden fresh racket of hoofbeats sounded from up the hillside. "What the fuck," Captain Ernie said.

The noise was quite close, and very loud. Captain Ernie and Long ran and peered past the cabin. "Holy shit!" Captain Ernie shouted. "The horses! The fucking horses are loose!"

He ducked back out of the way as first one and then another and then a solid mass of riderless horses charged past the cabin on both sides. Over the drumming roar of hoofbeats came a bang-bang-bang of gunfire and the shrilling of a woman's voice.

"Jack," Ann breathed, all unheard. "Oh, Jack."

Long was standing at the corner of the cabin, firing his weapon. A horse went down in a screaming kicking tangle, almost at his feet, and the oncoming wave broke around the fallen animal, but then a lunging brown shoulder knocked Long back and into the path of a big pinto, and next minute he vanished under the pounding hooves.

"Inside," Short shouted. "Everyone inside—"

But then all at once Jack was there, in among the stampeding herd, lying low along the roan's back, firing her pistol, and Captain Ernie's face went blank and the back of his head exploded. Short started to swing his weapon around but Fat Bob slammed into him, knocking the muzzle downward. Ann saw Fat Bob's body jerk and his mouth fly open, and then Jack was reaching down for her. She grabbed the extended arm, feeling a familiar steel-trap grip close over her own forearm, and she leaped upward high as she could and next instant she was seated behind Jack, arms wrapped around her waist, face pressed against her back, screaming in fear and joy, as the roan broke clear of the herd and carried them down the trail toward the road.

For a moment Ann thought they were going to make it. Down in front of Fat Bob's place, the jackers were herding the villagers into a rough line, and they turned and stared, open-mouthed, as the two women tore past. Ann saw Duncan Brady unslinging his rifle, and Ray going for his pistol, but too late for that, no chance of hitting a fast-moving target at rapidly lengthening range, and she almost laughed as the first few bullets popped past, not even close.

She was still almost laughing as the roan gathered himself to jump the little ravine that ran alongside the road, and that was when something went *thump*, quite softly, and the roan suddenly and instantly went limp beneath them and they went flying through the air, helplessly spinning and tumbling, like a couple of thrown-away dolls.

chapter
fifteen

Dreams again, and Jay woke screaming. Or hearing herself scream, though maybe that was only in the dream.

She rolled over and opened her eyes. Yellow spikes of pain stabbed through her pupils and out the back of her head, and she shut her eyes hastily, then opened them again more cautiously, squinting against the too-bright light.

New Mexico. Melissa's. Living room. Couch. Okay.

After a minute she heaved herself up to an approximation of a sitting position, clutching at the back of the couch for support. Agony bloomed in her skull and she covered her eyes with one hand, cursing.

When the pain had subsided a little, she took her hand down and looked around. Yep, living room, all right. Another night she hadn't made it to the bedroom and now her back and neck were stiff and her muscles ached from sleeping curled up on the couch.

She realized then that she was naked, and wondered vaguely why. Her skin was sweaty and stuck unpleasantly to the upholstery of the couch.

And the light was really *much* too strong, even though all the curtains were drawn. Squinting, she studied the clock on the

VCR atop the television set. Christ, nearly noon. Not that that was particularly late for her, but if she'd slept so late why did she still feel like recycled shit? But then the dreams always left her drained, tireder than if she hadn't slept at all.

This one had been a killer, too. Even though the details had already receded beyond recall, the fear was still there. Her heart was still pounding to rattle her ribs, and her hands shook.

She sat for a few minutes, rubbing her eyes and then the back of her neck, trying to think what day it was. Two days, now, she'd been on this particular bender? Or was it three? Everything was a big dark fog.

Of course that was the idea, wasn't it. . . .

She stood, finally, not wanting to, wanting in fact to lie back down and crash the rest of the day or better yet her life, but her bladder was making non-negotiable demands. She swayed, staggered, put a hand against the wall to steady herself, and waited till the room stopped wheeling about her. "Sonnabitch," she mumbled, and reached for the nearly empty Jim Beam bottle on the coffee table. Hair of the old dog, there, just a touch to settle her down—

Except it didn't. The bourbon didn't even get all the way to her stomach; just the smell and taste were enough to set off a violent reaction, and she dropped the bottle, clapped her hands over her mouth, and headed for the bathroom in a wobble-kneed run, barely making it down the hall and getting her face over the toilet before the first convulsive heave tore through her body.

It was some time before the last dry retching spasm died away, leaving her slumped on the bathroom floor, the tiles cold against her knees (praying to the great porcelain god, that Australian cyberpunk writer used to call it), her head resting sidewise against the sink. After a minute or two she forced herself to reach up and flush the toilet, but it took a lot longer to muster the strength to clamber gracelessly to her feet.

She found herself staring into the puffy red eyes of a gaunt, grayish face, framed with long stringy black hair. "Yo, Morticia," she croaked to the mirror. "You look like shit."

She stepped into the shower and turned it on, hot as she could endure, and stood for a long time letting the water dance on her skin, inhaling the steam, before finally reaching for the soap and the shampoo.

The bath made her feel a little better, but not much. Her head still felt ready to crack like an overboiled egg, her stomach churned and burned, and her belly muscles hurt from the dry heaves. The skin of her face felt too tight.

She toweled off, tossed the towel in the general direction of the shower door, and walked back up the hallway and into her bedroom. Reaching into the closet, she stopped and stared at her bare self in the long mirror on the inside of the closet door. Moved by some obscure impulse, she ran a hand down her body, between her breasts—the nipples still shriveled hard from the shower—and the long smooth still-flat flesh of her belly, to rest lightly atop her dark springy pubic bush. Still not bad, she thought, for an old babe, for a drunken old babe—

That was when it came back, all at once, the memory of the previous evening, and once more she put her hands to her eyes, but the pictures were inside, no shutting them out that easily, no shutting them out at all.

◄ ▲ ▼ ►

It had been just about dusk when Danny Santos showed up. By then she had been well and truly smashed, hadn't been even borderline sober for a couple of days. She'd had the CD player turned up to blaster levels, Jerry Jeff Walker's whisky baritone flooding the whole house and the backup band rattling the windows with shitkicker twang. Danny Santos had had to bang repeatedly on the front door before she noticed he was there; she hadn't heard his truck at all.

He'd stood in the doorway, looking at her, looking about the dirty and littered living room, looking again at her as she swayed before him. "Uh, no," he'd said in response to her repeated invitations to come in. "I better not. I just came by—"

"Oh, come on." Grabbing at his arm, trying to pull him inside. "Have a drink with me. Listen to some music. Don't you like this guy? Good ol' Jacky Jack. Wait, I know, it's too loud, I'll turn it down—"

Stumbling across the room, tripping on an empty bottle and almost falling, finding the control and turning the volume up even higher for a second and then, giggling, down to a more normal level. "There, now we can talk, come on *in*," moving in a zigzag course back toward the door, smiling brightly, "I'll even turn it off if you want, they don't have my favorites anyway. You know my favorite song?" She waved the Jim Beam bottle in her left hand. "'Why Don't We Get Drunk and Screw?' That's the one I like. Is it Jimmy Buffet who sings that one?"

Stopping in the middle of the floor, giving Danny Santos a different sort of smile: "Come to think of it, why don't we? Get drunk and screw, I mean. Of course I'm *already* drunk, but I bet you could get that way pretty quick. I'd help you. I'd help you with the other part, too, only I bet you wouldn't need it."

"I'm sorry." Sadness and embarrassment in his eyes, those gorgeous dark brown eyes. "I just came by to see if you needed anything."

"Well, I do." Her voice getting louder and harsher, demanding. "Right now I *do* need something, God damn it. You won't even have to make a trip to get it for me."

Setting the bottle on the end table, almost knocking it over, crossing her arms and skinning the none-too-clean T-shirt off up over her head, braless breasts dangling free as she bent and stripped shorts and panties down together. "Look," standing naked, running her hands over her nipples, rubbing herself between her legs, "pretty good for an old babe, huh? You want it, I know you do, come on, let's fuck, what's the matter, *come back here you son of a bitch blanket ass faggot—*"

◁ △ ▽ ▷

Remembering now, seeing once more the pain on his face as he turned away, hearing again the slam of the door through her own wild shrieking, she said aloud, "Oh, my God. Oh, my God."

She said it quite softly. And, a moment later, still in that same quiet reasonable voice, she added, "All right, then."

Thoughtfully, unhurriedly, she took down a gray skirt and her good cream silk blouse, both still in their plastic travel bags. She laid them carefully on the bed and went over to the dresser and got out a pair of white lace panties—one of the few clean pairs left—and the bra she hadn't worn since arriving. Hose? Why not, she decided, and dug those out too.

A little while later, fully dressed except for shoes, she studied herself in the long closet-door mirror. Not bad, but not very damn good either; her face desperately needed makeup, but there was no way in hell she was going to try to apply that with her hands shaking so badly. Better Morticia than Bozo.

Her hair was still wet from the shower but she didn't feel like fooling with the dryer; it was clean, that was good enough for present purposes. She took a deep breath and said, "Well."

Crossing the room, sitting down at the desk, she opened a drawer and got out a yellow legal pad and a black Bic pen. After a moment's thought she wrote:

> *And so I find myself trying my hand at yet another traditional literary form. I am not sure what one is supposed to say. They never covered this in any of the workshops. For starters, I should perhaps pass on my findings from some recent experiments: drinking oneself to death has a pleasant sound to it, but as a practical matter it leaves much to be desired. Time, then, to*

She stopped, stared at the shaky scrawl, and shook her head. Nobody was going to be able to read this. And why, after all, bother? It wasn't as if she were going to get paid for it, and only fools and wantabees wrote for free.

She ripped the paper from the pad, wadded it up, and tossed it in the general direction of the overflowing wastebasket. What a mess she'd made of this lovely home; Melanie would go into cardiac arrest if she could see it now. It looked as if a bunch of unusually rowdy fraternity boys had been using the place for their end-of-term party.

She thought briefly of cleaning the place up, as a last decent gesture. But she knew she'd never be able to do it; she'd make a start, and then she'd get to thinking, and then she'd take a drink, and pretty soon she'd be off again. No. Too bad, she thought, slipping into her dress shoes, but Melanie's house was just going to have to stay like this.

But then, on the way out to the garage, it occurred to her that at least she could refrain from making a new and even worse mess here.

And so, after she had gotten the little leather case from the trunk of the Toyota, she didn't take it back into the house as she had intended; but instead she unlocked the car and laid it carefully on the seat, on the passenger side, along with the bottle of Jack Daniel's she had brought from the house. A few minutes later she was swinging the Toyota onto the blacktop and down the winding mountain road, singing hoarsely to herself:

> "Hey, Jay,
> where you goin' with that gun in your hand?
> Don't know for sure
> but I won't be comin' back again. . . ."

She had not meant to go far, only to get clear of the house; but the road was narrow and there was little or no shoulder, no place to park the car without creating a hazard for any other vehicles that might come this way. She kept going, driving slowly, looking for a suitable spot.

She almost drove past the turnoff without seeing it. It wasn't much, just a gravel road, even narrower than the blacktop, curving off to the right and disappearing between groves of tall pine. By now she was well down off the big mountainside, crossing the flank of a foothill that would have counted as a full-scale mountain in most parts of the country.

She slowed to a stop, studying the side road. A memory stirred in her still-throbbing head, something Richard had said on a previous visit, driving past this point; but she couldn't retrieve it and she didn't really care. Without waiting to think about it, following a suddenly overpowering impulse, she hauled the Toyota around and headed up the gravel road.

A couple of miles on, the road emerged from the pine woods and went angling up across a rocky, almost treeless slope. Next to the road was a deep ravine, across which someone had built a solid-looking little bridge. On the other side of the bridge stood what appeared to be the remains of some sort of gate, though there was no fence or wall on either side of it. A big metal sign dangled crazily from a no-longer-vertical post, its lettering faded, part of it shot away by passing sportsmen:

FUTURE SITE OF SPANISH HILLS MENTA

Now she remembered; Richard's voice came back to her: "We almost had a mental institution up here, if you can imagine it. These people from Albuquerque acquired some land, up that road there, leased it from the tribe that owns it—most of this land around here is Native American property, you know, they lease it to ranchers and developers. The plan was to build a fancy private psychiatric hospital. Even did a little preliminary work, but apparently their funding somehow failed—"

Perfect, she thought. Absofuckinglutely perfect. In the words of that evil old fraud Brigham Young, this is the place.

She stopped the car, not bothering to pull over—it was obvious this road got almost no traffic—and got out, taking the leather case with her. A brisk cool wind was blowing down the hillside, making low whining sounds in the scrubby brush nearby, riffling her nearly dry hair. Overhead a big hawk wheeled and soared in an otherwise vacant blue sky.

She laid the leather case on the Toyota's fender and opened it and took out the revolver. Her hands were almost steady, now, as she swung the cylinder out and thumbed cartridges into the chambers. She wondered why she was bothering to load it fully; it wasn't as if this would take more than a single round. Yet she finished the job, for no reason but sheer compulsiveness, and clicked the cylinder back into the frame.

She laid the pistol on top of the case, very carefully, and went back and got the bottle of Jack. It was unopened; she'd been saving it for a special occasion. Which, she considered as she broke the seal and unscrewed the cap, this certainly was.

"Here's to you, Jay," she said, raising the bottle. "You fucked-up old bitch."

Remembering, she took only a very small cautious swallow to begin with. Even so, it hit her empty and aching stomach like a gasoline explosion, and she leaned against the Toyota for a couple of minutes, breathing through her mouth and clutching her belly, before she was sure it was going to stay down. But she knew from experience that the next one wasn't going to give her nearly as much trouble, and sure enough it didn't.

She made herself stop after a few more sips; having a last little taste was one thing, but she didn't want to be seriously drunk at the Big Moment. Besides, this was going to require a certain degree of coordination. Get shitfaced and shoot herself in the foot or blow off a tit, that would just about make the nut. She screwed the cap back on the bottle and set it on the fender and picked up the pistol again.

She walked around to the front of the car and stood in the middle of the road, facing uphill. She raised the .44 and hesitated. Head or heart? Head was surest, probably quickest, but the thought of doing anything to make hers hurt worse, even for a moment, was too awful to consider.

She held the muzzle against her body, experimenting with different angles. Where the hell *was* the heart, anyway? Remembering something she'd heard, she stuck the barrel under her left breast, angling a bit upward.

Close enough for rock and roll.

She took a deep breath and started to take up the trigger slack, and that was when the two women appeared, absolutely out of nowhere, flying through the air ass-over-elbows, to crash hard into the gravel roadway.

The shock was so great that Jay stood for a minute with her mouth hanging open, the gun in her hand sagging forgotten to her side. There was nowhere they could possibly have come from, no trees or rocks close by that could have hidden anything bigger than a ground squirrel; and yet there they were, lying in the middle of the road, no more than a dozen feet away, beginning to move now, rolling over and raising their heads, groaning aloud.

She watched as they sat up, looked at each other, and then

simultaneously reached out and touched hands. After a minute they got to their feet, moving surprisingly fast despite their obvious pain, and began looking around, first back across the ravine in the direction they'd come (except they hadn't, of course, but they had all the same) and then up the road, and finally turning around and at last seeing Jay standing there staring at them.

They were a sight to stare at, too, even discounting the impossible manner of their arrival. The one on the left wasn't too strange, barring her patched and faded clothing—denim shorts, khaki shirt with ripped-off sleeves—and the weird look in her eyes. The other, though, was something out of a bad action movie: camouflage pants, high-topped black boots, heavy leather gunbelt—though the holster appeared to be empty—and cartridge bandoleer. Even, for God's sake, a black patch over one eye.

They were about the same height and general build—about her own size, Jay realized, though the one-eyed one looked more muscular—and, as best she could guess, about her age too. Certainly much too damn old to be dressing like that.

The one on the left said, "Oh!" and took a step backward, hand going to her mouth. The one-eyed one said, "Jesus!" and slapped at her hip; and then paused, her windburned face going pale, as she groped frantically at the empty holster. "Oh, shit," she said, much more softly, and began to look about her, at the surface of the road. "*Oh*, shit—"

The other one said sharply, "Look out, Jack, she's got a gun!"

I do? Jay thought stupidly, and then: oh, that's right, I do. She moved back and laid the revolver on the hood of the Toyota. "It's all right," she said, speaking slowly and clearly. "Don't be afraid—"

She hadn't realized a human being could move so fast.

Suddenly the one-eyed woman was right on top of her, pressing her back against the car, holding an enormous shiny knife up in front of her.

"Don't move," the one-eyed woman said. "Don't even fucking breathe . . . get the piece, Ann!"

Out of the corner of her eye—she didn't dare turn her head—Jay saw the other woman scoop up Richard's pistol. "Got it?" the one-eyed woman said, and stepped back, releasing Jay. "Sorry about that," she added. "Lost my own when we—"

She stopped, a strange expression coming over her face. She and the other woman exchanged looks. The other woman said, "Oh, no. Don't tell me. . . ."

They began looking around again, this time in a wholly different way. The one-eyed woman said, "Ann, look at this car. Look at those tires, those fresh marks in the gravel." To Jay she said, "You drove here, didn't you? Just a little while ago?"

Jay nodded. The one-eyed woman said, "Uh huh. Give me the piece, Ann."

She took the pistol and examined it. "Another make I never heard of before. Nice, though. You got any more ammo on you?"

Jay pointed at the leather case resting on the fender. The one-eyed woman flipped the case open and whistled. "Man, look at all that nice clean brass. Brand new, if I know anything, these aren't reloads. God damn it, I'm starting to think it's happened again. Do you fucking *believe* this?"

The other woman was walking around the car, studying it. "Let me check the license sticker—good God, Jack, you're right."

"Well, kick my ass." The one-eyed woman scratched her

head. "How—no, never mind, we can talk about it later. Right now we need to get our butts out of here. If we're back in your world, then we're both hot. Got to be some serious people looking for us, after that scene at the motel."

"I'm not so sure we're in my world either," the other woman said. "Look at that sign. And look around, here. I think I know where we are, only we're not there. You know?"

The one-eyed woman seemed to understand this string of gibberish; she nodded thoughtfully. "Why not? If there's two, no reason there couldn't be more. But we still better haul ass, till we find out the score."

She looked at Jay. "You live around here?"

"I'm . . . staying nearby. Some friends let me use their house while they're out of the country."

After she'd said it Jay wondered why. Might as well get down on her knees and beg to be taken hostage. If Xena and Louise, here, didn't simply murder her; and why, for the love of Christ, did that thought frighten her so badly? They'd merely be doing for her what she'd been about to do for herself.

Yet so it was; she didn't, she realized with profound annoyance, want to die now.

The one-eyed woman gestured with the revolver. "Okay, you take us there. Careful," she said as Jay moved toward the car. "One funny move, it'll be the last thing you ever do."

"Please do what Jack says," the other woman put in. "We don't want to hurt you."

Jay opened the door and slid in under the wheel, keeping all her moves slow and obvious. The two women came around the car on either side—the one-eyed one keeping the revolver pointed at Jay's head, the other one pausing to collar the bottle of Jack Daniel's that still stood on the fender—and got in behind her. "Drive," the one-eyed woman growled.

Jay started the engine and began the ticklish business of getting turned around on the narrow road. She heard the one-eyed woman say, "That stuff any good, Ann?"

There was a soft brief gurgling sound. A whiff of sour-mash aroma drifted to Jay's twitching nostrils. "Excellent," Ann replied, her voice a bit choked. "Outstanding, in fact."

"Let me have a taste." Then, a moment later: "Oh, fuck, yeah—"

Straightening the car out, about to head back the way she'd come, Jay said, "May I have a drink too?"

"Sure, why not?" The bottle appeared beside her face, held in a strong-looking hand. "Just a little, though. Don't want you wrecking this thing."

Jay took the bottle, saw that the cap was off, and took a quick swallow. "Thanks," she said, passing it back.

"Hell, it's yours, after all." Jack sounded a bit friendlier now. "You got good taste in booze. Good taste in guns, too, this one's a real beauty."

"Are you some sort of police officer?" Ann asked as Jay put the car in motion.

Jay laughed. "Me? That's funny. No, I'm just a free-lance science fiction writer."

"No shit?" Jack sounded genuinely interested. "What's your name? Or what name do you write under?" Jack snorted. "What the fuck am I thinking? Unless you're a lot older than you look, how would I have heard of you?"

What did that mean? "I write as Jay."

"Jay who?" Ann wanted to know. "Maybe I've heard of you. My husband read science fiction occasionally."

"Just Jay. Kind of a corny gimmick, huh?" Her literary career and its affectations were very high on the list of things Jay didn't feel like talking about just now, but anything to distract these two from the idea of shooting her. "But I thought it was really cool at the time I was starting out, and then pretty soon it was too late. By now that's what everybody calls me. I imagine most of my friends only know me by that name."

She swerved to miss a pothole. "See," she said, "it's a made-up name, from my initials. J.A.Y., you see. For Jacqueline Ann Younger."

Jay's head still hurt. She really, *really* wished they wouldn't scream like that. . . .

chapter
sixteen

J ay said, "Bullshit."

She had said it quite a number of times, that afternoon and evening. Ann didn't think she'd ever heard a person use the word so many times in a comparable period.

"But the fingerprints," Jack said. "We showed you. That proves it."

"Bullshit. Doesn't prove doodly." Jay shook her head decisively and a little drunkenly; she and Jack were both getting pretty buzzy by now. "All you did was waste a lot of Melanie's dusting powder and make a mess on her bathroom mirror. It takes a trained expert to compare fingerprints, like at the FBI. Anyway, that's only theory, about no two people having the same prints. Nobody really knows. It could happen."

"Maybe two. Not three."

"Bullshit. Not saying it wouldn't be *unusual*, but it *could* happen. Whereas what you're saying," Jay took the bottle from Jack's hand and raised it, "couldn't.""

Jack said, "How come we know all about how your parents met, how your daddy was in the Marine Corps—"

"You could have gotten all that from interviews," Jay said stubbornly. "Fan magazines, maybe."

"Never heard of you before," Jack told her.

"Bullshit."

Ann said peevishly, "You know, for a supposed literary professional, you certainly seem to have a limited vocabulary."

She got up out of the big chair and walked away from where
the other two sat on the couch, over to the big front windows. It
was late afternoon now, and the descending sun was turning the
sky blaze red over the mountain crests to the west. The spectacle
did nothing for Ann; she felt only a dull dog-kicking irritability,
and her head hurt. Drinking whiskey on top of all those pills had
been a really bad idea. Not, she thought sourly, watching Jack
take the bottle back from Jay, that she'd gotten much of it.

"Jesus fucking Christ." Jack pushed her forefinger under her
eyepatch and rubbed the scar tissue. "Do we *look* like a couple of
fucking science fiction fans?"

"Actually," Jay said, "yes. Especially you. Give me back that
bottle."

"I think you've had enough."

"Bullshit."

Ann turned back to the window, closing her eyes against the
red glare, wishing she could close her ears against the bickering
voices behind her. Why was Jack arguing with this irascible lush?
If Jay was yet another self, she was one Ann would just as soon
not have known about.

Behind her she heard Jack say, "All right, then, answer this.
How do you explain—"

"Shut up," Ann said suddenly. "For God's sake, shut *up*."

She spun about and crossed the room in a few quick strides,
coming to a stop in front of them, holding out her hand, while

they stared up at her with wide eyes and open mouths. They looked, she thought, like scolded children, and she almost laughed. For the first time she could actually see the resemblance. She said, "Give it here. You've both had enough."

Meekly, Jack handed over the bottle. "Cap," Ann said, snapping her fingers, and Jack located it on the coffee table and passed it up.

Ann raised the bottle to her own lips and took a long deliberate pull, watching the two of them past the gurgling neck, silently daring them to speak. They didn't. She screwed the cap on tight and tossed the bottle into the big chair behind her.

"You're allergic to tomatoes," she said to Jay. "Your left breast is slightly smaller than the right. Your period, unless you've managed to fuck it up with all that drinking, runs on a twenty-six-day cycle. Stand up."

"What?"

"Stand up, damn it."

Looking confused, Jay got to her feet. Ann's hand shot out, grabbing at the front of the gray skirt, pressing the material back against her lower belly and groin. "Here." Ann's fingertip jabbed at Jay's pubic area. "You've got a dark brown mole, about the size of a pencil eraser, just above and to the left of your vagina. It doesn't show because your pubic hair covers it."

"Hah!" Jay grinned triumphantly. "That's how much you know. I had it surgically removed, back when I was—"

She stopped. "Shit," she breathed. "How did you know?"

"Want to see mine?" Ann put her hands to the waistband of her own shorts. "And Jack's?"

"Hey," Jack cried, "that's right! I remember noticing you had one too, first time I, uh . . ."

She flushed slightly. "Wait a minute, I just thought of something—" Getting up off the couch, she grabbed Jay's left hand and held it up. "Look there, that little white scar on your thumb. You got that when you were nine, when you managed to snag it with a fishhook and Daddy had to cut it out. Remember?"

She held her own thumb alongside Jay's. "See? We both got one. Ann doesn't, because her world split off before ours did, and in her world Kennedy wasn't killed and our mother got her shit together and dumped Daddy and so Ann never had the pleasure of the bastard's company."

Jack dropped the hand and put her hands on Jay's shoulders. "You wet your pants at your fourth birthday party," she said, "and Aunt Velma said you were too old to do that and made you go to your room. When you were living with Aunt Lois you watched through the hedge while the kid next door jerked himself off behind their garage. Kenneth, that was his name. Little turd offered you fifty cents, a few days later, to show him your pussy. Made you so mad you sneaked over and let the air out of his bicycle tires."

Jay's face was papery white. "You," she said helplessly, "no, you can't—"

"When you were ten you played with yourself for the first time." Jack had her face up close to Jay's now, gripping her shoulders tightly, looking into her eyes. "You were looking at a new art book in the school library and you saw the picture of Michelangelo's David and it got you excited and you sneaked the book into the girls' room and hid in a stall and rubbed yourself nearly raw, looking at the nude dudes—and women, you looked at them too, you really liked that Titian Venus. Two days later you got your first period and it scared the shit out of you because you were certain you'd damaged yourself."

Jay sat down suddenly on the couch. "Jesus," she said, and put her face in her hands. "Please," she said a moment later, "can I have another drink? Just a little one?"

"Forget it," Ann told her. "Listen to Jack."

"That fall," Jack went on, "when Daddy came to take you camping, you didn't want to go with the son of a bitch but—"

"Don't." Jay's voice was muffled by her hands, and by something else; she seemed to be having trouble breathing. "Don't talk about him like that. That was the last time I ever saw him."

"No shit?" Jack sat down beside her and put an arm across her shoulders, which were beginning to shake. "What happened to him?"

"He went back to Vietnam. By then all the American combat troops were supposedly out of the country, but he was attached to the embassy in Saigon. He was killed by a VC bomb," Jay said, still without looking up. "At least that was the official story. I always wondered what he was really doing, how he really died."

Daddy's fate, Ann mused, would seem to have been immutable in any possible world. Live by the sword, and all that. Interesting that he'd survived longest in Jack's world.

"I know he was a son of a bitch," Jay went on. "But when he got killed all I could think about was silly things like the presents he'd brought me, like that stuffed dog—"

"Cat," Jack said. "It was Uncle Mac who gave you the dog. Daddy got the cat in Thailand. Had a rhinestone collar."

"Oh, yeah." Jay looked up and pushed her hair back from her face. "That's right, don't know why I got it mixed up—" Her red-rimmed eyes went huge. "Shit! Fucking *listen* to me!"

"Here." Ann picked up the bottle from the chair and passed it to her. "Just one, though."

While Jay took a long shaky pull at the whiskey, Jack said, "I know it's a hell of a thing to handle. We've both been through it, but we had a little more time. And a lot of proof in front of our eyes, that we couldn't ignore or argue away. You're having to take the whole thing just on our word."

"And seeing you materialize like that," Jay said, lowering the bottle. "If I hadn't seen that I still wouldn't believe any of it. You just appeared, like Nimoy and Shatner on the old *Star Trek*."

"Shatner?" Ann retrieved the bottle before Jack could collar it. "Who the hell's Shatner? You mean Jeffrey Hunter, don't you?"

Jay stared at her and then, unexpectedly, she burst into a loud hoarse laugh. "Believe it or not," she said when she could speak again, "you've just done it. I give up. I'm sold. Nobody would have thought to make that up. Nobody's that warped. Not even me."

After a moment she added, "Unless this is a wish-fulfillment dream. Be nice to think there's a world somewhere where Kennedy didn't get killed and they got somebody else to play Kirk."

Ann said, "Just out of curiosity, who's the president of the United States in this one?"

Jay told her.

Ann said, "Bullshit."

◀ ▲ ▼ ▶

That evening, after dinner, Jay said, "What was she like? Mother, I mean."

Ann paused, about to wipe the dining room table. "Hm." She thought for a moment. "You want the truth, don't you?"

Standing in the door to the kitchen, hands full of empty microwave-dinner trays, Jay nodded. "Please," she said. "I never knew her, you know."

Ann put down the cloth and straightened up—a little painfully; the bruises were starting to hurt, from the fall onto the gravel roadway—and said, "To be honest, I didn't know her all that much better than you did. Oh, hell, that's not fair, I've got some good memories. She didn't neglect me, didn't completely ignore me."

She shrugged. "It's just that she was sort of wrapped up in herself. Had to be, at first, learning to deal with depression—she finally got on antidepressants, but at first she was just trying to do it herself, seeing self-appointed therapists and taking classes in yoga and transcendental meditation and even Scientology."

Jay made a face. "I know what you're saying. I've had friends who got into that kind of thing. It does tend to make people self-centered, doesn't it?"

"Yes. But I can't really blame her," Ann said. "She was desperate, ready to try anything, and do I know how that feels. You really can't think about anything beyond your own problems."

"Oh, sure," Jay agreed. "Hell, I'm nobody to talk, hiding at the bottom of a bottle. I'm just trying to understand."

"But even after she got past that phase," Ann went on, "and you understand, most of that was when I was pretty small, I don't remember too much about it . . . after that, I don't know, maybe she got a little too carried away with her new-found self-esteem. She built herself a career—"

"What did she do?"

"Photography. Turned out she had quite a talent for it, too. She became very successful, very much in demand, especially with the travel industry. So she was gone a lot," Ann said. "I'm afraid I did the boarding-school thing too. Back East, though."

"I'll be damned. So she was—is?" Jay's face changed expression. "Is, uh, is she still alive?"

Ann shook her head. "She died two years ago. Lung cancer." She snorted. "Chain smoker. We had some pretty good fights about that."

"Sorry."

"It's all right. As I say, we . . . weren't close."

Jay nodded again. "Well. I better get rid of these." She turned and disappeared into the kitchen, carrying the cardboard trays. Three of me, Ann thought, and none of us knows how to cook. No, that was wrong, Jack wasn't a bad cook at all if you gave her an open fire or a wood-burning stove. She just didn't know how to use a modern kitchen.

Jay came back, empty-handed, and stood leaning against the door frame while Ann finished cleaning the table top. "What you said just then," she said. "About not being close to your, to our mother. Were you ever really close to anybody? Because I don't think I was. I was married for two years, to a certain charming bastard, and sometimes I'd look at him across the table or asleep—when he remembered whose bed he was supposed to sleep in—and I'd think who *is* this?"

"I was married longer than that," Ann told her, giving the table a last swipe, "and I know exactly what you're saying."

"Guess we're just not a getting-close girl," Jay mused.

From up the hallway came a sudden blare of off-key song:

"Oh, I wish I had someone to love me
Someone to be mine alone

Oh I wish I had someone to play with
Cause I'm tired of playing with my own."

Ann said softly, "Never before."

Jay laughed. "Oh, right. You two—" She shook her head. "You two of me? Fuck, this is going to make me crazy . . . you two, you're, umm—?"

"Yes." Ann smiled. "Very umm indeed."

A yelp drifted down the hallway, coming from the half-shut bathroom door. Jay said, "What's she doing in there, anyway?"

"I believe," Ann said, "she's trying to shave her legs."

Jay grinned. "Why don't you go give her a hand?"

"I thought about it," Ann said calmly.

They looked at each other for a moment, and then Jay said, "Oh, hell, don't mind me. I think I'm jealous."

She pushed her long black hair back off her face; it was a gesture Ann had seen thousands of times in mirrors. "Look," she said, "whatever there is between the two of you, it's nothing to me. God knows I don't have any prejudices that way—if I did I'd have a hell of a rough time in my line of work nowadays, believe me. Far as I'm concerned, people can do what they want, up to and including necrophilia between consenting adults."

"But you're about to tell me something."

"Right. Just that it's not my thing, all right? I tried it a couple of times, a long time ago, and it didn't do anything for me. I'm afraid I'm a raging heterosexual. I like guys."

She stopped and looked thoughtful. "At least I used to, till I got into a committed relationship with bourbon. Lately I've been getting itchy again. Wonder why."

Ann said, "We're not going to try to seduce you, if that's what you're getting at."

"Sort of." Jay looked embarrassed. She made a two-hands gesture that took in her face and body. "Not that I really think anybody's going to make a pass at me, the way I look now."

Ann looked at the red eyes and puffy grayish face and said nothing. Jay looked, in fact, like hell. She hadn't had anything to drink for a few hours—unless she'd been getting at a hidden supply, that was very possible—but she was still a long way from sober; she moved unsteadily and her voice was a little too loud at times, and her hands shook visibly. But she'd stopped begging for a drink; Ann didn't know whether that was a good sign or a bad one.

"All I meant about being jealous," Jay added, "I just envy you having somebody, that way. Man, woman, or whatever."

Up the hall, Jack sang:

> "Well, the last time I seen her and I ain't seen her
>   since
> She was suckin' off a mutie through a bob-wire
>   fence—"

Ann winced. Jay laughed. "Okay," she said. "Just wanted to get the arrangements straight. You two can bunk in together in Richard and Melanie's room. I'll just continue to sleep alone."

◄ ⏶ ⏷ ►

But late that night Ann awoke to strange sounds coming through the wall near her head. She sat up and realized that Jack was already awake, lying propped up on one elbow, her eye shining in the near-darkness. "Jay?" Ann said.

"Uh huh." Jack threw back the covers and swung her legs over the side of the bed. "We better have a look."

They found Jay on all fours on the hallway floor, crawling clumsily toward the bathroom. Behind her, a trail of reeking stains showed that she hadn't made it in time.

Jack half-lifted, half-dragged her into the bathroom and held her head over the toilet, while Ann went back and got a roll of paper towels from the kitchen and began cleaning up the mess. From the bathroom she could hear the sounds of heaving and gagging and, a couple of times, Jack's voice, though she couldn't make out the words.

In the guest bedroom, lying on the floor beside Jay's bed, she found an empty bourbon bottle. The room smelled like a distillery. The sheets were soggy with sweat and not only sweat.

She went back to the bathroom in time to see Jack shoving a naked and shaking Jay into the shower. "Wet herself," Jack told Ann. "Puked on herself, too."

In the shower, Jay began screaming, a long high wordless howl that the drumming water didn't even begin to drown out. Ann and Jack looked at each other.

"We'll have to take her in with us," Ann said. "For tonight, at least."

Jack nodded slowly. "Right. Won't be much fun, but we sure don't dare leave her alone."

Jay was still screaming. Jack sighed.

"Gonna be a long night," she said, and it was.

chapter
seventeen

Jack awoke next morning with an instant and very clear knowledge of what she was going to do.

She pushed back the blankets and got up off the floor, moving quietly, watching the sleeping faces of the two women on the bed. Over by the wall, Ann stirred slightly, and next to her Jay muttered something indistinct into the bunched-up pillow, but neither opened her eyes and a moment later Jay began snoring again.

Jack rubbed her hip, wincing—the floor had been harder than it looked—yawned, and lifted her gunbelt off the chair beside the bed and slung it over her shoulder. Otherwise naked, she picked up the box of cartridges from the nightstand and padded out and down the hallway to the guest bedroom.

Stepping over the litter on the floor, wrinkling her nose at the sour smell that filled the room, she looked through the contents of the closet and the bureau drawers. Everything was in a mess, naturally, but she picked out a pair of sky-blue satin panties and stepped awkwardly into them and hauled them up, to find that Jay was in fact as skinny as she looked. But she tugged the too-small briefs into the semblance of a fit—damn woman didn't have any ass at all, she thought, must have dissolved it in booze—and decided she liked how they felt against her skin.

She picked up a lacy bra, looked at it, and sighed. The truth was she didn't even know how to put it on. Probably too small anyway, she told herself, and tossed the bra on the bed.

Moved by a sudden impulse, she took a long red dress from the closet and held it up in front of her, studying herself in the closet-door mirror, turning her head and shoulders this way and that. Then she grinned, gave herself the finger, hung the dress back up, and went back to the bureau.

A few minutes later, clad in khaki shorts and a dark-blue T-shirt, feet shod in fancy white sneakers, she checked herself out again. Not bad at all, she decided. Well, if you didn't notice the half-dozen Band-Aids stuck here and there to her bare legs. Funny that she'd remembered how to use Band-Aids.

She hoisted her gunbelt off the bed, started to buckle it on, reconsidered, and slung it over her shoulder again. According to Jay, people in this world—at least this part of this world—didn't go in for wearing iron out in public. It wouldn't make any difference out here, with nobody around, but she might as well start getting used to going without. It felt funny, but no funnier than a lot of other things.

Time to get to work.

Ann woke to the sound of gunfire, loud and very close. She sat up in bed, throwing the tangled sheets aside with one hand and scrabbling at the bedpost with the other, before memory kicked in. She stopped groping for the gun that wasn't there, blinked a couple of times, and started to lie back down; but then the rest of her brain finally came awake and she said, "Shit!" and sat up again.

She got out of bed, climbing carefully over Jay, who twitched and mumbled but didn't open her eyes. Jack was nowhere to be seen. Ann wondered whether she ought to wake Jay, but then more gunshots sounded outside and she turned and ran for the door, grabbing the rumpled white terry robe off the doorknob as she passed, throwing it on and clutching it about her without bothering with the belt.

Jack was standing in the front yard, holding the revolver out in front of her in a two-handed grip. Twenty or thirty feet away, a little row of brown bottles glinted in the morning sun. The ground around them was dark and damp-looking, scattered with shiny fragments of glass.

The pistol went off with a loud deep boom, bucking briefly in Jack's hands. One of the bottles exploded in a spray of straw-colored liquid and flashing glass shards. "Outstanding," Jack said aloud, apparently to herself.

Standing on the porch, leaning over the railing, Ann said, "Jack, what are you doing?"

Jack glanced around. "Oh, hey. Sorry if I woke you up . . . the fuck's it *look* like I'm doing?"

"But—" Ann started down the steps. "I mean, why?"

"After last night," Jack said, "you can ask?"

She aimed and fired again. The bottle on the end suddenly lost its neck. "How about that?" Jack said. "Don't guess you'd believe I did it on purpose?"

"All right," Ann said, "but why this way? Why not just pour it all down the sink?"

Jack shrugged. "I needed to find out where this thing shot. Figured I might as well combine both jobs." She lowered the .44

and looked at it. "Nice piece, but damn, I'm going to miss my three-fifty-seven."

She snapped the cylinder open and tapped the ejector rod. "Man," she said over the small tinkling of empty brass on the rocky ground, "I don't believe how much booze she had around the place. Part of a case sitting in the living room, still in the box, but there were bottles all over the house, all the way from nearly empty to nearly full."

"I suppose you're right," Ann said. "About getting rid of it, I mean. No other way to keep her away from it."

"Her?" Jack grimaced. "Come on, Ann. Jay's got the biggest booze problem around here, but she's not the only one. You know how I get, for God's sake. Or no, you don't, not really, but trust me, you don't want to."

She dug in her shorts pocket and came up with a handful of fresh cartridges. "That's the other reason I did it this way," she added. "Pour it down the drain, shit, I didn't trust myself to do that. Even this way, it's not easy."

"I'm sorry. I didn't realize you had that much of a problem."

Jack paused, thumbing fresh rounds into the chambers. "Oh, yeah, like you're the one who's okay? You don't have any more of your nice little pills now, do you? How long do you figure you can go before you start looking around for some kind of a substitute?"

Before Ann could digest that the front door banged open and Jay's voice called, "What the fuck's going on?" Then, in a totally different tone, "Oh, no. *No*—"

They both turned and looked up as Jay came charging naked down the steps, all white skin and black hair and huge wild eyes, waving her hands and yelling: "No, stop, what are you, crazy, you can't do that—"

Jack clicked the cylinder shut and raised the .44. "Sure I can," she said, and snapped off a quick one-hand shot, finishing off the neckless bottle. "You just watch."

Jay rushed across the yard, making a horrible dry noise in her throat, arms flailing. Ann tackled her and hauled her to a stop before she could get to Jack, pinning her arms down at her sides. "Don't," Ann said in her ear. "Don't ever touch Jack while she's shooting. She'll hurt you."

Jack fired three rapid-fire shots. Two bottles exploded. A puff of dust appeared just beyond the row of targets. Jack said, "Fuck!"

Jay quit struggling, sagged against Ann's arms, and let out a low despairing moan. "Please," she said pitifully. "Please don't do this. You don't know—"

"Yes she does," Ann told her. "That's why she's doing it."

Jack fired again. Jay's whole body jerked as if the bullet had hit her. "Please," she said again. "Let me have just one."

Jack lowered the pistol and looked at her for a moment. "You're really hurting, huh?"

Jay licked her lips and nodded. After a minute Jack said, "Okay."

She strode over and picked up one of the remaining bottles and held it up to the light. Stuffing the pistol into the waistband of her shorts, she unscrewed the cap and slowly poured whiskey out onto the ground, while Jay whimpered softly in Ann's arms. "All right," Jack said, coming back and holding the bottle out to Jay. "There's about a shot left. Should be enough to steady your nerves a little."

Jay grabbed the bottle and raised it greedily to her lips. Jack said, "Enjoy it, girl. It's the last you're gonna get."

She frowned. "Unless you've got some stashed around here, that I missed. God help your skinny ass if I catch you with it."

She turned back and fired again. Now only a couple of bottles remained.

"Look," she said, breaking the revolver open again and fumbling for more cartridges, "we've got to stop fucking around. We're in a hell of a situation and we've got to figure out how to deal with it. Just because people aren't shooting at us any more, doesn't mean we're out of danger."

She paused in her reloading, looking at Ann. "Not that there's any guarantee how long that no-shooting part's going to last. Those fuckers in the gray suits—they found you before, how do we know they can't find you again?"

Ann clutched the robe around her; the breeze suddenly felt colder on her bare skin.

"Yeah," Jack said, resuming her reloading. "And from what you say, this little old wheelgun isn't even going to slow them down. That's something to think about. If they do show up, how the hell do we fight them? *Can* we fight them?"

She slapped the cylinder back into the frame. "We've got to get our shit together," she said. "We haven't got the time to waste sitting around getting lushed, trading sob stories like a bunch of old whores. Let alone any more scenes like last night." She looked at Jay. "You finished with that?"

Jay nodded jerkily. "Thanks." Her voice was still rough but a little steadier; there was a bit of color in her face now. "I don't suppose—" She looked longingly at the remaining bottles. "I mean—"

"Nope." Jack swung around and stuck the gun out at arm's

length and fired twice, very fast. The two bottles exploded almost simultaneously. "There," she said. "Ann, if you ever have to use this piece, it shoots high and a little to the right."

She reached out and took the empty bottle from Jay's hand and tossed it skyward, left-handed. As it reached its apogee and started to fall, she emptied the .44 at it. Undamaged, the bottle spun to earth and smashed against a rock.

Jack said, "Shit," and then, "Well, I scared the hell out of it, anyway. Come on, let's go back inside. You two need to get some clothes on."

◀ ▲ ▼ ▶

But, of course, it wasn't that simple. Jay was quiet and reasonably calm through the rest of the morning, but at lunchtime she sat staring at her untouched food and then began shaking and crying, not making a sound, her face white and crumpled as thrown-away paper. After a minute or so she got up and ran out of the room. Loud hiccuping sobs came back down the hall.

Ann started to move, to follow her, but Jack put out a hand. "Leave her. Right now she's got to deal with this herself. Besides, you'll just make her even more ashamed, seeing her like this."

After a moment's hesitation Ann sat back down. "Trust me," Jack said. "I know a little about it. Never been where she is, but I been in the neighborhood."

"Alcoholism, you mean?"

"Wouldn't say that, no. Always been able to quit and go without if I needed to—like if I'm going hunting or something, where I need a clear head. Damn well *got* to be able to do that, in my world . . . but," Jack said, "I sure used to drink too damn much when I did drink."

She glanced in the direction of the door, where Jay's weeping was still audible from down the hall. "Never went at it as long and hard as she has, though," she mused. "So I don't really know how long it'll take before she settles down."

"If she ever does."

"Oh, she will," Jack said confidently. "If we can just keep her off the juice long enough to dry her out, she'll be all right. I'm pretty sure of that."

She turned back to look at Ann. "See," she said, "there's two main reasons people become drunks. Fat Bob explained it to me. Some people, they've got something wrong with their body chemistry, they can't handle it and they can't leave it alone, you know? For them it's like that Mexican poppy juice they sell in Taos. They have to just stay clear away from it, it's not easy. Even in my world, and it's got to be even harder here, where people can just walk into a store and buy it."

She shrugged. "The other kind, they drink because there's something eating them and booze helps turn it off. That's what it usually is with me, when I go on a lush, and that's what we got here."

"How do you know?"

"She's me," Jack said, "and that means her body can't be hooked up all that different from mine. And, like I say, I can leave the stuff alone any time I need to, been doing it for years. Besides, she's you, too, and you told me once you never had a drinking problem at all."

"I'm not sure your thinking is scientifically sound."

"Maybe not, but I bet I'm right. And," Jack said, "that means she should be okay, once she gets her system cleaned out and her nerves quit acting up. Because I'm pretty sure I know what's been making her drink."

"Really?" Ann's voice came out drier than she'd intended. "What's your diagnosis, Doctor Jack?"

"You mean you haven't figured it out yet? Shit, and you're the smart-ass scientist . . . you were right there when she said it: she started drinking because she was having these dreams that were making her crazy. Just like me," Jack said, "and just like you, only you were having crazy thoughts while you were awake. Don't you get it? Some way, *we were picking each other up*. Thoughts and dreams and stuff, leaking through, getting into each other's heads."

Ann said, "Good God."

"Uh huh. I know it sounds loony, but is it any more impossible than what we already know? If there can be three of us in three different versions of the world, if that's not impossible, then who's to say what *is* impossible?"

"It could be," Ann said reluctantly, after a moment. "There have been accounts of people, siblings usually, having shared dreams—mostly in the literature of parapsychology, so I've always been a bit skeptical, but it could be . . . and I've heard of shared hallucinations and delusions, that's pretty well established. *Folie à deux*, I believe is the term."

She was trying to remember; there had been references, in the psychology books and journals she'd borrowed from Dr. Peters—trying, vainly, to get some sort of handle on her own problems—but she hadn't really paid attention.

"Whatever," Jack said with a dismissive gesture. "I probably got the scientific part wrong, but you know what I'm saying.

We've been picking up thoughts, head pictures, from each other, and that's what's been making us all three crazy."

She pushed a finger under her eyepatch and rubbed. "Some of the dreams I had," she added, "were about being locked up in strange places, and having people doing weird shit to me, asking me questions and I didn't know what the fuck they were talking about. That hospital where they had you? I *recognized* that place. . . ."

She made a face. "Maybe that's taking it too far, I don't know. But the feelings, anyway—like you kept having all these violent thoughts, wanting to hurt people, I bet you were picking that up from me. All the real violence in my life."

"You're seriously suggesting," Ann said, "that thoughts and emotions and images could travel from one person to another, from one alternate world to another?"

"Why not? *We* sure as hell did," Jack pointed out. "If our butts can cross the line, why not our thoughts?"

She leaned forward over the table. "And that's why I say she's going to be all right. We're *all* going to be all right, long as we're together." She reached out and put a hand on Ann's. "Didn't you tell me you hadn't had any more of your crazy attacks, after that night I showed up at the hospital?"

Ann nodded. "Right," Jack said, "and me, I haven't felt all wild and fucked up the way I used to. Just kind of depressed and nervous sometimes—you too, huh?—and ten gets you one we were picking that up off Jay."

"Jay did say she'd taken a turn for the worse," Ann said, "had some really bad dreams, just about the time I was getting stressed out waiting for you."

"See?" Jack leaned back and folded her arms. "You don't really believe it yet, I know, but you'll see. Long as we're together, we're all right."

From the hallway came the sound of unsteady footsteps. The bathroom door slammed, too hard.

Ann said, "Doesn't sound as if she's all right. For that matter I'm not feeling all that wonderful myself." She hugged herself and shivered. "Nerves on edge, feel like crying myself to tell you the truth."

"That's just the drugs wearing off. You two are going through some chemical processes, got to just hang in there and get past it. You'll be okay," Jack said once again. "Both of you."

"Got it all worked out, do you?" This time Ann didn't even try to keep the sarcasm out of her voice.

"Yep. I know you think you're smarter than me," Jack said, unruffled. "You might keep in mind, though, my brain's exactly the same as yours. I just been using it for different things."

Ann felt her face go hot. "Jack——"

"And," Jack went on, ignoring her attempted protest, "that's what I was really talking about, this morning, about needing to get our shit straight and think about where we go from here. God damn it, Ann, this is the biggest break I've ever had. Not just because I like it better here—and I do, I *like* water that I don't have to haul from the spring and chop wood to heat it, I like these clothes and I like not having to worry about jackers and muties and wild dogs and all that shit, I like the idea that I might not get killed any time soon."

She shook her head. "But even more than that, I like feeling the way I do now. I feel more, hell, how do I say it, more together inside myself—you know?—than I've ever felt in my whole life. And by Christ I'm not letting anybody fuck it up for me now."

She stood up. "I better go check on her," she said. "She's been in the can a little too long . . . we better clean that room of hers up, too. Damn if I'm sleeping on the floor again tonight."

◄   ▲   ▼   ►

They took turns, that night, staying with Jay, keeping an eye on her while she tossed and threshed in what looked like very unsatisfactory sleep, talking with her during the longer periods when she couldn't even manage that.

"Talk about anything," Jay said, "just talk to me," and so they did, or tried to, maybe getting a little thick and more than a little repetitious as the night passed and the small hours began to get bigger, but Jay said that was all right, anything to give her something to think about besides how bad she wanted a drink.

"It's in my head now, mostly," she said, "no real physical craving left, nothing I couldn't handle anyway, no worse than quitting smoking. It's just that I keep thinking about how good it would feel, that first swallow going down and the way it warms you up inside—" She went on about that until Jack, who would have liked one or two herself by now, finally told her to change the subject or shut the fuck up.

Somewhat surprisingly, she had no great difficulty with Jack's latest theory. "Why not?" she said. "Once you buy the primary premise, of who we are and what's happened to us, your idea doesn't sound all that wild. I've done some reading up on dream studies and paranormal research, doing background for a novel I wrote a few years ago. For that matter I knew a pair of twin sisters in college, they swore they sometimes had the same dreams, or one of them would answer a question before the other asked it."

Jack rubbed her bad eye and then her good one. It was really late and she was starting to fade; she wondered if she should go wake Ann and ask her to take over. "I just hope I'm right," she said. "Be nice to think there's a chance I could get myself straightened out."

"Me too." Jay sat down on the edge of the bed; she had been pacing the floor. "I do feel better in a way," she said. "I know it doesn't look like it, I've sure got a long way to go, but I think I know what you mean about feeling more . . . complete."

She gave Jack an uneven smile. "Stronger? That's a funny thought, but I think I do feel stronger with you two around."

From the hall doorway Ann said, "Oh, we're just the wind beneath your wings, aren't we?"

She came into the bedroom, making a one-hand gesture. "Go on, Jack, get out of here, go get some sleep. I'll take over." And, when Jack began an automatic and not very heartfelt protest, "No, really, I may as well. Wide awake, a little bit wired—withdrawal from all those pills, probably."

"Thanks," Jack said, rising from the bedside chair, stretching and yawning. "Me for Z City, then. Holler if you need me."

When she was gone Jay said, "You don't have to do this, Ann. I'll be all right. In fact think I can get back to sleep now."

"Lucky you, then. I wasn't just sparing Jack's pride, I really couldn't sleep now, not if I had to." Ann gestured at the bed. "Go ahead and turn in if you'd like. I'll just be around."

Jay nodded and stretched out on the bed, dragging the blanket more or less over herself, not bothering to get properly under the covers. "Thanks," she said, and closed her eyes. "Could you get the light, please?"

◀ ▲ ▼ ▶

Ann wandered into the kitchen and poured herself a cup of

coffee—fresh pot since she'd last been up, Jay must have made it, Jack wouldn't have had a clue how to use an electric coffee maker—and carried it back up the hall to the living room. Gray morning light was already coming in through the big windows.

She sat down on the couch and flipped on the surviving end-table lamp. The other still lay on the floor, a victim no doubt of one of Jay's drunken rages; the whole place was a shambles, they definitely had to clean things up today. She considered turning on the TV but decided the sound might wake the others. Besides, she couldn't figure out how to operate the unfamiliar remote control unit.

Instead she took a magazine from the stack under the coffee table and stretched out, sipping her coffee—it was dreadful, but she'd expected no more—and began to read.

She lay there reading for a long time, while the light grew stronger outside; she studied the pages carefully, even the ads, trying to form a picture of this world, which had seemed so similar to her own but which now appeared almost as strange, in some ways, as Jack's. The United States was still recognizably the same country, but it had clearly taken a different road in many respects. Social programs were sketchy and in disarray—incredibly, there was, according to what she read, no national health care system at all—even though the disparity in the distribution of wealth was like something out of Dickens. A staggering number of people were homeless, many of them veterans of that Vietnam business, which in this world, as in Jack's, had apparently escalated into a full-scale and calamitous war that went on clear up into the seventies.

Science and technology seemed to be roughly at the same level in most areas, but there were major differences—for one thing, the space program was a joke; as far as she could learn, there wasn't even a manned base on the Moon.

On the other hand, references to "the former Soviet Union" and "the all-volunteer armed forces" definitely sounded encouraging, as did the absence of any indications of current American military adventures overseas, or any references to the bloodbath in South Africa. Maybe somebody had gotten something right here, anyway.

At last the stack of unread magazines dwindled to two, a *New Yorker* and a rather ragged-looking *Time*. She reached for the *New Yorker*, paused, and decided she needed more coffee. She sat up and picked up her cup and got to her feet, and that was when she heard the vehicle pull up in front of the house.

She stood absolutely still, mind gone blank, while a door opened and shut and then footsteps sounded on the porch steps, and then there was a knock. In the quiet house it sounded very loud.

Ann started to move, to go and look out the big window, but then she stopped: best not to be seen, keep quiet, hope whoever it was would go away. She waited, then, holding her breath while the knocking continued, letting it out with relief when it stopped.

Then, after a moment, she heard the unmistakable grinding click of a key being inserted into the lock. Before she could even begin to think what to do, the door swung open.

The morning sunlight backlit the figure in the doorway, and for a moment Ann could make out only a dark silhouette; but her eyes adjusted after a second, and she saw a husky, dark-skinned young man, dressed in T-shirt and jeans and a purple bandanna headband.

"Miz, uh, Jay?" he said uncertainly, looking at her. "I just came by to see if you were okay. I mean, after, you know—"

He stopped; his heavy black eyebrows went up and then down. "Uh," he said, "what—"

Idiotically, involuntarily, Ann said, "Hi."

chapter eighteen

Jay opened her eyes and stared at the bedroom ceiling, not quite awake yet but with a sense of something wrong. A moment later she heard the voices in the living room.

Awareness returned all in a rush; she sat up and muttered, "Christ," and slid out of bed, reaching for her robe and wrapping it around her before heading for the door and up the hallway to the living room; where, sure enough, there was Danny Santos, standing in the doorway staring at Ann. Who was looking back at him with her mouth not quite hanging open.

Jay said, "Hello, Danny," and they both turned to look at her. "So," she said with what she hoped was a bright smile, "what brings you out here?"

"Uh—" Danny Santos shook his head, evidently with the idea of clearing it. "Well, you know, like I was just saying to—"

He stalled out again, looking back and forth from Jay to Ann and back. Jay said quickly, "Oh, I'm sorry, Danny. I'd like you to meet my—sister," the pause barely perceptible or so she hoped. Sister, yeah, that's the ticket. She walked over and stood beside Ann. "Danny, Ann. Ann, Danny."

"Hi," Ann said. "Pleasure to make your acquaintance."

Danny's face registered several different reactions in quick overlapping succession. "Oh," he said, and then after a moment, "I didn't know, I mean, Miz Scott didn't say anything about anybody else staying with you."

"Ann just got here yesterday," Jay told him. "She'll be here for a while. Melanie knows," and God help us if you've got any way of contacting her. "I—"

Behind her, Jack's voice said, "Everything all right?"

Jay turned, sensing the others doing the same. Jack stood in the hall doorway, stark naked unless you counted the gunbelt slung over her left shoulder. And the revolver in her hand, which wasn't exactly clothing but certainly was an eye-catching accessory. At least she wasn't pointing it at anybody. Yet.

Ann said, "Everything's fine. Just a friend of Jay's, come calling."

"Okay," Jack said, and shoved the gun back into its holster. "Sorry about that."

She turned and strode unhurriedly back down the hallway, her bare buttocks and legs flashing attractively in the light from the still-open front door. They all watched in attentive silence.

After she had disappeared into the bedroom Jay cleared her throat. "My other sister," she said, trying not to sound as desperate as she felt. "Jacqueline."

"She, um," Ann said, and gave up.

"She was mugged some time ago," Jay said, "and she's still a little on edge. I'm trying to get her to get rid of that pistol."

"Looked like Mr. Scott's gun," Danny said. He looked really unhappy.

"Oh? I wouldn't know. Probably a common make." Jay heard herself talking faster now; any minute she'd be babbling hysterically. "Danny," she said, forcing herself to slow down and speak calmly, "I'll level with you. My sisters flew out here to stay with me and help me deal with my drinking problem. I called them after—you know. The other day when you were here."

"Oh." Danny's face cleared immediately; he even smiled, a quick white flash against that wonderful brown skin. "Oh, well, hey, that's really good. I'm glad to hear it."

He ran his hand over his face. "See," he said, "that's why I came by. Because, you know. The other day." He was starting to look uncomfortable again. "Thought maybe I ought to check," he said, "see if you were all right."

"I'm fine," Jay assured him. "I'll be just fine. Now my sisters are here. My two dear sisters, we're very close, you know. Like sisters. Haha."

"Haha," Ann echoed weakly.

"Well, that's sure a relief," Danny Santos said. "So is there anything you—"

He crunched to a stop as Jack reappeared, dressed this time and, *Deo gratias*, not carrying her damned gun. Or at least not carrying it openly, though there was a suspicious bulge under the loose-hanging tail of her shirt. She'd put on her eyepatch, too.

"Hey," she said to Danny Santos. "My name's Jack. What's yours?"

"Short for Jacqueline," Ann put in quickly. "You see."

"This is Danny," Jay told her, experiencing that losing-it sensation again, like feeling all four tires sliding on a patch of black ice. "Danny, my *other sister*—"

Jack went over and shook Danny's hand vigorously. "Any friend of Jay's," she said. "How's it hanging?"

Danny seemed to be having trouble meeting Jack's eyes, or rather eye; his own eyes seemed to be trying to drift downward. "Pleasure," he mumbled.

He looked at Jay again. "What I was going to say," he said, "is there anything you need me to do? Like get you something from town? I'll be in class till this afternoon, but I could bring you whatever you wanted after I get done."

"No, we're fine." Actually there was quite a lot they needed— the supplies on hand wouldn't be nearly enough for three— but they could take care of that later; no way in hell did they need this kid coming around right now.

"Well, okay, then," he said, backing toward the door. "You've got my number if—"

"Yes." Following closely, not actually crowding him out the door but pretty near it, inexcusably rude behavior—especially to an Indian, they had a thing about body space—but never mind, get him *out* of here. "I'll call you if we need anything, Danny. Promise."

Then out on the porch, suddenly and crazily and without any thought whatever, throwing her arms around him and squeezing tight, laying her face up against that big barrel chest: "Danny," she heard herself say, "thanks for caring. It's really sweet of you."

She let him go and watched him hurry down the steps— looking back up at her once, grinning uncertainly—and climb into the pickup cab. She raised a hand as he drove away, but she couldn't see whether he responded.

When he was out of sight she went back inside, to meet the broad grins of Ann and Jack. "All right," she said, "God damn it, go ahead. Have fun."

"Why, *sis*-ter." Jack's good eye went wide in mock shock. "Would we make fun of our dear sister?"

"Our dear cradle-robbing sister," Ann put in. "My God, I thought you were going to start humping his leg. Have you no shame, sister dear?"

"Hey," Jack said, "he did have a nice tight butt. Great shoulders, too. Can't say I blame you, sis."

"All right," Jay said as they both began laughing, "all right, I didn't hear either one of you coming up with anything better, did I? Any suggestions as to what I should have said? 'Danny, I'd like you to meet my other selves, they just dropped in from the alternate worlds they inhabit.' Sure, why not?"

"She's got a good point there," Jack said to Ann. "Woman's got a good point."

"You've got some good points yourself," Ann told her with a leer. "Showed them all to our visitor, too, didn't you?"

"Right," Jay said, "not to mention coming in holding that fucking gun—Christ, you're a *menace*—"

"I've told her that," Ann said. "I swear I can't take her anywhere."

"Shit," Jack said, "I was the one who saved the day and you know it. After he got a look at my goodies he wasn't thinking straight enough to realize what a crock of bullshit you were handing him."

"Possibly true," Ann agreed. "There was a pronounced bulge in the front of his pants for the rest of the conversation. I was impressed."

They all three broke up, then, falling together onto the couch, laughing like madwomen, clutching at each other for support.

"Jesus," Jay said when she could speak again, "I needed that. I swear I feel better than I have in days. Years."

Wiping her eyes, Ann said, "Why don't you go back to bed, then? You can't have gotten much sleep."

"No, that's all right." Jay stood up and stretched. "I think I'll just stay up. Then tonight I shouldn't have any trouble getting to sleep."

"Good idea," Jack said. "Guess I'll do the same. Maybe we'll all get some Z's tonight. Then tomorrow we can start thinking what we ought to do about the situation."

"Oh, yes," Ann said. "We definitely do need to think things out. We can't stay holed up here forever, we're going to have to deal with other people and we've got to work up some kind of credible story and get it straight. Judging by our efforts just now, I'd say we're not very good at improvising."

"*I* thought I did rather well," Jay said with exaggerated dignity. "As a writer of fiction—"

"As a writer of fiction, I hope that wasn't a typical example of your dialogue." Ann rolled her eyes. "'My dear *sisters* and I—'"

"'—are *very close*,'" Jack finished for her, and they fell into each other's arms, hooting and cackling and tickling, giggling like girls.

"Hey!" Ann's voice was muffled by Jack's shoulder. "Is that a gun or are you just happy—no, damn, it *is* a gun."

"You two." Jay shook her head. "God, you two, I swear."

They looked up, still giggling. "We'll be good," Ann promised.

"I don't doubt it," Jay said. "But I'll never know."

◄   ▲   ▼   ►

That night, though, she didn't fall asleep as readily as she'd expected; tired as she was, badly as her mind and body craved rest, she couldn't seem to relax. She turned from side to side, unable to settle into position; her fingers twitched and now and then an arm or leg jerked spasmodically. She felt as if someone had inserted a key into the back of her neck and tightened all her nerves like piano strings, clear past what should have been the snapping point.

It's not that I want a drink, she told herself, I just want something to loosen me up enough to let me sleep, the AA tells you nobody ever died from not sleeping, but Christ, it can sure make you wish you were dead.

She recognized the trap; she'd been here many, many times before. Tell yourself you just need a little something to get to sleep, that's all—but then you lie there in the dark having just one more sip to put you to sleep and just one more because that one didn't quite do it and finally you pass out, but you wake up four or five hours later because by then the booze has worn off and whatever was keeping you awake is still there inside your head, so you reach for the bottle and do the whole thing all over again, and in the morning you wake up with a cement mixer going in your head and you look at the bottle and can't figure where it all went, you just had a little bit to help you sleep. . . .

Well, at least there was no danger of that this time, thanks to Jack and her damn Annie Oakley act, not a drop left in the place—she'd already checked, while they were outside cleaning up the broken glass in the yard; Jack hadn't missed a single bottle, God bless the magnificent woman and God damn the meddling bitch.

Gradually the twitching and jerking subsided; consciousness began to slip away, and she snuggled her face against the pillow and sighed as the fog of sleep at last rose behind her eyes.

And, naturally, that was the moment when she realized she had to go. Right then.

Cursing through her teeth, she got up and barefooted down the hall to the bathroom. The cold tile floor was enough to wake her up again; she'd known that was going to happen, though, she'd been through this particular cycle many, many nights before.

On her way back she paused, for no conscious reason, next to the closed door of the other bedroom. And stood listening, suddenly unable to move from the spot.

The sounds that came through the door were nothing all that extraordinary: a few soft thumps, such as a person might make trying to find a comfortable position to go to sleep, and a couple of low grunting moans. A woman's voice said something; she couldn't recognize whose, or catch the words, but it was followed by a laugh.

Jay's skin felt suddenly very warm, all over. Her right hand, she discovered, was trying to creep between her legs.

Not thinking, not allowing herself to think, she reached for the doorknob.

The bedroom was dark, but the moonlight through the window fell squarely on the bed. Jay stood for a moment in the doorway, watching the two writhing bodies, the tangle of intertwined arms and legs, dark hair and pale hunching hips. Then they stopped, and two faces turned up to look at her.

"Um," she said, "is this a private party, or . . . ?"

The pause that followed felt very long; that's it, Jay thought, I had to fuck things up again—

But then they both laughed, and Jack's voice cried, "Come in, ourself!"

◄ ▲ ▼ ►

Sunlight, striking through the window, warmed Jay's face and made her blink as her eyes reluctantly opened. She moved slightly and immediately heard a protesting groan from somewhere near her left shoulder blade. "Sorry," she said.

"What time is it?" Ann's voice came from over against the wall. "Never mind, I don't want to know."

Nobody moved or spoke again for a minute or two. Finally Jay said, "Well. This has certainly been . . . interesting."

"Certainly *crowded*," Jack said peevishly. "Whoever belongs to that elbow in my short ribs, do you mind . . . thank you."

Jay sat up and rubbed her eyes. The light was very strong; it must be well into the morning. Crowded or not, they'd all slept soundly when they'd finally gotten around to sleeping. Memory came back in a quick flood of amazing images; she felt her face prickle.

"I'll go make coffee," she said, and as Ann started to protest, "No, really. I'm all right. I can do it."

◄ ▲ ▼ ►

Some time later, sitting down in the living room, she said, "Is the coffee all right? I'm afraid my taste buds aren't in great shape—"

"It's fine," Ann assured her, sipping. "Better than mine."

"Couldn't tell you," Jack admitted. "I'm still learning to drink this stuff. Don't guess I've had coffee a dozen times in my whole life—Daddy said I was too young and by the time I wasn't it was all gone. Now and then somebody finds a can in some ruins or something, and they can name their price—if they don't get killed for it. Real coffee's worth a lot more than gold."

Jay lifted her own cup and tasted. Ann was being kind; it was almost bad enough for an AA meeting. Well, she thought, I said I could do it, I didn't say I could do it right.

She cleared her throat. "Ah, look, last night—as I say, it was interesting."

They looked at each other and then at her. They did that a lot. She wished they wouldn't.

"Okay," she said, "so it was *very* interesting. Downright fascinating, in fact. Oh, hell, I enjoyed it, all right?" Christ, yes, she didn't think she'd ever come so many times in a week, let alone a single night. Flushing, she said, "It was great."

"It did have its moments," Ann murmured. "Yes indeed."

"No shit." Jack grinned. "We're all going straight to hell, but who cares?"

"And," Jay continued, "I'm glad we did it. Maybe we'll do it again some time."

Watching her face, Ann said, "But?"

"But, well. I guess I'm trying to say that it's a fine place to visit but I can't see myself living there. Sorry," she said. "I mean—"

"It's all right," Ann said gently. "Our feelings aren't hurt."

"Yeah," Jack said, "you get a chance to do that Indian kid, go for it. Get him back up here, we'll clear out and let you jump his bones."

"No way," Ann said. "I want to watch."

Jay snorted. "Get real, you two. I'm not out to seduce Danny Santos, for God's sake."

"Then can I have a crack at him?" Jack asked eagerly. "He's really cute."

"Definitely," Ann agreed. "Hunk City."

"Hey," Jack said, "we could—"

"No we couldn't," Jay told her. "Don't even say it. Bad enough that my life's turned into something out of the kind of books I write. Damn if I'm going to let it become a scene from a tasteless adult video."

"Bit late for that, isn't it?" Ann remarked dryly. "After that little triple-X-rated scene last night—"

Jack got to her feet and walked over to the window and looked out, just as tires sounded on the gravel outside. "Hey," she said. "Speak of the handsome devil. Guess who just arrived?"

chapter nineteen

D anny Santos said, "Good coffee."

He set his cup carefully down on the coffee table. "Nice and strong," he added with apparent sincerity. "Not many people make it strong enough, the way I like it. Never could stand weak coffee, you know?"

"More?" Ann asked, but he shook his head.

"Better not," he said. "Supposed to be bad for you, drinking too much coffee."

He sat back and looked off out the window. They all waited patiently. They had all known enough Indians to understand what was going on; it would have been unconscionably rude, by the rules of his culture, for him to come straight to the point.

Finally he sighed softly and looked at Jay. "I did some thinking," he said, "after I left here yesterday."

He paused. Jay refrained from saying, "Yes?" or anything of the sort. A part-Cherokee mystery writer had told her once that this was something white people did that got on Indians' nerves, the automatic little interjections that served only to assure the other person you were listening. Among Indians you kept quiet while the speaker organized his thoughts.

Danny's mouth curved into a half-embarrassed grin. "I told

you," he said, "I'm a big fan of yours. Got all your books, all the magazines with your stories in them. Got a lot of stories about you, too, interviews, you know."

Jay suddenly realized where this was going.

"I went home," he said, "after my last class, and I dug out my little collection, and sure enough, I was right. Remember that interview you did in *Locus* magazine, couple of years ago? When you told about being an only child and how you thought that was a big influence on your personality and your work? Growing up with no brothers or sisters to talk with, you said, you got in the habit of making up imaginary people—remember?"

Jay said, "Oh, you know how those interviewers are. Can't get anything right—"

"Stop it." Ann's voice chopped Jay's fumbling words off like an axe blow. "For God's sake," she said angrily, "can't you see how hard this is for him? Don't make it any worse by insulting his intelligence."

"You're right," Jay agreed. "Sorry, Danny. It's just that, well, there's an explanation, but . . . Jack, don't even think about it."

Over by the door, Jack took her hand off the butt of the pistol under her shirt. "Sorry." She rubbed at her bad eye. "You're going to tell him? Are you sure about this?"

Danny began waving his hands in a little time-out gesture. "Hold it, hold it. You don't have to tell me anything. That's what I came to talk about . . . see," he said, "after I thought about it some, I went and told my grandfather."

"Shit," Jack said. "Should have known—"

"No, wait, it's okay. My grandfather, anything you tell him

like that, it's like you told it down a well, you know? Never goes any farther. Believe me," Danny Santos said. "He's—well, I don't know how to explain it. He's kind of a special person."

"A shaman?" Ann asked. "Medicine man, whatever you call it?"

"Not exactly," Danny said, a little reluctantly. "I mean, I guess partly, I don't really know how you'd say it in English. He's really old, anyway, and he knows a lot of stuff. Knows things sometimes before they happen, know what I'm saying?"

He looked at Jay. "And he asked me, when you first came out here, to keep an eye on you, and let him know if anything unusual happened."

"He what?" Jay blinked. "How did he know—well, I suppose you told him, but why—"

"No," Danny said, "that's just it, I never said anything to him about you. He was the one who brought it up. Like I said, sometimes he just knows things."

Jay and Ann glanced at each other, eyebrows going up. Jack, however, said only, "So what did he say when you told him?"

"He wants me to bring you to see him," Danny said. "All of you. Today."

That stopped everything for a few seconds. Finally Ann said, "Okay, huddle time. Excuse us, Danny—"

◄ ⏶ ⏷ ▶

In the hallway, standing close together with the others and talking very low, Jay said, "How the hell do we get out of this? I don't want to offend him, but—"

"What do you mean, get out of it?" Jack asked. "I say let's go see his grandfather, like he wants. We can use any help we can get."

Jay said, "You're kidding," but Jack shook her head.

"These old Indians," she said seriously, "they can surprise you. There was this one, I don't know what tribe he was, came around Fat Bob's every now and then, treated sick people—he knew stuff, all right. Like he came up to me, first time he ever met me, and looked me in the face for a minute, and then he said, 'You have bad dreams.' How the fuck did he know?"

Jay snorted. "I'll let that one go by . . . Ann, how about you? Don't tell me you're buying into this silly shit too."

Ann shrugged. "I don't know what I believe any more. I've seen so many impossible things lately, my disbelief circuits seem to be burned out. Jack's right, though," she said, "about our needing any help we can get. Right now we're so alone it's frightening."

"Help?" Jay put her hands on her hips. "What makes you think Grandpa is going to want to help us? Three weird-looking white women babbling a lot of crap about alternate worlds, he's going to think, 'Oh, fuck, more New Agers,' and get rid of us as fast as he can. Or maybe try to sell us some quartz crystals."

"So?" Jack said. "If that's the worst that can happen, then what's the big deal? He runs us off, we come back here, we're no worse off. What's it hurt to try?"

"If nothing else," Ann said, "we're going to have to start dealing with people sooner or later. This might not be a bad place to start. After all, even if he talks about us, who's going to listen? If this world is anything at all like mine, nobody listens to Indians."

"You go, then." Jay leaned against the wall, looking away. "You two go talk to the old weirdo. I'll just stay here and clean house. Sure needs it, just look at it."

"Fuck that," Jack said. "For now anyway, we go everywhere together or we don't go. What's your problem, anyway?"

Ann was studying Jay's face. "What *is* your problem with this? There's something you're not saying."

"Damn it," Jay said, swinging around and glaring at Ann, "I don't *want* to 'deal with people'!"

Her voice was too loud and she stopped and glanced toward the living room, where Danny Santos stood carefully looking out the front window. "Don't you get it?" she said after a moment, in a lower voice. "I can't deal with people right now." She held out her hands, which trembled visibly. "Look at that. I'm a fucking wreck. God knows how long it'll be before I can face other people, but I know I'm not ready to do it now."

"All the more reason you need to do it," Jack said. "People need to do what they don't think they can do. That's one thing Daddy was right about."

"Bullshit. Please," Jay said, her voice changing, starting to break up, "don't make me do this. Don't you see? I can't do it. I can't face *anybody* now. Even one old Indian."

"Then," Jack said, "you better figure on backing your ass up to him, because we're going." Her hand flashed up and clamped down on Jay's upper arm. "Now. No more argument. Come on, let's go get dressed. We're going visiting."

◄ ▲ ▼ ►

Out in front of the house they all paused, looking at Danny Santos' old pickup truck. "Huh," Jack said. "How are we going to work this? Want me to ride in the back?"

"Unnecessary," Jay said, pushing back her hair and not looking at any of them. "We can take the car."

"The car?" Danny Santos looked uneasier than ever. "You're not, uh, I mean, I'm, uh—"

"Yes, yes, I know. I wasn't supposed to drive Melanie's precious little environmentally correct Japanese roller skate. But you know I've been doing it, you knew all along I would, didn't you? If you didn't you must not know very many drunks."

She fished in her jeans pocket and held out the keys to Danny, still not looking at him. "Here. I'm sure you're a better driver than any of us. You're the one who wants us to meet Grandpa. Take us to him."

◄ ▲ ▼ ►

On the way down the mountain Danny said, "Tell you the truth, it was Grandfather got me to go to work for the Scotts in the first place. I'd just as soon you didn't tell them that, though."

Sitting beside him, watching him drive, admiring the ripple of arm and shoulder muscles as he steered the Toyota down the winding road—he really was an excellent driver, despite his protests that he'd never operated anything with an automatic transmission before—Jay said, "What do you mean, got you to go to work for them? Melanie said you were one of her students."

"Well," Danny said, "he got me to sign up for her class, too. It was last year—I guess around the end of summer—when all of a sudden he wanted me to get close to the Scotts. Said they most likely needed somebody to do errands, work around the place—most of these white people with money, around here, they've got somebody like that. Generally Mexican or Indian. Hey, no offense," he added quickly, raising a hand from the wheel in an apologetic gesture. "I mean, I've got nothing against—"

"It's all right," Ann said from the back seat. "As long as you come watch us dance and buy our beadwork."

Danny laughed. "Okay, okay, you got me. Anyway," he said, "I did need some kind of a part-time job, so I did like Grandpa said. Now and then he'd ask me questions, but I just figured he was curious about how people like that lived. He's interested in all kinds of stuff."

"And now you think he may have been setting you up for this?" Jay tried to keep the skepticism out of her voice.

Danny's shoulders lifted and dropped. "Who knows? You don't question an elder."

Ann said, "Danny, what are you studying at the university?"

"Quantum physics. Well," he said, "I'm just a physics major right now. But that's what I want to do for my graduate work."

"Oh," Ann said, rather faintly.

"Listen," Danny said as the road flattened out onto the open land of the valley and the dark line of the main highway appeared up ahead, "I have to stop somewhere, get some stuff Grandpa needs. Okay if I do it at this little town up here?"

"That's fine," Jay told him. "Whatever you want."

"All right, then," Danny said, starting to slow down as they passed the first speed-limit warning sign. "There's a supermarket out by the highway, ought to have everything."

◄ ⋀ ⋁ ►

"I've been here before," Jack said, staring this way and that as they rolled through the small town. "Ann, I was here that last day, just before the night I met you. I killed—*ow!*" She rubbed her ankle, looking more surprised than hurt. "Why'd you—oh," seeing Ann's face, getting it. "I mean, I was going to say, I killed some time here."

The "supermarket" was on the far side of the highway underpass, at the eastern edge of town. It didn't amount to much, really nothing but a smallish grocery store, the dusty windows plastered with hand-printed signs advertising specials on produce and paper towels and dish soap.

The parking area was virtually deserted, and Danny started to stop in front, but Ann said, "Pull around to the side, please," and, looking puzzled but saying nothing, he did so.

"I'll just be a little while," he said, opening his door and looking around at them. "You ladies need me to get you anything?"

"I'll go in with you," Ann said. "Now you mention it, we do need some supplies."

"We do?" Jay said. "I mean, there's plenty of food left—"

"Not food," Ann said impatiently. "Haven't you looked at the calendar lately? And there are three of us, and I'll be very surprised if we don't start just about simultaneously. Have you got enough *supplies* to take care of that?"

"Shit," Jack said, counting rapidly on her fingers, "that's right, I lost track there. Just a few more days. No wonder I've been feeling so damn edgy."

"You're right," Jay told Ann. "There's not enough at the house. Not for three of us. Here." Moving awkwardly in the confined space, she got her wallet out of her hip pocket and passed it back to Ann. "Think you can manage?"

"You're not coming in?"

Jay shook her head. "I couldn't handle it right now. Sorry."

"All right." Ann took the wallet and started to get out. "I'll be all right. Things aren't that different . . . here."

Jack said, "Hang on. I'm going in with you."

"What? Jack, I don't think—"

"I've got to start some time," Jack said, opening the door on her side. "Might as well be here and now."

Ann said something too low for Jay to hear. "Oh, all right," Jack said. "I'll leave it in the car, okay?"

A couple of minutes later, watching the three of them vanish around the corner of the little store, Jay sighed and scooted down in her seat. At least it was quiet, now. She hoped they'd take their time.

Something tickled her nose: a stray bit of dust in the air, perhaps. She sneezed, and then sneezed again.

"Shit," she said, rubbing her nose with her fingertips, popping open the glove compartment to look for Kleenex.

And there it was, shiny and pretty in the sunlight that filtered through the windows: the bottle she'd stashed there, back when she'd made that last run, and completely forgot until now.

She reached out a trembling hand and touched the gleaming glass, gently, almost reverently. After a moment she lifted the bottle free, very carefully, and held it up in front of her face. "Thank you, God," she whispered. "I owe you."

Her hands were shaking so hard now she could barely get the cap off, and when she did she dropped it on the floor, but she hardly noticed. Gripping the bottle in both hands, she raised it to her lips and took a long gulping pull.

She closed her eyes and shuddered almost ecstatically as the first swallow went down. Quickly she chased it with another, drinking rapidly, anxiously watching the corner of the building for the others' return. No sign of them so far; no sign of anyone except a big fat Mexican man who came out and got in a pickup truck and drove away.

She rolled down the window one-handed, still swigging, thinking to dissipate the whiskey smell. A dry dusty breeze came in, carrying the boom of traffic from the nearby highway. Jay leaned back in her seat, smiling slightly. I can handle it, she thought. Now.

She turned and half-lay against the door, tucking her feet up under her, snuggling into place, cuddling the bottle in her arms while she got comfortable. With any luck Ann and Jay would get in an argument over pads versus tampons or something, anything to slow them down in there, just a little bit longer. . . .

She was lying there like that, drinking, enjoying the sun on her face, the bottle now over a third gone, when the big blue Buick came tearing into the parking lot, going much too fast and weaving all over the place. She raised her head and peered over the dash as it squealed to a rough stop in front of the store.

Drunks, she thought fuzzily, hell of a time of day to be drunk, and then she laughed out loud and raised the bottle again, watching, as the Buick's doors opened and two extremely strange-looking men got out.

chapter twenty

Jack said, "I don't know, Ann, I've never used those things." She took the box of tampons from Ann and looked at the label. "I just barely even remember store-bought pads," she added. "I'd only got my first a couple of months before it all went down."

"What did you use?" Ann asked. "I wondered about that."

Jack shrugged. "Whatever I could get, same as all the other women back there. Old rags, when you were lucky enough to have them. When you didn't, well, you don't really want to know."

"Probably not." Ann looked around and laughed softly. "We're embarrassing Danny," she said.

Danny Santos was standing several aisles away, at the front of the store, giving his full attention to the label on a packet of flashlight batteries, under the suspicious stare of the blue-haired white woman behind the counter. His back was to them and his shoulders were ever so slightly hunched.

"Hey," Jack said, "he's an Indian, all right? They've got a thing about women's stuff."

"We're unclean?"

Jack shook her head. "No, not that. More like sacred, holy.

That old medicine man told me about it. We've got so much power we're dangerous."

"Well," Ann said, "now I think of it they're right, I know what I'm like sometimes. My God, you realize we're all liable to start PMSing at the same time, that's a frightening thought . . . better tell him to relax, we're not there yet. Just being prepared, like good little scouts."

"Were you in the Girl Scouts?" Jack asked. "Daddy wouldn't let me join. Said they didn't have any discipline and they didn't know shit about wilderness technique—"

Ann had stopped listening. She was looking out the dust-blurred front window, through the space between a couple of sale posters, at the blue car that had just come to a remarkably inept stop in front of the store. Or rather she was looking at the two men getting out.

It took a second to recognize them; the gray suits were covered now, more or less, by ill-fitting work clothes—Short's jacket sleeves were rolled up to his elbows, and a good six inches of gray material showed below Long's pants cuffs—but there was no mistaking those two store-window faces. Especially since they were making no attempt to conceal the weapons in their hands.

Ann wanted to scream, tried to speak, choked, and instead whacked Jack hard on the shoulder. Jack said, "What," and then turned to look where Ann was pointing. "Oh," she said then. "Oh, fuck. It's them."

Ann nodded. "Fuck," Jack said again. "Weird-looking sons of bitches, all right. I didn't get a good look before." She moved closer to the window, peering out. "And you had to make me leave that piece in the car."

"It wouldn't do you any good," Ann said, finally able to speak again. "Trust me."

"Maybe not, but I could try." Jack was looking around. "Where's the back way out of this place?"

"How far would we get?"

"I don't know, but we—"

That was when the Toyota appeared, tearing around the corner of the building, tires screaming, engine blatting, headed straight for the two men. Who stopped and spun around, weapons coming up, just as it slammed into them.

There was a loud sickening thump and a tinkle of broken glass as the left headlight shattered, and Short went flying through the air, arms and legs flailing, while Long went down and disappeared under the wheels. Jack said, "Holy shit!"

The car's horn began a rapid insistent hooting. A window slid down and Jay's face appeared. Her mouth opened and she seemed to be shouting, but the horn drowned her out. She stuck her arm out the window, making vigorous beckoning motions.

"Let's go," Ann said, unnecessarily. Jack was already halfway to the door.

The woman behind the counter was staring, open-mouthed, out through the doorway. So was Danny Santos. "What," he managed to say as Jack and then Ann dashed past him and out of the store, the rest of his words drowned by the bang as Jack's shoulder hit the heavy glass door and knocked it open.

Jay was gunning the engine impatiently as they piled into the car. "Go," Ann said, sliding in beside her, "go, go!"

"Those guys," Jay said, "were they the ones you were telling about?"

"Yes. Come on, get going." Ann twisted in her seat, looking this way and that, seeing Danny Santos standing in the door of the store, his mouth open. "Never mind him," she told Jay. "Just go."

"Right," Jay said, releasing the brake. The Toyota lurched forward, tires and various other components registering audible protests at her clumsiness. "You think they'll come after us?"

"Bet on it," Ann assured her.

"They're getting back in their car," Jack said from the back seat.

Jay hauled the Toyota around in a brutally tight semicircle, throwing Ann hard against the door, and accelerated toward the exit. She paused to let a couple of cars pass and then pulled out onto the blacktop. "I'm just glad I didn't fuck up," she said as they headed for the overpass. "Been a hell of a thing, they'd been the wrong guys, you know?"

Ann said, "You mean you weren't sure? You—"

"Hey, I never saw them before, did I? It was just a guess. They had those things that looked like weapons, and I remembered what you said." She glanced around. "Hang on."

She swung the wheel suddenly to the left, cutting across the road, barely missing an old station wagon, jamming hard up the southbound ramp and onto the main highway. Ann said, "Jay, for God's sake—"

Jack said, "What's that smell?"

"Oh, no." Ann's nostrils twitched, picking up the familiar sour reek. "Jay, you've been drinking again!"

"Yep," Jay said, cutting in front of a horn-blaring cattle truck, "sure have—*look* out, you stupid son of a bitch!" She made a one-finger gesture at the white-faced driver of a Jeep. "You two can preach at me later on. If we live that long."

Ann spotted the neck of the bottle sticking up between Jay's thighs, and thought about grabbing it. But she didn't dare do anything that might distract Jay. By now they were clear of traffic and picking up serious speed, the view blurring and streaking past on either side. She glanced at the speedometer and wished she hadn't. "Jay, you're going to kill us. Pull off and stop, and I'll take over."

"Huh uh," Jack said behind her. "No time for that. Those guys are right back there, coming up fast. They're all over the road—shit, I think I could drive better than that—but they're moving ass."

Jay cursed and glanced in the mirror. "Fix that," she muttered. "Belt up and hang on. This is gonna get hairy."

Ann hastened to do up the unfamiliar seat harness. As the buckle tongue snapped into place she said, "What are you—*akk*!"

The Toyota was slowing even more suddenly than it had accelerated, fishtailing sickeningly, tires howling as Jay pumped the brakes. The nylon webbing dug painfully into Ann's flesh as she was thrown forward against the seat straps. From the back seat came a heavy thud and several pungent curses.

The back end broke loose and came around as the Toyota skidded to a near-halt, its nose pointing off to the left, a good ninety degrees to the highway. Ann caught a glimpse of an unpaved turnoff and a sign: EMERGENCY VEHICLE USE ONLY. Then Jay stepped on the gas again and they were bumping over rutted dirt, rocks rattling against the car's underbody, and a moment later they were slewing wildly onto pavement again, heading back northward. "There," Jay said with satisfaction. "Let's see the bastards follow that."

"Then," Ann said weakly, "maybe now you should let me drive?"

"What for?" Jay grinned, not taking her eyes off the road, which was once again streaking beneath the Toyota's wheels at increasing speed. "I'm doing okay. Lost 'em, didn't I?"

"Not really," Jack told her. "They—holy *fuck*, look at that! Turned around somehow, now they're coming back on the southbound side, going the wrong way, I can't believe this—"

Ann twisted around in her seat and looked back. She couldn't see anything. But Jack said, "Uh oh. Big cloud of dust, looks like they just found that crossover."

"Or they crashed," Jay said hopefully. "Easy to see they don't know what they're doing—"

"No, they made it," Jack reported. "Here they come. Go faster, they're gaining on us."

"I'm standing on it," Jay said through her teeth. "That Buick's got lots more power than this thing. On a straight road like this, they can just run us down, no matter how badly they drive."

A green-and-white sign flickered by, too fast to read. "Ha," Jay said. "Interchange coming up. I'm going to get off this slab. If we can't outrun them maybe I can outdrive them. Hang on again."

The hump of the overpass appeared ahead. Jay said, "Here goes," and swerved sharply into the exit lane, braking hard but still going too fast, almost losing it on the tight curl of the offramp, the Toyota heeling way over on its shocks. Ann's hands were white against the dash, her nails digging into the vinyl. "Jay," she said, "for God's sake look *aaaaAAAAAAAAA!*"

There was a truck at the bottom of the ramp, stopped dead, turn signals blinking; it was enormous and it completely blocked the ramp, no way past it and they were going much too fast to stop or even slow down enough to do any good. They were all yelling now, bracing themselves for the impact, as the shiny square rear of the truck rose up and filled their vision—

And then, just like that, the truck wasn't there. For a moment *nothing* was there, nothing outside the windows but a kind of strange bright shimmering fog; then the view cleared and they shot through the space between a couple of rusting burnt-out cars and down the sand-blown main street of the little town, past shattered windows and shot-up signs and more wrecked cars and trucks, while a big flock of buzzards rose flapping and squawking from what almost looked like a couple of human bodies in the middle of the street.

From the back seat Jack shouted something about not stopping but it was wasted breath; Jay was standing on the gas now, accelerating hard down the ruined street, the Toyota's tires bouncing violently over the cracked and potholed concrete. In almost no time they were clear of the town, heading up the road toward the mountains, tires sliding dangerously on the patches of drifting sand that covered the gnarled blacktop; and then they all screamed again as the view once more went momentarily blank. A moment later the shimmering grayness cleared away, the car stopped jumping, and there was clean smooth pavement under the wheels. A big sign by the road side announced:

```
SPANISH HILLS MENTAL HEALTH CENTER
            12.5 MILES
```

There was barely time for that to register before the strange fog closed in again; and this time when it cleared they were speeding along a familiar-looking road across open rolling desert, foothills coming up very fast ahead.

After a minute Jay said, "Jesus! What the fuck was *that* all about?"

She glanced sidewise at Ann. "Or rather, was what just happened what I think it was?"

Her voice was high and ragged; her face was even whiter than usual. Her hands were gripping the wheel so hard the long tendons stood out on her wrists and forearms.

"Probably." Ann wasn't surprised when her own voice came out shuddery and thin. "Jay, you better pull over now. Let me drive."

"You got it." Jay slowed the Toyota and pulled off onto the narrow gravel shoulder. "What the hell," she said as the car crunched to a stop, "we've lost those guys for sure now."

She opened her door and got out and started around the front of the car. Sliding over behind the wheel, watching her through the windshield, Ann noticed that she was clutching her whiskey bottle. As she got back in the car Ann said, "Don't you think you ought to get rid of that now?"

"Nope." Jay unscrewed the cap and took a long swig, holding the bottle with both shaking hands. "Now's when I really need it."

Privately Ann recognized the feeling; she wouldn't have minded a drink right now herself. But as she swung the Toyota back onto the blacktop she said, "Jay, after all you went through getting off that stuff—"

"Listen," Jay said, "you better damn well be glad I fell off the wagon when I did. I hadn't, you'd be dead by now."

Her voice was stronger now; she waved the bottle for emphasis. "What I did back there, you think I'd have done something like that sober? Run over a couple of total strangers with my best friend's car, just because they looked a little bit like some guys in a bullshit story this couple of crazy women told me? Shit, I still don't believe I did it."

Jack said, "Ann, you better move this thing faster. I hate to tell you, but I don't think we lost your buddies after all."

"What?" Ann checked the mirror but all she could see was road and desert. "Are you sure?"

"Saw something—there!"

Ann caught a glimpse, now, her eyes registering a quick flash that might have been sunlight reflecting off a windshield, still nothing solid: something back there, though, and coming fast. She saw it again now, as the distant vehicle crested a rise and then disappeared once more into a long dip. "You think it's them?" she said dubiously, accelerating all the same. "How could they have followed us?"

"Can't make out the car that well," Jack said, "couldn't swear that's who it is. But somebody's sure coming fast up this road. You want to hang around and find out for sure?"

"Wouldn't be that hard," Jay observed, "for them to figure out we must have gone this way. This is the only road out of that little town, except for the fourlane."

Ann didn't think that was the whole answer. The gray-suited men obviously had some means of locating her and tracking their movements at a distance; they might even know about the house. She felt a flicker of despair: why was she running? They'd get her, this time or next, if something else didn't get her first—

"Who *are* those guys?" Jay mumbled, and took another drink.

They were climbing now, the road swinging right and then left as it entered the foothills, still easy driving but Ann let up on the gas a bit all the same, not yet sure of the unfamiliar car's handling. "Don't slow down," Jack protested. "They'll catch us."

"Not on this road," Ann said. "Not the way they drive. Going to be all they can do just staying on the pavement. Especially with a big heavy car like that."

"They don't have to catch us," Jay said. "This road doesn't really go anywhere. Just wanders off into the mountains, turns into gravel a few miles beyond the house, and I don't know where it finally winds up but we haven't got enough gas to make it."

Ann dropped her eyes to the gas gauge. "For God's sake, Jay!"

"Well," Jay said, "nobody was supposed to be driving it, were they? And I wasn't exactly planning for the future, the only trips I made." She held up the bottle. "Not exactly," she repeated, her voice starting to blur a little on the consonants: "ezzackly" was more how it came out.

They passed the turnoff—still gravel, Ann noticed with relief, and no signs; definitely back in Jay's world, then, she hadn't been quite sure—and the road began snaketracking in earnest up the side of the big mountain. More confident now, or maybe just not caring, Ann pushed the Toyota hard on the sharp curves and felt the tires clawing for a grip on the worn asphalt, faint squealing sounds coming from beneath the rear wheels. Not that there was any real point in going fast, they were going to be caught anyway, but it made her feel better; the fox knows she can't outrun the hounds but she runs all the same. . . .

"Almost to the house," Jay announced, pointing. "About a half mile beyond this next turn."

Ann let up on the gas and braked lightly as she took the turn, which was a really nasty one, with a vertiginous sheer drop just beyond a guardrail that wouldn't have stopped a bicycle. Suddenly she felt a tapping on her shoulder. "Stop here," Jack said, "and let me out."

Wondering why, knowing better than to ask, Ann pulled the Toyota to a stop just past the turn. "Here?"

Jack already had the door open. "Go," she said as she jumped out. "Don't wait for me."

Ann twisted around in her seat, about to object, but Jack said, "God damn it, *go!* You can wait for me at the house."

The door slammed shut. In the mirror Ann saw Jack trotting back down the road, pistol in hand. A moment later she had vanished behind a rock outcrop next to the road, on the inside of the hairpin. Ann took a deep breath and put the Toyota in motion again. "It's all right," she said, as much to herself as to Jay. "Jack knows what she's doing."

"Yeah?" Jay said. "Glad somebody does."

◀ ▲ ▼ ▶

Standing behind the rock outcrop, watching the Toyota disappear up the road, Jack sighed with relief. She'd been afraid

Ann would want to argue or ask for explanations, and there was no time for that.

Or so Jack had believed; but now, as she leaned back against the rock and rubbed her bad eye and tried to steady her breathing, she realized she still couldn't hear anything but the wind through the scattered pines. The suits must be farther back than she'd thought. She hoped they weren't going too slow; this was going to be iffy at best.

Finally she heard it, the distant note of a big engine laboring on a steep grade, growing rapidly louder. She wiped her right hand on her shorts and fitted it carefully around the .44's grip and then wrapped her left over it, watching the road, listening to the note of the approaching motor.

When the blue car finally stuck its nose around the curve she saw that it was indeed moving pretty slowly but still fast enough for her purposes. She couldn't see inside for the sunlight glinting off the windshield, but that was all right; it was the same car and that was enough.

She stepped out onto the road shoulder and began firing.

Her first shot went high and the blue car's windshield went suddenly opaque with a crazy network of white cracks. Before the driver could react she shot again, remembering now that the .44 shot high, holding down at six o'clock. The blue car started to slew and skid as the driver slammed on the brakes. Jack kept shooting.

She didn't know which of her shots finally hit the front tire. Suddenly there was a sharp bang, almost as loud as her revolver, and the blue car tilted and swerved wildly to the left, just as the .44 snapped empty.

She made no move to reload. Either there was no time or there was all the time in the world. She stood and watched as the driver fought for control.

The car was going quite slowly, no faster than a trotting horse, when it went off the road. It still had enough momentum, though, to crumple the ridiculous guardrail. It went over the edge at a sharp angle, left front wheel first, then the right, the back end swinging skyward; and for an instant it hung there, rear wheels spinning uselessly in midair, before sliding inexorably forward and downward.

Jack walked unhurriedly across the road and peered over the edge of the precipice. Far below, she could just make out a little blue toy car, still falling. Then it hit something and bounced, and as she watched it turned over and bounced again, rolling and caroming down the steep rocky slope at the foot of the cliff, pieces flying off, to come to rest at last upside down amid a patch of fallen boulders. There was no explosion.

After a moment a big metallic boom drifted up to Jack's ears, along with other satisfying sounds. Smiling slightly, she turned and began walking up the road.

Halfway to the house she stopped, seeing the Toyota coming back down the road. "Shit," she said to herself, not really angry or even surprised.

She waited while the car rolled up beside her and Ann stuck her head out the window. "Are you all right? We heard shots—"

"I'm all right." Jack yanked the rear door open, gesturing with her free hand toward the wrecked guardrail. "But you ought to see the other bastards."

"You mean—oh." Ann stared at the guardrail, and the big emptiness beyond. "Amazing," she murmured.

"All *right*," Jay said happily. She sounded drunker than ever. "So much for the bad guys."

"I don't know," Ann said. "I wonder. You wouldn't think any living thing could survive something like that, but—"

"Come on," Jay said. "We better go back and get Danny."

"Is that safe?" Ann asked, starting the car.

"No," Jay said, "but neither's anything else. Not with you two."

◄   △   ▽   ▷

Driving back down the mountain, taking it easy now, Ann said, "I still can't believe what happened. What we did."

"You mean when we came off the highway, and—what the hell *did* we do, anyway?" Jack leaned forward and rested her arms on the back of the front seat. "And how did we do it?"

"It didn't happen," Jay declared. "I've already decided. Drunks may have our limitations but we're hell at denial."

"We've done it before," Jack pointed out. "Or rather it's happened to us. You think it's something we're doing?"

"At some level, I think so. Think about it," Ann said. "It always happens when at least one of us is in danger. And it seems to help when one of us has been drinking or taking drugs. I don't know how that last part fits in," she added, "but it's too consistent a pattern to ignore."

"Jesus. Then we could do it again."

"I don't see why not. Especially now." Ann tilted her head toward Jay, who was once again applying herself to the bourbon bottle. "Now there are three of us, it's become much stronger. Our combined . . . power, for want of a better word, must be exponentially greater. That's the only possible explanation of how we were able to take the car along this time."

"Huh. That's right," Jack said. "Always before, all we ever took with us was small stuff we had on us, like clothes and weapons. A car, man, that's something else."

"Yes, isn't it? And we made it back," Ann said, "that's something that never happened before either. We always ended up in a different—whatever, world or plane, somewhere else on the reality continuum—"

"I can make a sentence using continuum," Jay proclaimed. "'Masked Man wait here by trail, Tonto continuum to fort.'"

Jack reached forward in a swift movement and took the bottle out of her hand and tossed it out the window. "*Hey*," Jay protested.

"That's it," Jack told her. "It's been a long fucking day."

◁ ▲ ▽ ▷

As they approached the town they saw a solitary figure walking slowly along the shoulder. Ann slowed the Toyota and then stopped. "Danny," she called. "Are you all right?"

Danny Santos broke into a wide grin and started to cross the road. Halfway across he paused, looking at the front end of the Toyota, and his grin got a lot less enthusiastic. But he came on, while Jack opened the door for him, and scrambled in back next to her.

"So you're okay," he said. "I was really worried."

"Sorry to drive off and leave you like that," Ann said. "But we were in a hurry. Anyway, there was no point in endangering you. You weren't the one they were after."

"You mean those guys in the Buick? What happened to them, anyway?"

"They had an accident," Jack told him.

Ann said, "Did anybody call the police?"

"Nah. That old lady who runs the store, she was pretty shook up, but she said she wasn't getting involved. She didn't even realize I was with you. I just did the dumb-Indian act and walked off, just in time to see you guys come tearing back down that ramp. Then you sort of . . . disappeared, it looked like. Never saw anything like it."

"Danny," Ann said, "I think we owe you an explanation—"

"No," Danny said decisively. "Don't tell me anything. Tell my grandfather. It's time for us to go see him."

chapter
twenty-one

Coming into the outskirts of the town, Ann said, "Danny, is there any place near here where we can gas up? I really don't want to stop here if we can help it."

Danny Santos leaned forward and looked over her shoulder, studying the instrument display. "Nowhere you can get to on what you've got left," he said. "You're just about running on fumes as it is."

"Yes. All right, then, we'll just have to hope nobody connects us with the high-speed antics of this morning. Or cares enough to call the law."

"There's a place right up there," Jack said, pointing. "Hey, have you still got the money? The way we were running around—"

Ann felt the bulge of Jay's wallet in the hip pocket of her shorts. She couldn't remember putting it there. "Yes, I've got it."

"Hurry up, then," Jay said. "I need to pee."

◀ ▲ ▼ ▶

The self-service pump almost defeated Ann, and she started to ask Danny Santos for help, but then she figured it out and ran half a tank while Jay trotted off to the restroom. Replacing the pump nozzle in its bracket, feeling a little pleased with herself,

she walked across the concrete drive and into the little convenience store and handed the bills to the chubby dark-faced girl
behind the counter. "Thank you," the girl said, giving her her
change. "Have a nice day."

So that particular bit of meaningless happybabble had survived
in this world too, Ann thought as she started out the door; and
then she saw the police car turning into the station drive, swinging around in a half-circle to stop dead in her path. It was an
ordinary black-and-white cruiser, not very new and not very
big, but at the moment it looked about a block long. The door
bore the emblem of the county sheriff's department.

The window slid down, revealing a round reddish face partly
concealed by large mirror shades. Brown uniform, gold badge,
big American flag patch on the left shoulder. "Hi," the cop said.

"Hi." Ann made herself smile.

The cop jerked his thumb in the direction of the Toyota.
"Yours?" he asked.

Ann nodded, without thinking, and then wished she
hadn't. But saying no would have been just as bad. What if he
asked to see her license and registration? She could probably
get away with using Jay's license—assuming it was in the wallet, she hadn't checked—but what about the papers for the
Toyota? She tried to think of a story but her mind seemed to
have crashed.

"You know you got a broken headlight?" the cop asked.

"Yes." A desperate inspiration made her add, "That's where
I'm going right now. On my way to Santa Fe. To get it fixed."

"Mm." He gave a noncommittal grunt, the sort they must
teach at police academies. "All right, then," he said after a

moment. "Make sure you do. I see you with it still broken, I'll have to issue a citation."

"I will. Promise," Ann said, feeling an urge to scream very loud. "Thank you," she added.

The cop didn't move to get out of her way. He continued to look at her. "You're not from around here."

"No." What now?

"Saw you stop up the road," he said, "to pick up that Indian. He giving you any trouble?"

"No. Oh, no," she said quickly. "He—"

"Is he drunk? Maybe I need to take him in, let him sleep it off?"

"No, no." Ann shook her head. "Nothing like that."

"You want to be careful," the cop went on. "Best to stay clear of those people. You don't know what they can be like."

He paused, still looking at Ann; then he shrugged and turned away, while the window slid back up. A moment later the cruiser was rolling back down the ramp and turning up the street, to disappear around the next corner.

Ann exhaled unevenly and walked on over to the car. Opening her door, she saw that the seating arrangements had been revised: Jack was now up front, while Jay sat in back with Danny. Jack's gun was lying in her lap.

"What was that all about?" Jay asked as Ann started the car.

"Just a visit from our friendly neighborhood bigot," Ann said. "Nothing to worry about. Jack, put the damn gun away."

"I know that guy," Danny said. "Bad news. Better get out of here before he comes back."

"Which way?" Ann asked, easing the Toyota down the ramp.

"North," Danny Santos said.

◀ ⏶ ⏷ ▶

Driving north, Ann said, "What reservation does your grand-father live on?"

"Oh, he doesn't live on the rez. See," Danny said, "my grand-father's not from my pueblo. He's Apache, from over in Arizona. Didn't go over too well when my grandmother married him. Pueblo people generally don't care for Apaches, you know? And, well, it's kind of a closed society in a small pueblo like ours. If you're not from there, you're just never going to fit in. Or if you're . . . different."

His voice changed slightly on the last words; he paused for a moment before going on. "So," he said then, "they went and lived with his tribe for a few years, but my grandmother wasn't happy there and finally she came back home, bringing my father with her. Of course he was just a little boy at the time."

"Your grandfather lives in Arizona?" Ann looked at the gas gauge. "We can't possibly—"

"No, no. He left too, not long after my grandmother took off. Had some trouble with some people in his own band, I never have known what it was all about. My grandfather," Danny said, "he's a strange sort of guy, got his own ideas about a lot of things and doesn't mind saying what he thinks. Sometimes he pisses people off."

"Nobody likes a smart Athapascan," Jay remarked, and then, as Jack turned and glared at her, "Sorry."

"So," Danny said, "he went up to Vegas and worked con-struction and then as a casino security guard, till he had enough money to buy himself a little place of his own."

"Then you're a quarter Apache?" Jay asked.

"I guess," Danny said. "The way white people figure it, yeah.

My tribe, though, we're matrilineal. You're whatever your mother's mother was."

"Makes sense," Jack said.

"Up ahead," Danny said, "where that sign is. That's where we have to turn off."

◄ ▲ ▼ ►

The mountains came down close to the highway here; the blacktop road began climbing almost immediately after the intersection, winding steeply across pine-forested slopes and between jagged gray rock formations. Up near the crest of the first big ridge, Danny directed Ann down an unmarked gravel side road, and then along a confusing series of increasingly rough little one-lane tracks until she was thoroughly disoriented.

But at last they came out onto a small open space, maybe half the area of a football field—natural meadow or clearing, Ann couldn't guess—and Danny said, "Here we are."

Ann wasn't sure what she'd been expecting; some sort of small cabin, perhaps, of logs or rock or adobe, or even a hogan or whatever the Apache equivalent might be. What she saw, however, was a big shiny trailer tucked up under a couple of tall pine trees. An old but clean-looking Jeep was parked nearby. Next to the trailer was a large satellite dish.

Ann pulled the Toyota off the dirt trail and stopped next to the Jeep. "Well—"

She glanced around and saw that Jack had turned in her seat and was looking back over her shoulder in the direction of the back seat, grinning. Jay was asleep, her head nestled against Danny's shoulder. "I suppose we should let her sleep it off," she said dubiously. "Danny, do you think you can get out without—"

But Jay opened her eyes just then, blinked a couple of times, and muttered something that might have been "Fuck," and then, seeing them looking at her, she said, "What?"

"Have a nice nap?" Jack asked dryly. "Come on, girl, time to move it. We're there."

As they got out of the car Danny said, "Actually we're not so far from the Scotts' place, if you measured it in a straight line on a map. Typical New Mexico situation, though, no direct route, can't get from Point A to Point B without going through the rest of the alphabet."

He pointed. "It's right over on the other side of that ridge. I hiked it once, a few years ago, just out of curiosity. Took me all day, pretty rough going in places, but—"

He fell silent as the trailer door opened and a short, stockily built, white-haired man appeared, looking at them with no particular expression. "Hello," Ann said after a moment.

Danny said something in a language Ann didn't recognize. The old man responded briefly in kind, and then in English: "Welcome. Glad you made it."

He came down the cinder-block steps and strode toward them, moving quickly and with the easy grace of a much younger man. He wore new-looking jeans and a fancy blue Western shirt, with a red bandanna holding back his shoulder-length white hair. His face was heavily lined; his skin was the color of an old penny.

Danny started to speak again in that same dry-sounding language, but the old man cut him off: "Speak English, boy." His voice was high-pitched and soft. "Very rude to talk in front of guests in a language they don't understand. Besides, your Apache is so bad it makes my teeth hurt."

Danny said, "These are the ladies I told you about."

"Of course." The old man was looking them over one by one. "Yes," he added after a moment, "I see. Or I'm starting to."

He stepped forward and put out a hand as Danny said, "Ann, my grandfather—"

"George Santos. Call me George." The old man studied Ann's face as she took his hand; his eyes were those of an inquisitive ancient turtle. His grip was gentle, but it was still like shaking hands with a pine tree. "Ann," he repeated, and nodded, and turned to Jay. "And you're the writer?"

"Guilty." Jay took his hand, looking self-conscious. "Although some critics wouldn't say so."

"Don't know anything about science fiction," he admitted. "Haven't read much of it, mostly I read history. But I read a couple of your books that Danny loaned me, and some stories in these magazines he had, and I really liked them. You have a great gift for storytelling."

"Thank you." Jay was very nearly blushing.

He took Jack's hand. "Ah," he said, looking at her face, the tone of his voice changing. "You were right, Daniel. This one is a warrior."

Suddenly he raised her hand to his face and sniffed. "Been shooting a gun, huh? Not too long ago, smells like."

Jack nodded. George Santos said, "For real?"

Jack didn't ask what he meant. "Yes," she said.

"Huh. Gone that far already, has it?" He shook his head. "All right, then, you all better come in. Looks like there's some talking to do."

◀ ▲ ▼ ▶

The trailer's living room was surprisingly spacious, partly because of the neat and efficient arrangement of its furnishings. A leather-covered couch sat against the front wall, with a matching chair facing, and in between a low table of some dark carved wood. The windows were curtained with big colorful blankets, obviously hand-woven; the walls were hung with framed photographs and several well-executed paintings. "My brother Louis," Danny said, seeing Ann looking at the paintings. "He's the artist in the family."

Jack said, "Wow. Nice place you got here," and Ann and Jay made sounds of agreement. "Looks like you're doing all right for yourself," Jack added.

"I get by," the old man said. "Got my Social Security, make a little from stock."

"Stock? Cattle, you mean?" Ann asked. "Or sheep?"

"No, no, *stock*. Investments. Mostly mutual funds, these days," George Santos said. "Open market's getting a little squirrelly, but I still play some."

"Who do you think's putting me through the university?" Danny said, and got a shut-up look from his grandfather.

"Oh." Embarrassed, Ann turned and began examining an assortment of items on a long shoulder-high shelf: arrowheads, a small stone carving of a bear, various rocks and mineral specimens. In the middle stood a dark stone, big as half a loaf of bread. Some sort of crystal, Ann thought, though its smooth-faceted surface might have been cut and polished by human hands for all she knew; her knowledge of geology was shamefully sketchy. It looked black at first, but then she saw it was actually a very dark purple, the color of deep shadow. Without thinking, she extended a finger.

"Excuse me," George Santos said, "but I'd rather you wouldn't touch that."

"Oh. I'm sorry." Face ablaze, Ann pulled her hand back. "I don't know what . . . I'm sorry," she said again, stupidly.

"It's all right. Handle anything else you like. Didn't mean to snap at you."

Jack was admiring a framed collection of military medals. "Bronze Star," she murmured. "Purple Heart, Combat Infantry Badge—Korea?"

"Okinawa. Long time ago, when I was young and crazy." The old man made a dismissive gesture. "So," he said, "you ladies care for something to eat?"

Ann started to decline politely, but then her stomach cast a vigorous protest and she realized with surprise that she was seriously hungry. They hadn't, after all, had a chance to eat since breakfast, and that had consisted mostly of coffee.

Before she could reply Jack spoke up. "That would be great. I don't know about everybody else but I'm starved."

"Don't go to any trouble on our account," Ann said, without real conviction. Now the subject had come up, she felt almost dizzy with hunger.

"No trouble. I was just getting ready to fix my own dinner. Just as easy to fix more." George Santos paused and put his hands on his hips, looking thoughtful. "Unless . . . any of you vegetarians? I know a lot of white people are, nowadays."

"No, no," Ann and Jack said almost in unison.

"Definitely not," Jay affirmed. "Good thing, too." Then, innocently, as Ann and Jack glowered at her: "What?"

"All right, then. Make yourselves comfortable. Won't be too long."

◀ ▲ ▼ ▷

"Coffee?" George Santos asked, quite some time later.

Jay said, "Yes, please," and Jack, wiping her mouth with a paper napkin, nodded vigorously.

Ann shook her head and smiled, not sure she could speak just now. She stared in stupefied amazement at her plate, at the few remnants of what had to be the biggest steak she had ever eaten. A childhood memory popped into her mind, a tag line from an old commercial: *I can't believe I ate that whole thing.*

The old man gestured to Danny, who was standing beside the table holding a big silver coffee pot. "All right," he said as his grandson poured, "if everybody's had enough, it's time to talk."

Ann didn't want to talk; she wanted to lie down somewhere and sleep and digest for a couple of weeks, like a python. But Grandfather Santos was looking at her, as were the others, so she took a deep breath and said, "Danny, I think I'll have that coffee after all . . . well. Well, I'm not sure how to begin, this is going to sound very strange—"

"Can't be any stranger," George Santos said gently, "than some of the things I've seen with my own eyes. Take your time and tell it your own way. I'll listen."

◀ ▲ ▼ ▷

He did, too. He listened like no one in Ann's experience, with total attention to every word. He sat absolutely still, looking at Ann—and then at Jack and Jay, as they got in on it—without ever making direct eye contact; his hands were folded in his lap.

Only occasionally did he interrupt with brief, insightful questions; usually the question had the effect of guiding the speaker, drawing out some important point that had been overlooked. He could, Ann thought, have been a great police detective; and certainly she had never had a psychiatrist who listened one hundredth as well.

What he thought of what he was hearing—that was another matter. Neither incredulity, nor surprise, nor any other identifiable reaction registered on that creased rawhide face; his eyebrows went up a couple of times, just a tiny fraction of an inch, but in a way that could mean anything or nothing. It was a little unnerving; Ann wished she knew what he was thinking. It occurred to her, though, that maybe he didn't think anything yet; maybe he was simply reserving judgment until he'd heard the whole story.

Danny, sitting beside him, wasn't doing inscrutability nearly as well. Despite an obvious effort—you could see the strain lines from across the table, at the corners of his eyes and mouth and along the sides of his neck—it was clear that he was listening with mounting unhappiness. Especially when Jay spoke; he stared at her with such visible pain that Ann half expected to see tears in his eyes.

When at last the long recitation was done, he turned to his grandfather and began speaking in that brittle-sounding language. Whatever he was saying, he didn't get to say much of it; George Santos raised an imperious hand. "Daniel, you're being rude again. I told you about that."

He looked at the three women in turn, and suddenly his face cracked open in a smile. "My grandson wanted to apologize," he said, "for bringing you up here. I think he was about to say he had no idea you were crazy."

"Grandfather—" Danny began in English.

"Hush, now. That's all right. Most people would have the same reaction." The old man snorted softly. "Of course most people aren't studying that quantum physics business. After some of the stuff you've been telling me over the last couple of years, I don't see how there's *anything* you can't believe."

Danny frowned. "Okay, good point," he admitted. "But—"

"Butt's a short cigarette. You're studying to be a scientist. A scientist is supposed to be ready to consider new ideas. You used to tell me that back when you were still a little kid in gradeschool."

"You really believe—this?" Danny glanced around at the women. "You think it's possible?"

"Why not? Like I said, according to what I've been hearing from you, anything's possible. It's all just probabilities." George shrugged minutely. "And after all, our traditions tell us that there are other worlds next to ours."

Danny leaned back in his chair, his face thoughtful. "All right," he said after a moment. "I hear what you're saying about keeping an open mind. But why do I have this feeling there's more to it than that? Why do I think you know something you're not telling?"

George Santos laughed out loud. "By God," he said, "for a boy who's three-quarters Tiwa, now and then you show signs of real smarts. Must be your Apache blood."

He pushed his chair back from the table and got to his feet. "My, just look at the time. Gone and got late, hasn't it?"

Ann noticed suddenly that it was dark outside the windows. When did that happen? The clock's hands were swinging up toward midnight.

"You're not going to answer me, though." Danny's voice held a mixture of annoyance and amusement. "Are you?"

Jay said, "So you believe us. Or you don't disbelieve us. Fine, but where do we go from here?"

"Well," the old man said, "I don't know about you, but where I'm going next is to bed. Be a good idea if you'd all do that. Come morning, we can see about answers."

He waved a hand. "Afraid you'll have to work out the sleeping arrangements for yourselves, but you ought to be able to manage something. That couch opens out to make a bed—Daniel, take care of that, will you, you know how it's done. I'll get some blankets and pillows from the hall. Oh, and Daniel, you better sleep out front tonight. Give these ladies some privacy. You can use that sleeping bag you left here."

"It's all right," Jay said quickly. "I mean, he doesn't have to do that. We don't mind."

"Maybe not," George Santos said. "But it might not hurt to have somebody out there, all the same. You never know."

◄ ▲ ▼ ►

Ann was just dropping off to sleep when she felt the couch shift slightly beneath her. She opened her eyes in time to see an indistinct form moving quickly across the darkened room. The trailer's front door opened just long enough for Ann to recognize Jay's profile as she stepped silently outside.

The door closed again, with almost no sound, and Ann sat up and pushed back the blanket curtain to look out the window. Beside her Jack said, "Umhmf," and then, "What's happening?" She pushed herself up, her face alongside Ann's.

They watched as Jay walked across the moonlit open space, toward the shadowy area beneath the trees. They saw her bend over the dark oblong shape on the ground.

"I'll be damned," Ann said. "She's doing it."

"Go for it, girl," Jack breathed.

Out under the trees, Danny Santos sat up very fast and started to get to his feet, but Jay appeared to be pushing him back down. A moment later she sat down beside him.

"We shouldn't be watching this," Ann said. She didn't move, though. Neither did Jack.

It was hard to see details; Danny and Jay were only a couple of vague dark objects amid the shadows. It wasn't long before they moved together and then there was only a single larger shape, which, not long after that, tipped over and assumed a horizontal position. "All *right*," Jack said.

Ann let the curtain fall back and they lay down again, laughing softly together, snuggling together under the warm blankets, holding each other, falling asleep in each other's arms; and so they lay through the rest of the night, till early morning, when they were awakened by the terrible voice from outside:

"You in there! Everybody out, now!"

chapter
twenty-two

You people in there! Do you hear? Outside, now!"

Ann sat up with a violent convulsive motion, pawing at the blanket curtain. Sunlight blinded her; she blinked and flinched, covering her eyes with one hand, and then peered out again more cautiously. Jack was already crouching beside her, looking out at the other side of the window.

Jay and Danny were standing in the middle of the open space, a short distance from the trailer. Both of them clutched blankets about their bodies; they didn't appear to be wearing anything else. On either side of them, weapons aimed, stood the gray-suited men.

"We see you." It was Long doing the shouting; Ann could see his mouth open. *"Come out now."*

"Left the fucking gun in the car again," Jack said. "Didn't think I'd need it any more."

"No matter," Ann said. "You couldn't hurt them with that thing."

"I guess you're right. If they survived that crash they wouldn't mind a few forty-four slugs." Jack looked at her. "What, then? Run for it?"

"We'd never make it. And even if we did, they'd just kill Jay and Danny."

"This is your last warning," Long called. *"Come out or we shoot one of these people."*

"Better do as they say." George Santos was standing over by the door, fully dressed. "I don't think they're bluffing."

"No," Ann said. "I don't think they'd know how."

Quickly she jerked on shorts and shirt, not bothering with underwear, while Jack did the same; the old man turned his head politely away until they were more or less dressed. "All right," Jack said. "Time to get it over with."

She reached across the bed and squeezed Ann's hand. "Whatever happens—"

"Yes," Ann said, squeezing back. "Me too."

Following Jack down the steps, hearing the old man coming along behind them, Ann felt a deep sadness, but there was no fear left in her. Jack was right: time to get it over with.

"We could all run for it," Jack murmured as they walked barefoot across the pine-needle-carpeted space beneath the trees. "Break in different directions, they might not get us all." She didn't sound very confident.

"Forget it," Ann told her. "We go together. One way or another."

"Don't try anything," George Santos said. "Not yet, anyway. Do what they say, and wait."

"I'm sorry," Jay said as they approached. Her eyes were huge and full of pain. "I'm sorry—"

"Be quiet," Short said, and jabbed her in the small of the back with his weapon. "No talking unless we speak to you."

"This is all?" Long asked. "No one else inside?"

He made a quick gesture with his weapon. Short made an

affirmative sound and began walking toward the trailer, his own weapon at the ready. Long took a quick step backward, covering them. "Keep still," he said.

"Please," Ann said, "let these men go. Whatever you want us for, they have nothing to do with it."

"If they are irrelevant," Long said, "then there is no reason to keep them alive."

There was a sudden muffled shout. A moment later they heard running feet behind them, and then Short appeared. His weapon was slung under one arm; he held something in both hands. "*Vi!*" he cried, and Long looked. Stared, actually, with an unmistakable look of shock: the first real expression Ann had ever seen on that usually blank face. That was so surprising she didn't register, at first, what Short was holding.

"*Vi,*" Short said again, holding up the object, and Ann recognized it then, the dark stone from the shelf in the trailer's living room.

Short added a string of fast syllables; Long replied with what sounded like a question. Both men's voices were slightly but distinctly higher in pitch now, and a little louder; their faces showed definite signs of agitation, and their eyes darted back and forth between the stone and the prisoners. Not much of a display, by normal human standards—it wouldn't have gotten them a second glance on a city street or in a busy office—but for these two, from what Ann had seen so far, this was the equivalent of running in circles and screaming. It would have been funny if it hadn't been so terrifying.

Long looked at the prisoners. "Which of you had this?" he demanded.

"Me," George Santos said. "It's mine."

"Where did you get it?"

"Found it in the desert." The old man's voice was calm, even casual; he might have been answering questions from a passing tourist. "Down south of here. Brought it home just because it looked pretty. Why, is it worth money?"

"Are you lying?" Long raised his weapon. "If you lie—"

"If you shoot me," Grandfather Santos said reasonably, "you'll never know, will you?"

"We can shoot the others," Short said. Holding the dark stone in his left hand, he unslung his weapon and pointed it one-handed like a pistol. "One by one until you tell us the truth."

"Go ahead," Jay said. "You're going to shoot us anyway. So fuck you."

Ann wished she hadn't said that. These two were obviously close to some sort of edge; push them and they might do anything. But then Jay was probably right about their final intentions, so what did it matter?

"Yes," she heard herself say, "get on with it, will you? I'm tired of looking at the two of you."

"Etgay eddyray to unray," Jack muttered.

Danny Santos remained silent. Ann glanced quickly at him, not moving her head, and saw his face and the set of his shoulders under the blanket, and knew immediately why. He's going to do it, she thought, this is it—

Then everyone stopped moving, everyone stopped speaking, as the air began to glow and shimmer in the space between the suits and the prisoners. Within the glow appeared the outlines of a human figure, and for a moment Ann thought, oh, God, not more of them; but then the shimmering faded away and they were all looking at a tall, strikingly handsome woman with short-cropped white hair, dressed in a long blue gown.

"Good morning," the woman said in a low musical voice. She was looking at the prisoners. "Will everyone please be quite still for a moment? Thank you."

She turned to face the gray-suited men, who were standing rigid, looking even more like store-window mannequins. Her right arm came up, bent at an odd angle in front of her face. The sleeve of her blue gown slid back and sunlight glinted on something shiny on her forearm. Long and Short stared at it with the same near-human fascination they had given the dark stone.

The woman lowered her arm and spoke a couple of words in what sounded like their language, her pleasant contralto now clear and hard as quartz.

They moved, then, quickly and almost in unison, doing something to their weapons and then slinging them over their backs, their movements jerky and mechanical. The woman extended her left hand, pointing, and Short stepped forward and carefully laid the dark stone on the ground at her feet. Then both men stood with their hands down at their sides, staring straight ahead, like soldiers at attention, while she spoke again.

Long put his hand inside the front of the gray suit—Ann couldn't see how he did that, there didn't appear to be any sort of opening—and took out a small black device, about the size and shape of a remote television control. He did something with his thumb and almost immediately the air around the two men began to glow and shimmer. A moment later they were gone.

Jack said softly, "Holy shit."

The woman turned back to face them. She was smiling now. "George," she said, and held out her arms.

George Santos stepped forward and they embraced. It was a pretty warm-looking embrace. "Cut that pretty close, didn't you?" he said, when they finally separated. "Thought you were coming yesterday."

"Sorry." She was still holding both his hands in hers. "Believe it or not, I got held up in a meeting."

Danny Santos cleared his throat. The old man and the woman looked around then, still smiling. "Let's see, Kala," George said. "I guess we better wait out here while these young folks go inside and get dressed. Soon as they're done I'll fix some breakfast, and a fresh pot of coffee. Then we can talk."

Jay touched George's shoulder. "Excuse me. Have you got anything to drink around here? You know."

"No." The old man shook his head. "Afraid not."

"Good," Jay said, and trotted off after the others.

◄ ▲ ▼ ►

A little while later, sitting on the couch that was still a pretty messy bed, Jay straightened up from tying her shoes and said, "Hey, you guys. I'm sorry."

"Don't worry about it," Jack told her. "It wouldn't have made any difference. There wasn't a damn thing any of us could have done, or not done, that would have made any difference. I'm glad you got to have some fun."

"Jack's right," Ann agreed. "All that matters is that we're alive and they're gone and I don't think they'll be back."

"I think you're right," Jack said, buttoning her shirt. "Who *is* that old babe? Man, I thought those two bastards were going to shit when she showed up."

Danny emerged from the bathroom, dressed now but still not looking very happy. "Good question," he said. "I'd like to know too."

"Well," Ann said, "somebody tell those two they can come in now, we're all decently clad. Danny, give me a hand with this trick couch."

Jack went over and opened the door and looked out. George Santos and the white-haired woman were standing under the trees, talking and laughing. They looked up and saw her and returned her wave, and began walking unhurriedly toward the trailer, arms around each other's waists. The woman carried the dark stone balanced in one hand.

"I tell you," she heard the old man say, "I'm just not worth a damn in the morning till I've had my coffee."

"Oh," the woman said, "I wouldn't say that."

Jack stepped back as they came up the steps. "Hello," the woman said, looking around. "I suppose introductions are in order. My name is Kala."

They all introduced themselves; she took their hands in turn, smiling, flashing white even teeth. Up close she was really fine-looking, even beautiful in her way. No one would mistake her for a teenager—Ann guessed she was somewhere in her mid-to-late fifties—but she wore her years well; the lines about her eyes and mouth only added to the strength of her face. Her white hair was cut close to her head, no more than half an inch long; the effect was surprisingly attractive. Her skin was deeply and evenly tanned, almost as dark as the old man's.

Jay said, "Whoever you are, thanks. I thought we were already history."

"Those guys," Jack said, "it seemed like they recognized you. If you don't mind me asking, are you from, uh, wherever they're from?"

"In a way. And no," the woman said, "I don't mind if you ask questions. I just don't guarantee I'll be able to answer them in any way that will make sense to you."

"Right." Jack rubbed briefly at her bad eye. "Well, you can't get me any worse confused than I already am."

Kala set the dark stone on the coffee table and seated herself gracefully in the big chair, tucking her long blue skirts neatly about her ankles, while the three other women sat down on the couch. "As for their recognizing me," Kala said, "it's possible, but very unlikely. They recognized my authority. That was enough."

"What was that you showed them?" Jay asked.

Kala raised her right arm and slid back the loose sleeve of her gown. A silver band, thick as a finger, spiralled around her forearm from elbow to wrist. It had been worked into the stylized likeness of a snake; the flattened head rested next to the back of her hand.

Ann said, "It's beautiful. Is it an emblem of your—authority?"

"It can be. When one is needed."

"What are you," Jack said, "some kind of priest? Priestess?"

The woman burst out laughing. Back in the kitchen nook, George Santos chuckled. "Kala's a lot of things," he called over his shoulder, "but not that. Huh uh."

"Merely a public servant," Kala said. "Part seeker after knowledge, part bureaucrat, with the latter part growing ever larger despite my best efforts."

George came back into the living room. "Coffee ought to be ready pretty soon," he said. "Kala's being modest. You wouldn't believe the rank she's got, where she comes from."

Kala shrugged. "It's true my status is quite high. My family is very old and powerful. Where I come from, as you put it, we are not as democratic as you."

Jack said, "Where *are* you from? The future?"

"No. But that's a natural guess, considering." Kala put her fingertips together. "You three already know of the existence of alternative planes of probability."

"You come from an alternate world?" Ann said. "Like mine and Jack's?"

"Yes. But a very different one," Kala said. "The point of divergence lies much farther back, in ancient times. To give you an idea, in my world there was never a Roman Empire. Rome, and eventually the western world, were conquered by the people you call the Etruscans, and their empire lasted considerably longer. The Christian religion never appeared, nor did Islam. At any rate," she went on, "for whatever reason or reasons—and there's still a great deal of scholarly debate as to that—our civilization is in many respects much more advanced than yours."

"So much so," Jay said, "that you might as well be from the future?"

"That is a very good way to put it."

"And you not only know about alternate worlds," Jack said, "you know how to travel between them. On purpose, not the way we did. Wow."

Ann gestured at the dark stone. "That's some sort of beacon? A homing device?"

"It can serve as a navigational aid, yes. Its primary function, however, is to record certain phenomena—for which," Kala said, "I'm afraid I know no terms in your language. I don't believe the concepts are known to your science."

Over by the door, Danny said, "I can't believe I'm listening to this. Even worse, I can't believe I'm *buying* it."

"You saw what happened out there," Jay pointed out. "She just appeared, and then those suits disappeared, right in front of us in broad daylight."

"I know I saw it," Danny said sourly. "Doesn't mean I believe it."

He looked at his grandfather. "She's been here before, hasn't she? More than once, I bet."

"My first arrival in your world," Kala said, "didn't go all that well. The navigation was a bit off. I materialized in the wrong place and fell down a steep hillside into a rocky ravine. George found me while I was still trying to sort myself out."

"Thought she was some kind of a foreign tourist," George said. "She couldn't speak English as good then as she does now."

"That was almost five years ago. And yes, I've been here many times since. Don't be angry at your grandfather. He wanted to tell you, wanted to introduce us. I wouldn't permit it. There are, after all, rules. Which I was already breaking in talking with him."

Her mouth quirked. "And which I am now flagrantly disregarding. Oh, well, let's just call them guidelines. After all, I wrote half of them myself."

She reached out and patted the old man's arm as he stood beside her chair. "At any rate, it was a lucky error that landed me there. I don't know what I'd have done without George."

"Think that coffee's about ready," George said abruptly. "I better get started on breakfast. Hope everybody likes bacon and eggs." He turned and went back to the kitchen and began doing something noisy in the sink. Kala watched him fondly.

"Dear George," she said. "I'm embarrassing him . . . but he really has been invaluable. I can't think what he's gotten out of it. Perhaps he simply likes older women."

"Older?" Jay said. "Come on, now—"

"I am one hundred and twelve years old," Kala said. "As I say, we are in many respects more advanced than you."

"Oh," Jay said faintly.

"She mothers me," George said from the kitchen.

"Now," Kala said, "after we have had breakfast I'd like to ask the three of you a few questions—"

chapter
twenty-three

Kala's idea of a few questions turned out to take up the rest of the morning and then some. At George's insistence they broke for lunch, around midday, but the interrogation resumed immediately afterward.

It was well into the afternoon when Kala finally said, "Well, enough for now. Thank you for your patience, and my apologies for tiring you. You've been through a great deal."

"It's been kind of interesting lately," Jack agreed.

"Yes. I apologize, too—both personally and officially—for what you were subjected to. It will not happen again."

"You mean the guys in the gray suits?" Jay asked. "What the fuck was that all about, anyway?"

Kala looked away for a moment. "You do have a right to know," she said finally. "Yet I'm not sure I can explain it in terms you can understand. This is an area in which we don't even have a common language."

"Here." George Santos bent down and rummaged in the storage space beneath the coffee table. After a moment he grunted and produced a pack of cheap-looking playing cards. "Show them the way you explained it to me."

He handed the cards to Kala. She looked dubious. "Hell," he

said, "don't worry about the cards. They're old and ratty and I'm not even sure they're all there." He chuckled. "At least a lot of folks on the rez say I'm not playing with a full deck."

"All right. Thank you." Kala took a deep breath. "Please understand that this will *not* be an actual description of the reality. Merely an analog, a simplified model—oversimplified, in fact—to give you some idea of the basic concepts."

She dumped the cards out of their box onto her lap. Taking a card at random, she held it up. "Like all physical objects," she said, "this card exists in three dimensions. However, for purposes of illustration, let us pretend it has no thickness. Imagine it as a two-dimensional plane."

She turned it over: the nine of clubs. "Also," she continued, "let us imagine that these little trifoliate symbols are sentient beings—people, if you like—but they too exist only in two dimensions."

"And if you poke a pencil through the card, they'll only see it as a circle," Jay interrupted. "Because the rest of it lies in a dimension they can't perceive in Flatland."

Kala paused. "You are familiar with the theory?"

"It's a very common one," Ann said. "In school geometry classes, and educational television programs."

"They even taught it at the Indian school," Danny put in.

"It's one of the standard gimmicks in science fiction," Jay said. "In fact it's become a cliché."

"Shut up, you guys," Jack said. "Not all of us are so damn educated. Go on, Kala."

"Well, I'm sure you see what I'm—getting at, isn't that the idiom? Suppose there exist dimensions other than those we can perceive with our three-dimensional senses—"

"You're saying probability is a dimension?" Ann said skeptically.

"Strictly speaking, no. But you can think of it as such, for present purposes."

"This dimension business," Jack said, "I'm really confused about that. Ann's tried to explain it, but—"

"Direction, then," Kala told her. "Think of it as a different direction, if that's easier for you. A direction that lies ninety degrees from all the ones you can see."

"Yeah?" Jack tilted her head. "Okay, that works for me. I got you. I think. Keep going."

Kala picked up the deck of cards, tapping them into a neat stack. She looked around. George Santos said, "Don't worry about that coffee table, either. I already got a new top made for it." He looked sourly at the table top, which bore several oblong black scars. "My daughter-in-law and her damn fool cigarettes."

Kala nodded, placed the deck in the center of the table and slid back her right sleeve. With her left hand she touched the head of the silver snake around her forearm. The snake went instantly limp, sliding off her arm like a length of silver rope. She did something else to its head end and it snapped out straight and rigid, a silver spike at least two feet long. The tail end, they saw now, came to a very sharp point.

While they were still taking that in, Kala switched hands, holding the extended snake in her right now, point downward like a stiletto. Her arm went up and then down again, much too fast for their eyes to follow. There was a solid *thunk*.

She gave the snake a quick wrench and pulled it back upward. The entire deck of cards came with it; the pointed tip stuck out half an inch below the bottom card. There was a neat round hole in the table top, like a bullet hole.

"That," Jay said after a moment, "is what I call a unique accessory statement."

Kala held up the snake and pointed to the impaled deck. "Now," she said, "if we imagine each of these cards as we did the first one—"

"Wait, wait." Jack stood up. "I think I get it. All those cards, they're worlds like mine and Ann's and this one, all these different possible ways things might have gone, and they're right next to each other, all stacked up, like that deck of cards. Only the people that live in them can't see the other cards, because they're in a direction their heads can't register."

"Very good. Except that the 'worlds' you talk about are not really separate or separable, like the cards, but rather—" She paused, thinking. "Cross-sections, you might say, of the same overall reality. At least that is the generally accepted theory at this time." Kala smiled at Jack. "But yes, you have the basic idea."

"I do? Okay, then." Jack considered the cards again. "And that's how the three of us keep winding up in each other's worlds? We've been sliding up and down the snake?"

"No." Kala shook her head vigorously. "No, that's not it at all."

"Shit." Jack sat back down, looking deflated. "Well, I was rolling for a minute there."

Kala was sliding the cards off the silver shaft, leaving only two, several inches apart. "As you say," she said, "the inhabitants of these two planes are unable to make contact, even unaware of each other's existence, because they lie in a direction they cannot perceive. But—"

Again she touched the snake's head, a quick stroking motion of one fingertip. There was no immediate visible change, but then she grasped the snake at both ends and gave a tweak, and it bent easily as soft wire. She held it up: a U shape now, with a card on either leg of the U. The cards lay side by side; their edges were almost touching. "You see? Now they are in the same plane."

Ann said, "Good God. You mean that's what's going on? The probability line is bent?"

Kala held up a finger. "Not so fast. The line in question extends, as far as we know, to infinity or nearly so. It can't be simply doubled back on itself. At least I certainly hope it can't."

She picked up another card and threaded it onto the snake's body. With a twist of her wrist she bent the snake again, back the other way, so that the U became an S. Now there were three cards side by side, edge to edge. "See? All three are in the same plane, yet they intersect the line of the snake at three separate points."

Jack said, "I'll be God-damned. It's *kinked*?"

"Kinked?" Kala looked unsure for a moment, but then her face cleared. "Oh, yes, kinked. Yes, that is what it amounts to. Somehow a kind of kink has developed in the probability continuum."

"And our worlds are side by side, and we've been sort of leaking across." Jay was staring at the three cards hanging on the bent snake. "That's so crazy it actually makes sense."

"That was how we finally came to understand the phenomenon," Kala said. "It was noted that there were always three planes involved. Never two, never four."

"This has happened before?" Ann asked.

"Oh, yes. It's not common, but it happens. We still do not know the cause, though there are various theories. Usually the duration is quite brief, but now and then it lasts long enough to be studied. This one," Kala said, "has been exceptionally long-lived. We have been observing it for slightly more than five solar years, now."

She slipped the cards off the snake and wrapped it again around her forearm. "But," she said, "this is the first case, in our knowledge, of people crossing over physically from one world— to use your term—to another. Even when they are in the same plane, there still seems to be some sort of barrier or resistance. This is something that is not yet understood."

"Then," Jay said, "what's different about us?"

"Ah! Some of us would very much like to know the answer. It seems you have some special ability that you yourselves don't understand—and, at the present time, neither do we."

Kala grimaced. "As for your having somehow shared each other's thoughts and dreams, and that business with the automobile—I am almost afraid to think about these things."

Ann said, "Wait a minute. You say we're the only people who've done it. What about you?"

"I'm sorry. I should have said, you three are the only ones to cross directly in this way, making use of such a distortion. A short cut, isn't that the phrase? My people have indeed developed what you might call probability travel, but only the long way, along the continuum."

She indicated the pile of cards in her lap. "To return to our analogy, we have to travel up and down the snake. And the process requires a whole complex of equipment, the size of a small factory, and the expenditure of enormous amounts of energy. Whereas you simply . . . do it." She shook her head. "As I say, we would really like to know how."

"We?" Jay asked.

"My organization. We study the probability continuum," Kala said. "That is our purpose, to try to understand the workings of probability, which we believe may hold the key to understanding the universe. Actual travel is merely a tool, and a limited one. And there is no way for me to explain to you, here and now, the things we study or the ways in which we study them."

She touched the pile of cards. "Nor do I have any further childish illustrations that would help. I'm sorry."

"How'd you find out about us?" Jack asked.

Kala laughed softly. "That wasn't difficult. When you crossed over—you were first, weren't you?—you created a major anomaly, a disturbance in the field. And it grew stronger with each crossing. Nothing like it had ever been observed before."

"But then," Ann said, "why were those men ready to kill us? I'd think if we're of such great interest—"

"Oh, yes. At last we come to that." Kala's face went grim. "I said we were more advanced than you. That doesn't mean all of us are equally so. We have our share of stupid people and even outright lunatics. Sometimes they rise to high position," she said. "Ours is a very old and complex society, infested with factions and riddled with intrigue. Influence can count for more than competency."

She made an impatient gesture. "In any event, one such person took an interest in your case, when it was first detected. He should not even have had access to the information, but—"

"You had a leak," Ann said.

"Leak? Interesting idiom. Yes, there was a leak. And a certain person," she said, in tones that would have etched glass, "concluded that nothing less than the fabric of the universe was at risk. He was convinced that your crossings were going to weaken the barriers, until your worlds began to slip together and collapse upon each other, with unimaginable consequences to the stability of the continuum."

Kala grimaced. "Bullshit, as George would say. The universe is much too enormous to be disrupted by the movement of the tiny collection of molecules you represent. But the fool panicked, and he had certain contacts, and—without going through channels—he took his fears to the head of a certain secret government agency. An agency which, though we did not know it yet, had been experimenting with probability travel for its own purposes."

"Jesus," Jay said. "Like the CIA? And they sent a couple of cowboys after us?"

"They were to bring you back—actually Ann was the one they were originally after, they got her name from the television news transmissions—if possible. Their orders, however, were to remove you, alive or dead."

"Evil fuckers," Jack said. "I just wish I could have killed them for what they did to Fat Bob."

"It would have made no difference to them," Kala said. "And it would have been pointless. They are tools, no more. They obeyed orders because they are incapable of doing otherwise. Keep your anger for those who sent them. Who," she added with a tight little smile, "are even now being dealt with. Very severely."

"They're not human?" Ann asked. "Some sort of androids?"

"Closer to what you'd call cyborgs. Really, you don't want to know the details."

"That's okay," Jay said. "I'm just glad they're gone. Lucky for us you happened to be operating around here."

"Lucky? Happened? My dear, coincidence is a very dubious concept, in the light of probability theory. Some of my colleagues maintain flatly that there is no such thing. I'm not sure I disagree."

Kala waved a hand. "But in this case, there was no question of coincidence. It was because of you that I came here, five years ago."

Ann said skeptically, "Now you're telling us you can predict the future too?"

"Only in the sense that meteorologists do with their weather predictions. Like them, we can study certain factors, analyze certain patterns, and arrive at reasonably accurate general projections. And," Kala said, "there were strong indications that this geographic area, in the present world, would somehow be very important. Some major phenomenon was developing here— nothing more specific, but it was obviously worth investigating."

"This area?" Jay said. "You mean New Mexico?"

"In fact, the projections showed the main convergence would be centered on that area to the south of here, where the mental hospital is located in Ann's world, and the survivors' camp in Jack's. As I said, there was an error in navigation and I came down on George's land."

Danny said, "That's why Grandfather made me take that job with the Scotts? To keep an eye on the area for you?"

"Their house is the closest one to that place," George said. "Nobody else lives anywhere nearby. It was my idea, so don't get sore at her. Anyway, it's not like you didn't need a job."

There was a short awkward silence. Then Ann said, "This has all been very interesting, but can we can get back to here and now? I'd like to know what happens next. To us, I mean."

"Yes. You're right." Kala got to her feet, tossing the cards onto the coffee table and smoothing her gown over her hips. "Let's go outside, the four of us."

"If you ladies want some privacy," George said, "me and the boy can go outdoors. No need for you to get up."

"No, no. I'm tired of sitting here. I want to walk about, enjoy the fresh air and the view." She moved toward the door. "We'll be back soon."

◀ ⏶ ⏷ ▶

Outside, Kala led the way across the clearing, past the parked vehicles and the big pines, looking around and breathing deeply. "What a beautiful world," she said. "I hope its people appreciate it. I'm certainly going to miss it."

She glanced back at the trailer. "I'm afraid I've caused trouble here. No doubt Daniel feels used, and I can't blame him."

"They'll work it out," Jay said. "You had something to say to us?"

"Yes." Kala stopped and turned to face them. "It's time to talk about you and your alternatives. I have a real interest in this," she said. "You have been threatened and terrorized, and your lives put at serious risk. We—the people I represent—share some responsibility. There is therefore an obligation to help you. In my society we take obligations very seriously."

She raised her right hand. "However, we also place a high value on free will and the right of individuals to decide their own destinies. So I will give you the alternatives, as I see them, but the choice must be your own."

She folded her forefinger down. "One: we can return you to your respective worlds. Or rather Jack and Ann can return to theirs, with Jay of course remaining here."

"No way in hell," Jack said instantly. "I'm not going back there. I'll shoot myself first. I mean it."

"In my world," Ann said, "I'm officially an escaped psychotic murderer. Besides, we're not splitting up." She looked around; Jack and Jay were nodding agreement. "Wherever we go from here, we go together."

"Certainly. Merely informing you of all the options." Kala folded down the next finger. "Two: you can all stay here, and work out your future on your own. It won't be easy, it will require a great deal of thought and careful planning, and the risks are high. Still, you are extremely intelligent and resourceful, and courageous. I think you could do it."

"Damn if I know how," Jack grumbled. "Ann and I don't even fucking *exist* here. And how would we live? I guess we could learn enough to get around and deal with people, but how do we support ourselves? Everything I know how to do is probably against the law here."

"I'm not much better off," Ann said. "I doubt if the local scientific community recognizes degrees earned in alternate worlds. Talk about losing your accreditation. I'll probably end up washing dishes in a diner."

"We could give you a little help in establishing identities," Kala said. "Everything seems to be computerized here—at a very primitive level—and this cybernetic network would be laughably easy to manipulate. As to your other point, no doubt you could find some employment."

She smiled suddenly. "Perhaps you could collaborate with Jay in her writing. Given your scientific knowledge, and Jack's experiences, you should be able to add great authenticity to her creations."

"You think actually knowing what you're talking about is an asset in my line of work?" Jay said. "You don't know much about the writing business, do you?" She rubbed her face thoughtfully. "And yet it's an idea. Hm. Toughest part might be finding an apartment in New York big enough for the three of us."

Ann looked at her. "New York?"

"Oh, sure. We're all too conspicuous out here. In the city, you two wouldn't even be noticed."

Kala was waving her hands impatiently. "Please, please. You can discuss the details later. As I say, I'm only listing the alternatives . . . three," she said, "you can return with me, to my world."

"Hey," Jack said, "no offense, but why would we want to do that? So far you haven't made your world sound like a lot of laughs." She shuddered. "Specially if you got any more like those two guys."

"Don't judge us by our worst," Kala said. "We do have more positive things to offer. Medical science for one thing, we're far ahead of you in controlling the aging process—"

"That's obvious," Ann said. "If you're as old as you say you are, I wouldn't mind getting in on your secrets."

"Also," Kala said, looking at Jack, "we can replace your eye."

"You can?" Jack's face went pale. "Don't kid around, now. Are you sure? It's torn up really bad—"

"Routine procedure," Kala said dismissively. "Takes a little time—have to take cell samples and grow you a new one, the actual implantation is quick and straightforward. I'm amazed this world still hasn't developed it."

Jack's mouth opened and closed without any sound coming out. She looked stunned.

"In fact," Kala said, "now I think of it, we'll do that for you anyway, even if you choose to remain here. I don't want to use that as an inducement to influence your choice, that wouldn't be ethical. I can take the cell samples myself, and then when the replacement is ready I can send a field team here to do the implantation. Simple operation, they can do it in any reasonably clean location."

Jack was rubbing her scarred socket compulsively. "Holy shit," she whispered.

"But if you want to come with me," Kala went on, "you'd be most welcome. It's clear you have some sort of special abilities, which you yourselves don't understand, and we'd very much like a chance to study this. Besides, you represent a great store of knowledge about your respective worlds—"

"Ishi," Jay said.

"What?"

"Ishi. This Indian, last survivor of a primitive tribe, somewhere in California. They found him and brought him to the city and kept him in this big museum, and that was where he spent the rest of his life, showing them how he made bows and arrows and all that."

Kala winced. "I see your point. Well, you would certainly not be prisoners, or museum exhibits, or anything of the sort.

At the same time," she said, "I won't mislead you. I really don't know how easy it would be for you to learn to fit in—I'm sure you could quickly master the necessary technical skills, but our society is very different from yours in many respects. There are aspects you might find unpleasant, or even unacceptable."

She paused. "There is one more possibility, and I don't know how you'll react to this. Come back with me," she said, "but not permanently. Only for a period of training, before going to work for us."

"For your organization?" Ann asked. "What kind of work?"

"Field work," Kala said. "Along the probability continuum. Making observations, carrying out study missions—" She spread her hands. "Much the sort of thing I've been doing here, really. We've had great difficulty in finding people who can operate in worlds like this, so different from ours. It should be much easier for you. And," she said, "you've already demonstrated your adaptability."

"Wow," Jack said. "Sounds interesting."

"Interesting? You have no idea." Kala's face had taken on a rapt expression. "We've barely begun to explore the continuum, and already we've found amazing things . . . and our capabilities are still growing. Only this year we made our first contact with a world on which *Homo sapiens* apparently never emerged."

Her voice dropped. "I've seen a Neanderthal city. Like nothing you've ever imagined."

They looked at her and then at each other. After a moment Ann said, "We could work together?"

"Oh, certainly. Normally our people do work in teams," Kala said. "I really shouldn't have been operating solo on this mission, but I've got enough rank to bend the rules a bit. And George was worth any number of half-trained assistants."

She put her hands on her hips and looked at them, smiling. "And with proper training, you three would make a truly marvelous team. Of that I am certain."

"Huh." Jack was rubbing her eye again. "I don't know. What do you guys think?"

"As a scientist, my mouth is watering," Ann said. "As a human being, I think it's an utterly insane idea." She made a face. "Though not much crazier than staying here and trying to make it in this world. I don't know *what* I think."

"Wait a minute," Jay said. "You two, all right, you don't have much left to lose, and this isn't your world anyway. But I live here, damn it—maybe it's not much of a life, okay, it's gone to hell, but it's mine and I'm used to it. And I've got friends here, people I care about—"

She glanced in the direction of the trailer, caught herself. "I mean," she said, flushing, "it's not as easy for me as it is for you."

Kala reached out and touched Jay's arm. "It's all right. Please do voice your feelings. All of you, I want you to talk this over. I'm going to leave now so you can do so. But." She pointed a finger at each of them in turn. "You must come to a decision."

"How long do we have?" Ann asked.

"Until tomorrow morning. I am sorry," Kala said, over their sounds of protest, "but I can't give you longer. I'm afraid there are indications that this particular disturbance, this kink, is about to come to an end. I don't know how much time is left."

She folded her arms. The sunlight flashed momentarily on the silver snake on her forearm.

"In the morning," she told them, "I will return. You will give me your decision then."

chapter
twenty-four

Morning air glowed and shimmered briefly in the middle of the clearing. Materializing, Kala smiled at George Santos and said, "Good morning."

"Morning." George put out his arms as she came toward him. "You all right?"

"Yes." She laid her face against his chest and embraced him. They stood for a moment in silence, holding each other.

"I'm going to miss you," Kala said at last. "You're quite the nicest man I've ever known."

"Going to miss you too," George said. His hand came up and stroked her short-cropped hair. "You sure there's no way—"

"No." She shrugged slightly within the circle of his arms. "Though of course nothing is ever certain."

"It's all probabilities, huh?" he said, and they both laughed.

"So," she said, leaning back and looking at his face, "have they reached a decision?"

"Uh huh," George said. "They were up all night talking about it."

Kala nodded. Disengaging, turning toward the trailer, she took his arm.

"Then," she said, "let's not keep them waiting."

Printed in the United States
5058